Praise for the Washington Whodunit Series

HOMICIDE IN THE HOUSE

"A solid choice for   Maggie Sefton, Fred Hunter, a
—*Library Journal*

"Shogan does a good job depicting the creaky, squeaky wheels of government, and Marshall plays politics and sleuth with equal dexterity in this capital Capitol Hill mystery."
—*Publishers Weekly*

4 Stars: "The gang is together again in this exceptional murder mystery as Kit, her friend Meg, boyfriend Doug and rescue dog Clarence collectively work to solve the crime. Each distinctive personality shines as they bring the case to a close. Be prepared for another adventure."
—*RT Book Reviews*

"If you are looking for a great, can't put it down book, look no further than *Homicide in the House*."
—*The Open Book Society*

"Author Colleen J. Shogan has penned yet another riveting mystery set into a national political framework and continues to prove herself to be a master of the genre."
—MBR Bookwatch

"*Homicide in the House* is amazing. I was hooked from the first sentence, and read it in only two days. I recommend

Homicide in the House to all fans of cozy mysteries. I think it will particularly appeal to anyone who prefers fictional political shenanigans over the real ones in the news lately."
—Jane Reads

"A well-written mystery, with some political info mixed in to build the setting without bogging down the story. There is an excellent cast, some humor, some drama, and an edge of danger…. An excellent read for any mystery or chick-lit fan."
—Sarah E. Bradley for InD'Tale Magazine

"I love how the author describes Washington D.C. and the ins and outs of our government. I have not had the pleasure of visiting D.C. but really want to after reading this series. The author does a great job making her characters believable."
—Penny M. for Cozy Mystery Book Reviews

"I absolutely loved this whodunit that could have been ripped from the headlines!…. I like Kit, she is smart, thinks before she jumps, and she know Washington. "
—Escape with Dollycas

"An action-filled, suspenseful read that will keep you on the edge of your seat all the way to the exciting reveal!"
—Lisa K's Book Reviews

STABBING IN THE SENATE

"Readers who enjoy amateur sleuth mysteries written in the style of Agatha Christie will enjoy this promising debut mystery."
—Dorothy St. James, author of the White House Gardener Mysteries, for *Washington Independent Review of Books*

"[*Stabbing in the Senate*] features loads of inside scoop

about the workings of Senate offices—complete with all the gossiping, back-stabbing, and procedural maneuvering—plus an appealing young sleuth, sprightly pacing, and an edge-of-your-seat showdown on the Hart-Dirksen underground train. Apart from joining Kit on one of her Hill happy hours, how much more fun could you want?"
—*Literary Hill*, a Compendium of Readers, Writers, Books & Events

"A fast-paced blend of murder mystery and political intrigue.... *Stabbing in the Senate* is a page-turner that will keep the reader's rapt attention to the very end."
—Wisconsin Bookwatch, *Midwest Book Review*

"I have to say it is one of the best whodunits I have read this year. Colleen writes with clarity and wit and she knows her subject matter. She has done her research, turned her talent into one of the best new books to be on the 2016 market. *Stabbing in the Senate* is a look at Washington D.C. that is sure to be a memorable, page-turning bestseller. I give this one ten stars."
—Pamela James, *Mayhem and Magic Blog*

"What do politics, Washington intrigue and an everyone-for-herself outlook on life have in common? They all come together in the suspenseful, thrilling debut novel by Colleen J. Shogan titled *Stabbing in the Senate*.... It's hard to believe this is a debut novel.... Put [Shogan's] book on your shelf or ereader, and her future on your radar."
—LuAnn Braley, *Back Porchervations*

"A well-written debut novel. The author has been a part of the group of people she writes about, and her personal knowledge shows in her vivid descriptions of people and scenarios.... The story is filled with twists and turns. Just like the main character,

the reader is never quite sure who to trust or who to believe. Kit and Meg, her best friend, are a very likable duo as they try to get to the bottom of things."
—*Book Babble*

"From the discovery of the body, through pages and chapters of intrigue, to the action-packed reveal and take down of the killer, I was totally engrossed in this stellar mystery."
—*Lisa K's Book Reviews*

"I am not really a fan of politics or D.C. in particular, but the way Colleen J. Shogan presented this story drew me in and kept me excited about it."
—Caro, *Open Book Society*

"I am not a person who enjoys political novels but this was a pleasant surprise. The mystery, adventure, suspense, and intrigue are not to be missed."
—Penny M., *Cozy Mystery Book Reviews*

"Protagonist Kit Marshall is a breath of fresh air in a city of opportunists, and *Stabbing in the Senate* is a smart, snappy whodunit that kept me guessing until the end."
—Susan Froetschel, award-winning author of *Allure of Deceit*

"Political intrigue, mystery, and a rescue beagle named Clarence. What more could you ask for?"
—Tracy Weber, award-winning author of the Downward Dog Mystery Series

"In this smart, fast-paced mystery, Colleen Shogan gives a fascinating look at Washington, D.C., politics through a Senate staffer's eyes. She kept me turning pages until the surprising reveal at the very end."
—Mary Marks, author of the Martha Rose quilting mysteries

"A taut mystery, set in the halls of the Senate, a backdrop Shogan knows well. It kept me guessing until the end!"
—Carlene O'Neil, author of Cypress Cove Mystery series

"*Stabbing in the Senate* is filled with memorable characters and finds you rooting for Kit Marshall, an honest, smart and funny young woman, navigating a complicated city fueled by politics."
—Purva Rawal, health care consultant and former Senate staffer

"Shogan does a good job of describing the work of a staffer—unsurprising, since she herself was one in a former life. Also believable is Kit Marshall's confusion in being thrust into the role of suspect…. *Stabbing in the Senate* is a quick read, perfect for those commutes on the Red Line."
—*The Hill is Home Blog*

"I was so intrigued with the story and wrapped up in all the possible suspects that I wasn't sure who the guilty party was until very late in the story. I liked Kit. She was a character who was easy to relate to and she made for a good amateur sleuth."
—*Brooke Blogs*

Calamity at the Continental Club

Calamity at the Continental Club

A Washington Whodunit

COLLEEN J. SHOGAN

Seattle, WA

CAMEL
PRESS

Camel Press
PO Box 70515
Seattle, WA 98127

For more information go to: www.camelpress.com
www.colleenshogan.com

All rights reserved. No part of this book may be reproduced or transmitted in any form or by any means, electronic or mechanical, including photocopying, recording, or any information storage and retrieval system, without permission in writing from the publisher.

This is a work of fiction. Names, characters, places, brands, media, and incidents are either the product of the author's imagination or are used fictitiously.

Cover design by Sabrina Sun

Calamity at the Continental Club
Copyright © 2017 by Colleen J. Shogan

ISBN: 978-1-60381-335-8 (Trade Paper)
ISBN: 978-1-60381-336-5 (eBook)

Library of Congress Control Number: 2016958174

Printed in the United States of America

Acknowledgments

———

I WROTE THIS book as I made a major change in my career, moving within the Library of Congress from the Congressional Research Service to a newly created Library Division focused on public engagement and outreach. The plot of this book reflected my switch from managing policy analysis to raising the national profile of the Library of Congress. The new job has a lot of benefits, including the opportunity to spend more time at museums, archives, and historic places. It was a pleasure to feature several D.C. treasures in my story.

The people who work in our nation's cultural institutions are underappreciated. Modestly paid, they are nevertheless passionate about preserving American heritage and history. My colleagues at the Library of Congress are among the most dedicated public servants in the country. They are also enthusiastic supporters of intellectual creativity, including the "Washington Whodunit" series.

As always, I thank my family, husband, agent, and publisher for continued encouragement and assistance. Special kudos to the 2016 Writers in Paradise conference at Eckerd College. The feedback from Laura Lippman and novelists in my seminar was invaluable.

It takes a village to write a book. Much appreciation to everyone in my life who has made it possible once again.

Chapter One

———

"KIT, FOR HEAVEN'S sake, you'll see him in two days."

Doug stood next to our condo door with bags in tow. After years of dating and cohabiting, I was adept at estimating his general level of annoyance. No reason to sound the alarm yet.

I gave Clarence, our chubby beagle mutt, another hug. "Don't worry, buddy. Meg will be here soon to take care of you."

Clarence shot me a dubious look. My best friend and Capitol Hill colleague had many virtues, but the Humane Society wouldn't be nominating her anytime soon for canine humanitarian of the year.

I lowered my voice and whispered, "She knows where we keep the treats." His ears perked up immediately. Just as his canine ancestors had responded to the hunter's whistle, our dog knew the magic word. Clarence couldn't catch a rabbit if it was confined to our suburban Washington D.C. condo. Nonetheless, he'd learned food-related terminology at lightning speed after we brought him home from the shelter.

I presented Clarence with a Milk-Bone biscuit I had been hiding behind my back. After sitting and giving me his paw, he eagerly grabbed the treat and retreated to his favorite armchair.

"Ready now?"

The annoyance in Doug's voice had ratcheted up a notch. It was a slight uptick only discernible by someone who had witnessed the slow burn of the American history professor many times. We were slated to marry someday in the future. That was the nebulous timetable I'd privately adopted. Over the next several days, other interested parties would likely be weighing in.

Doug sighed, a reminder I hadn't responded to his question.

"Yes, just let me grab my purse, and we can go."

When Doug opened the door, Clarence must have realized he wasn't accompanying us. He put his head between his paws and gave us the saddest pout he could muster. Unfortunately, no amount of doggie protest could rescue me from my familial duties. We all had to do our time: Clarence needed to make nice with Meg, while I had to brace myself for the days ahead with my future in-laws.

Once we arrived at our condo building's carport, Doug left me with the valises to retrieve our car from the underground garage. I had a few moments to compose myself before my trials and tribulations began. Two precious vacation days were out the window, sacrificed so I could attend a glorified history conference with the Hollingsworth clan.

To add insult to injury, we weren't even escaping the city for greener pastures. The annual meeting of the Mayflower Society had brought Buffy and Winston Hollingsworth to Washington. Thanks to the Internet, I'd learned that the Mayflower Society had existed for over a hundred years and it consisted of stuffy, rich people who liked to talk about American antiquity. Not my cup of tea, and certainly not how I wanted to spend my precious spare time away from work. Expressing nothing but disdain for "small-minded" contemporary American politics, my future in-laws rarely visited our nation's capital. Doug had implored me to join him so I could get to know his parents better. In a moment of weakness, I agreed.

Absorbed in my thoughts, I jumped when Doug honked to let me know he'd arrived with the Prius. After shoving the suitcases in the trunk, we took off toward Washington Boulevard in Arlington. Next stop, the world-renowned Continental Club in the District of Columbia.

A positive attitude never hurt. In my most sincere voice, I asked, "Can you tell me more about the Mayflower Society?"

Doug managed a small smile. He was nervous, with good reason. His parents weren't exactly easy-going. I'd interacted with them over holidays and during other family functions, but not since we got engaged a few months ago. After all, I wasn't exactly a Boston Brahmin or New England aristocrat. The Hollingsworths probably imagined Doug would marry a Harvard graduate who worked at the Museum of Fine Arts or the Gardner Museum in Boston. In other words, not a woman who mucked about in politics for a congresswoman in the House of Representatives and somehow found herself involved repeatedly in high-profile murder investigations.

"My parents have been members of the Mayflower Society for as long as I can remember," Doug explained. "The same group of friends has attended the annual meetings for decades. My father is the history buff, of course."

My fiancé spoke the truth, which was more complex than it seemed. Winston Hollingsworth ran a profitable family law firm in the Back Bay. While his older siblings joined their father at Hollingsworth and Associates, Doug had opted for the academic route. He'd been tenured at Georgetown after writing several page-turners in American history, miraculously not an oxymoron. Doug's family celebrated his accomplishments with a restraint mastered by wealthy direct descendants of the New England Puritans. Outwardly giving a nod to his successes, they privately whispered it was a shame he hadn't become a lawyer.

Doug's father loved his life as a prosperous Boston counselor and was proud of the renown he'd achieved, but he privately wished he'd chosen the same path as Doug and devoted his life to studying and writing about history. Not many knew Winston's secret.

"How could I forget your dad's passion for history? He's lectured me about the Battle of Bunker Hill more times than I care to remember," I said.

Doug grimaced. "Try to cut him some slack, Kit. He relishes these four days immersed in history more than anyone can imagine."

"I don't understand why your father doesn't call it quits at the law firm and follow his passion. He's made more money than anyone could possibly spend."

Doug's knuckles turned white as he gripped the steering wheel. "Do us all a favor and don't mention that idea around my mother."

There were so many topics supposedly off limits with the Hollingsworths, it would be safer not to speak at all. No mention of murder. No political chatter. No money talk. Perhaps it was time for a vow of silence. I immediately dismissed the idea. After all, I was a Capitol Hill staffer. If I wasn't talking, I didn't exist.

Under regular circumstances, I could have excused myself repeatedly to attend to office business as the chief of staff for Representative Maeve Dixon from North Carolina. That would have definitely bought me serious time away from the Hollingsworths. But that excuse wasn't going to hold water this time. Maeve was thousands of miles away, happily visiting China on a congressional delegation trip. Twelve hours ahead of D.C. time, she was too busy meeting with foreign ministers, cultural attachés, and other important people to send important assignments my way. Nope, I was flying solo.

Rush hour traffic was headed in the opposite direction, with evening commuters escaping the city for their suburban neighborhoods in Virginia and Maryland. We'd just crossed the Potomac River into the District, which meant we'd arrive at the Continental Club in less than ten minutes. It was time to broach the prickliest topic of all: our impending nuptials.

In my most upbeat voice, I said, "Your parents are paying for us to stay two nights at a private, posh club that's seven miles from our condo. Do you want to tell me anything else about their motivations?"

Doug kept his eyes on the road ahead. This was a sticking point, and he knew it. He pretended to focus on the traffic and ignored my question.

I waited thirty seconds before changing my tone to "slightly annoyed" and trying again. "Doug, we're almost at the club. Don't you think we should talk about the wedding? Are your parents going to try to pressure us into getting married soon?"

Doug must have decided he couldn't handle midtown rush hour traffic and argue with me at the same time. At six thirty, the restricted parking spots became available. He parked the Prius in an open space and turned to face me.

Doug took my left hand and touched my engagement ring. "Would it be so terrible if we set a date?"

I resisted pulling my hand back. For as long as I could remember, I'd wanted to marry Doug. We'd only been engaged for two months and my new position as the top aide for Representative Dixon had consumed all my energy. There hadn't been any extra time to plan our wedding.

More importantly, I doubted my minimalist tendencies synced with the high-society expectations of Buffy Hollingsworth. Falling back on logistics was easy enough. "We could set a date, but we have no idea where we'll get married. First we need to decide on the venue."

Doug cleared his throat. "I'm glad you brought up the location."

My intuition was rarely wrong. There had to be an ulterior motive for our two-night stay at extravagant digs in the city.

Doug's parents had money to burn, but something was rotten in the state of Denmark. And it smelled like the Continental Club.

Again, in my sweetest, yet now strained, voice, I inquired, "You have a place in mind?"

Doug ran his hand through his bushy hair and adjusted his glasses. "Not really. Well, um, maybe."

My inkling about a grander plan went from a clever guess to full-blown DEFCON. Maybe it didn't reach DEFCON 1, but definitely DEFCON 2. Time to mobilize for nuclear war.

"And the place is …?" My voice rose in pitch at the end, despite my determination to mask my annoyance.

Perspiration was beading on Doug's forehead. Early spring in Washington meant that the heat wasn't the culprit. "It would be great if you'd consider the Continental Club. My parents—I mean, my mother specifically—would like to put it on the table."

I'd worked on Capitol Hill for years, now for a member of Congress whose reelection was anything but certain. She often voted with the opposing party to maintain peace in her congressional district and represent the desires of her moderately conservative constituents. Consequently, I was accustomed to controlling my temper. Considering our work environment, it was a challenge to stay on an even keel. After rising to the top position a few months ago, I often stressed the importance of "playing it cool during tough times" to our staff. That said, I could take a page from my own playbook.

"Doug, we've only discussed our wedding in passing. I'm not thrilled about a costly and sophisticated shindig. If the Continental Club isn't beau monde, then I don't know what is." I sighed. Not only was I not one for showy celebrations, but my laid-back, retired parents, who traveled the world in search of the perfect vineyard, were decidedly not Continental Club material.

Doug squeezed my hand. "I'm not expressing myself very

clearly. My parents have that effect on me." He laughed uneasily before continuing, "What I meant to say is that it would be nice if you'd humor my mother for the next several days. You know, indulge in her fantasy."

Raising my eyebrows and my voice, I asked, "Indulge in her fantasy? Of what? The possibility of my being featured in *Modern Bride*? No, thank you."

Doug raised his eyebrows in surprise. "Kit, you're misunderstanding me. All I'm asking is a little support."

His pleading eyes gave me pause. Typically my fiancé was a paragon of equanimity. He didn't get too angry or too excited or too happy or too anxious. His parents clearly had him over a barrel. My sense of duty kicked into high gear.

After a deep breath, I steadied my voice. "Okay. It's a deal. I'll indulge in the fantasy," I paused, "to keep the peace."

Doug brightened immediately. But I wasn't finished with my speech. "Don't get too excited. Just because I'm willing to humor the Hollingsworths does not mean I will consent to have our wedding at the Continental Club. Understand?"

Doug nodded vigorously. "No commitments. Just play along. Sort of like when you interrogate suspects while you're investigating a mystery, right?"

Doug had a point. From time to time, I'd bent the truth while sleuthing. Neither of us could have known how often we'd put those skills to the test during our forthcoming sojourn at the Continental Club.

Chapter Two

———

A FTER OUR HEART-TO-HEART chat, we proceeded along Massachusetts Avenue toward a neighborhood near Dupont Circle known as Embassy Row. It wasn't a misnomer. The foreign diplomatic core resided inside regal estates, and the enclave was generally considered the most picturesque in the entire city. I knew the neighborhood because it was home to many of the city's most prominent public policy think tanks, such as the Brookings Institution, the Carnegie Endowment for International Peace, and the American Enterprise Institute. We passed the Indian Embassy's famous statue of Gandhi on Massachusetts and made several turns through sleepy, shaded streets. Finally Doug announced that we'd arrived at our destination.

With sunset imminent, darkness surrounded the stately mansion, more like an ambassadorial residence than a social club. Like many Washingtonians, I'd heard about the Continental Club but had never visited it. The outer façade resembled the style of Parisian grand buildings, full of classical features and symmetry. It reminded me of the New York Public

Library and other imposing structures built at the turn of the twentieth century.

"I wouldn't necessarily describe it as homey," I muttered.

We pulled into the driveway leading to the front entrance. A valet quickly emerged to meet our car. Doug commented, "I suppose it will suffice for two nights."

Our suitcases were carried into the foyer, where we identified ourselves as Mayflower Society guests. Bonnie, the staff member assisting us, asked if we'd ever stayed at the Continental Club. Both Doug and I shook our heads. A smile spread across her face. "Splendid! While your bags are transferred to your room in the mansion, I can provide you with some historical background."

"Thank you, but my parents have already checked in, and we want to let them know we've arrived," said Doug.

Bonnie was undeterred. "Yes, the Hollingsworths are enjoying a beverage on our back patio. I'll leave you there after our brief turn around the club."

Having no apparent choice in the matter, Doug and I trailed behind Bonnie. The wall behind the main lobby was filled with photographic portraits of the most learned illuminati in the United States. Henry Kissinger, Elie Wiesel, Daniel Patrick Moynihan, Alan Greenspan, Paul Krugman, and Robert Caro were amongst the most famous. The vast majority were men, but I noticed Sandra Day O'Connor, Jean Kirkpatrick, Camille Paglia, Ruth Bader Ginsburg, and a few other women had each earned a spot in the display.

Bonnie explained, "We're a private club with members who have distinguished themselves in an intellectual pursuit or public service. This is a collection of Nobel recipients, Pulitzer Prize winners, and Continental Club awardees. We don't often speak in superlatives these days, but dare I say these are the best of the best?"

Without thinking, I commented, "Like best in show."

Bonnie blinked. "Y-yes," she stammered, "in dog terms."

Doug shot me a disapproving glance.

"Sorry," I whispered. "Subliminal. I miss Clarence."

Bonnie didn't believe in dawdling. She ushered us around the corner so we could follow her into a large, beautifully adorned dining room. Vaulted ceilings, ornate chandeliers, and formally set tables filled the space. Servers in crisp, pressed uniforms bustled across the aisles. I was reminded of a place I'd seen before, but for the life of me, I couldn't recall what it was. I'd never set foot in a fancy social club before, so its familiarity made no sense.

"This is our main dining room. We serve lunch and dinner daily, except for Sunday, when we host our legendary champagne brunch. Will you be joining us for brunch? I believe your reservation is only for tonight and Thursday evening."

I suppressed a scowl. When we'd entered into negotiations concerning the Mayflower gathering—akin to the Paris peace talks—I'd held my ground and insisted we return to Arlington on Friday. Clarence had been a convenient excuse. After all, he could only survive Meg's inferior dog handling skills for so long.

Doug answered, "Only two nights. We don't know if we'll join the others for Sunday brunch."

What was he saying? I'd agreed to Friday and that was it. I shot him a stream of daggers, but Doug refused to let them hit the mark. I was not happy. Just because I'd promised to play nice in the sandbox didn't mean the rules went out the window.

Bonnie was oblivious to dissension amongst the troops. "You must attend if at all possible. It's divine." She looked pointedly at me. "We serve delicious champagne with brunch." Props to Bonnie. She'd read me like an open book.

She shuttled us inside an area adjacent to the main dining room called the MacArthur Room. With a sweep of her arm, she explained enthusiastically, "This is where Sunday brunch is served. We have every possible entrée, along with carving, omelet, and dessert stations."

Doug's eyes lit up. We both liked to eat, and normally Bonnie's passionate endorsement would have sold us both. But there was no way I was agreeing to extend our visit until Sunday.

Doug must have finally caught my groove. "We'll have to see. Thank you very much for showing us around."

Bonnie nodded. "I'll take you to our bar and the outdoor seating where your parents are enjoying cocktails." She fell into lockstep with Doug, leaving me to trail behind. Still, I had no trouble hearing their conversation.

"Aren't you a tenured history professor at Georgetown, Dr. Hollingsworth?"

Ugh. I hated it when people called Doug "Doctor." Anytime he saw blood, Doug ran faster than a NFL running back headed for the end zone. To me, the title "doctor" should be reserved for medical doctors.

Doug nodded, which spurred Bonnie on. "I don't represent the admissions committee, but given your considerable achievements at a young age, I believe membership in the Continental Club would be attainable."

Doug's face lit up. This wasn't my scene, but once again, I'd done my homework. The club was a bastion of the Washington D.C. elite. Several social clubs of its kind existed within the city, each with its own flavor and notoriety. The Continental Club attracted the cerebral, smarty-pants crowd.

The exchange between Bonnie and Doug continued. She was laying on the hard sell, and Doug ate it up. Finally, we reached the bar, and my mood instantly improved. First, that meant drinks were in order, and I certainly deserved one. Second, the bar area met my standards. It had a rustic, hunting cabin feel to it, with high-backed booths and stately wooden tables. Unlike most popular bars in Washington D.C. or the inner suburbs, there was no annoying gaggle of twenty-somethings lined up trying to get the server's attention. Instead, two eager bartenders smiled and quickly asked for our order.

After Bonnie left, Doug asked me if I'd like a drink.

"Yes, and I'd prefer a stiff one."

The bartender closest to me laughed. I immediately liked him. At least someone had a sense of humor.

"Two gin and tonics, please, with Hendrick's, if you have it."

"Yes, sir."

Doug added, "You can put it on Winston and Buffy Hollingsworth's tab."

After the friendly bartender handed the drink over, I took a sip. It was perfect. Maybe the next few days wouldn't be so bad.

"Thanks so much. What's your name? I'm Kit Marshall. We live in Arlington but we're staying here with my future in-laws for the Mayflower Society meeting."

"My name is Charles. I hope you enjoy your stay." He winked at me.

"If you keep making me drinks like this, it will certainly help."

Charles laughed. "I'll be here, and I'm happy to assist." Then he added, "Good luck, Ms. Marshall."

As I turned to walk outside, I noticed a dartboard on the wall. It seemed out of place, since there was no room in the tiny bar to play the game. I pointed to the board and asked jokingly, "Does this help you pass the time?"

Charles shook his head. "It's a new addition. Like many items inside this building, it was a gift from a member. According to the donor, this dartboard was used at Camp David by several presidents."

I raised my glass in acknowledgment and followed Doug to the rear of the bar area. Beautifully adorned glass doors led to the outside courtyard.

The Hollingsworths were sitting at a large table, each sipping from a martini glass. They weren't teetotalers, thank goodness. As soon as Buffy saw us, she jumped up. "Doug, you finally made it!"

I stood awkwardly behind Doug as his parents made a fuss

over him. Buffy turned to me. "Kit, it's so good to see you. Congratulations! Let me see your ring."

Before I could demur, she grabbed my left hand and shoved it under her nose for a closer look. There was nothing ostentatious about my engagement ring, a simple one-carat diamond in a modern halo setting. Doug could afford a ring three times its size, but flashy wasn't my style.

Buffy grabbed the reading glasses around her neck and put them on. Her silence was telling, along with the disapproving wrinkle of her nose. After a long moment, she couldn't hold her tongue. "Doug, why didn't you consult with us? We have plenty of jewels in the Hollingsworth family collection that would have been suitable for an engagement ring."

We were off to a fantastic start. Doug ran his hand through his hair, a telltale sign of stress. "I wanted to shop for the ring myself. You don't approve?"

Buffy let go of my hand. "Lovely, darling. Not traditional, of course. I suppose that's the contemporary style." She returned to her seat and took a long sip of her martini.

Winston grinned, enveloped me in his arms, and guided me to a chair. "Don't mind her, Kit. She's just excited to plan a wedding."

He'd managed to confirm my deepest fear. Still, I remained quiet and took a seat. After giving me a look that could only be interpreted as a veiled warning to remain calm, Doug took a seat.

As Doug and his parents caught up on news of the never-ending successes of the extended Hollingsworth clan, I studied my future in-laws. In their mid-sixties, they had accepted their age with the grace and poise that considerable wealth provides. Buffy had embraced the trendy gray hair color phenomenon. Her chin-length locks were a silver hue that made her appear sophisticated rather than old. She'd paired a springy pastel suit, likely Chanel, with a pale yellow silk scarf and earth-toned makeup. Winston was no slouch, either. Of course, he wore an impeccably tailored suit. I'd never seen Doug's father in anything other than a suit. Hopefully he didn't wear one to bed. He'd perfected the distinguished gentleman lawyer look decades ago and wasn't messing with it.

Just as I was mentally preparing myself to rejoin the conversation, Buffy exclaimed, "Grayson!"

A tall man approximately the same age as my in-laws strode toward the table. He returned the greeting, "Buffy and Winston! Delighted to see you."

Buffy sprang to her feet and gave Grayson a polite hug. My future father-in-law remained silent. I couldn't help but notice that he stayed in his seat, and that a flash of annoyance tightened his features.

"Grayson, you've met Doug. He's a historian at Georgetown, remember?"

Doug stood to shake his hand. Grayson huffed, "I suppose we have a true professional gracing our presence for the next couple of days."

Doug narrowed his eyes but said nothing. Instead, Winston piped up, "That's right, Bancroft. Might be a good reason for you to stop talking and start listening. You might learn something."

Grayson tittered. "Now, Winston, there's no need for that. We're all here to learn, and I'm sure your son will be a valuable addition."

Grayson turned his gaze to me and offered his hand. "And who is this lovely creature?"

I squirmed uncomfortably. "My name is Kit, and I'm Doug's fiancée."

Grayson kissed my hand lightly. "Enchanting. At least we know the young Hollingsworth has good taste."

Never one to take a backseat to anyone, Buffy interrupted. "Grayson, will you sit and have a drink with us before dinner?"

"Unfortunately, I cannot. Duty calls, and I must attend to numerous details before we begin our proceedings. I shall look forward to seeing you shortly." With that, Grayson hustled back toward the entrance to the indoor bar area.

My plan for the next couple of days was to speak only when spoken to, but curiosity had already gotten the better of me. "Who was that?"

Doug answered, "Only one of the richest men in the Washington D.C. area. Grayson Bancroft, who owns Bancroft Multimedia, plus a dozen other investment companies. His net worth is in the billions."

"Billions? Like with the letter 'B'?" I asked.

"You got it," said Doug.

Buffy broke in, "He's also the president of the Mayflower Society. We've known him for decades, haven't we, darling?"

Winston huffed. "Unfortunately. The man is insufferable."

Buffy wagged a finger at Winston. In a scolding tone, she said, "Winston, stop it. Everyone knows you want to be president of Mayflower."

He grumbled, "Fat chance. He'll never give it up, even on his deathbed."

Doug raised his eyebrows and tried to suppress a smile. "Father, this is the most annoyed I've seen you in years."

Finishing off her martini, Buffy said, "He's frustrated. What Winston wants, Winston gets. Except when it comes to Grayson Bancroft. He's tried to wrestle the presidency of the Mayflower Society away from him for years, but it's impossible."

Winston's face fell. "The man has more money than God," he explained, "so the other members of the Mayflower board don't see any reason for him to give up the chair. There's no way I can compete."

"That's life, my dear. You'd best roll with it." To me, Buffy said, "Kit, I'm such a fool! This ridiculous business with Grayson distracted me."

She reached underneath the table and rifled through her large leather shoulder bag. I strained to see the Louis Vuitton label. They'd just returned from a week in Paris, and the purse had likely been a prized acquisition from her one-woman invasion of the Champs Élysées.

Buffy's eyes lit up as she proudly spread several glossy magazines on the table. "I've been doing my research."

Like a Floridian caught in a snowstorm, I froze. Did Buffy want us to page through these publications together so we could plan the wedding? The promise to behave myself suddenly seemed impossible.

After a long moment, Doug cleared his throat, signaling me to respond. I mustered a shaky smile. "Um, thank you. I've been so busy with work, I haven't had a chance to begin planning."

Buffy nodded sympathetically. "Just as I thought. You work too hard, Kit. Hopefully some day that will change." She gave me a knowing look.

This conversation had gone from bad to worse. The wedding planning was the tip of the iceberg. Apparently Buffy also engaged in career counseling.

"Not anytime soon, I'm afraid. My job on Capitol Hill is rather demanding."

Buffy ignored my comment. Instead, she opened up the *Town & Country* wedding issue. "What do you think of this color scheme for a fall wedding?"

Doug must have sensed it was high time we broke up our little cocktail party. "Plenty of opportunities to toss around wedding ideas in the coming days. Right now, we're due upstairs for dinner."

Saved by the bell known as Doug. I mouthed *thank you* to him as we walked inside.

He pulled me close and whispered, "These next couple of days are going to be murder."

If he ever grows tired of being a history professor, Doug might just have a future as a psychic.

Chapter Three

———

$\mathbf{B}$ACK INSIDE THE mansion lobby, we climbed a winding staircase, past a gallery adorned with gorgeous portraits and artwork. From there the staff pointed us in the direction of our dinner. I nudged Doug. "What's inside that room?" I pointed to a large ballroom entrance slightly to our left.

"Don't know." He looked nervously toward the stream of fellow Mayflowers headed into our assigned room.

"Let's check it out. It'll only take a second." I grabbed his hand and pulled him along.

The Continental Club staff glanced our way, but said nothing.

"See, they don't care if we check it out."

We walked into a huge ballroom that could only be compared to the palace at Versailles. We were both awestruck by the regality of the space, with its floor-length mirrors, sheer curtains, ceiling murals, and crystal chandeliers. The room stood empty for the evening, yet it didn't take much to imagine how impressive it would look for a formal event. Suddenly, it hit me. The Continental Club looked familiar because it was a landed version of the *Titanic*. I could almost imagine

Leonardo DiCaprio holding out his hand, asking Kate Winslet for a dance across the beautiful hardwood floor.

"May I help you?"

Not one to tolerate stragglers, Bonnie had tracked us down. I'd take the heat for this one. "I caught a glimpse of the entrance to this room, and I couldn't resist a peek."

To my surprise, Bonnie didn't appear one bit upset. In fact, she sounded excited. "It's hard to pass up a chance to admire our ballroom. It recently received a million-dollar renovation. Now it looks exactly like it did in early twentieth century."

"It certainly does," I said.

"What do you use this room for now?" Doug asked.

"Musical concerts, formal dances, and receptions." Then she added, "Plus private events, like weddings." She gave me a knowing glance.

That figured. Bonnie was in on the gig. She knew the Hollingsworths were checking the place out for our future nuptials. The baroque ballroom was beyond impressive. Yet not exactly what I'd envisioned for my wedding.

Bonnie's last comment spurred Doug into action. "Thank you for showing it to us. We should join the others for dinner now." He put his hand on the small of my back and guided me out of the room.

We walked down a short hallway and entered a wood-paneled dining room. Five tables were draped with crisp white tablecloths and adorned with ornate china and crystal glassware. Other Mayflower Society attendees were milling about, and a waiter offered me a glass of champagne.

"We won't go thirsty," I muttered to myself.

"No, indeed." I turned around to face the deep baritone voice.

"Sorry, I didn't know anyone was listening. My name is Kit Marshall."

I extended my hand, and my eavesdropper shook it politely.

"Frederick Valdez. Here's sage advice for you. Someone is always listening."

Winston must have overheard the last line. After a hearty chuckle, he joined our conversation. "You would do well to heed Frederick's words. He's made a fortune as an early designer of cellphones."

Now I got the joke. "I should know better. Where I work, the walls have ears. So do the doors, elevators, and pretty much everything in between."

"My future daughter-in-law is a Capitol Hill staffer," Winston explained.

Frederick, who I guessed was in his early fifties, leaned closer. "Now I'm interested. Maybe this soiree won't bore me to tears after all."

"You have to excuse Frederick. He's not much of a history fan," said Winston.

I was intrigued. "Then why on earth would you subject yourself to days of lectures and tours?" Certainly a man of Frederick's station in life had other options for entertainment.

The non-antiquarian sighed. "It's an easy explanation. My wife Lola is a history buff. We attend every year because she enjoys it so much."

"Did someone say my name?" A woman roughly the same age as Frederick entered our circle. She had on a flowing pastel blouse and matching skirt better suited to a '70s revival of *Hair* than the Continental Club. Dangling feather earrings completed the hippie chick look. My black Macy's pants and matching blazer seemed boring in comparison. I owned seven similar outfits, the Washington D.C. version of a mandatory Catholic school uniform. Hillary Clinton wasn't the only one with an extensive pantsuit collection.

Winston gave our new visitor a hug. "Good to see you, Lola."

After introductions had been made, Lola smiled warmly at me. "I hope to hear all about your work in Congress, especially since you're now in the employ of that vibrant young woman from North Carolina."

She must have noted the surprise on my face. Leaning closer, Lola lowered her voice, "Winston keeps me informed about your career. He's actually quite proud of you. Thank goodness we have a Democrat in that House seat." She sipped her champagne and ran her empty hand through her free-flowing blonde hair.

Despite her attempt to keep our conversation private, nothing escaped her spouse's ears. "Please, Lola. Stop with the politics. We don't need to hear your leftist views right before we eat."

"You don't share the same beliefs," I commented.

Before Frederick or Lola could respond, Winston interjected, "That's an understatement!"

Lola laughed. "My husband's pro-business, anti-tax beliefs are a constant source of entertainment for me." She wove her right arm around his waist and gave him a squeeze.

Frederick said, "She's right. There's never a dull moment."

Grayson Bancroft's booming voice filled the room. "Ladies and gentleman, I hope you have enjoyed the cocktail hour. Please find a seat so we can begin this evening's dinner."

Doug and I found seats next to his parents. Frederick and Lola joined our table, along with the Mayflower Society's fearless leader. While pleasantries were exchanged, another couple approached our festive group and asked if any available seats remained.

Grayson jumped up immediately. "Of course! Cecilia, you're always welcome at my table!"

The woman appeared the same age as the majority of the other attendees, but her partner was close to two decades younger. She'd made a good attempt at preserving the remnants of youth, sporting perfectly dyed chocolate brown, shoulder-length hair, a springy A-line dress, and strappy silver sandals. Toned arm muscles provided evidence of an impressive physical fitness regimen. Her keen fashion sense and killer body couldn't mask the crow's feet and fine lines, which had probably been subdued by Botox and a face lift. But she still looked damn good.

"You do remember my husband, Drake?" she asked.

Grayson's expression darkened. "Yes, I'm sorry we couldn't come to your wedding. Kiki had a prior commitment that weekend."

Cecilia nodded curtly. "We received your note. And your generous gift."

Drake perked up instantly. Tall and slim, he wore an expensive-looking linen suit with a trim Armani dress shirt and tie. His tanned skin matched his sun-bleached blond hair, which he wore slightly long, perhaps in an attempt to reclaim his earlier days as a teenage heartthrob. "Is this the guy who sent us the expensive vase?"

Grayson bristled. "You mean the Lalique sculpture."

Drake was apparently undeterred. "In the shape of a heart, right?"

Grayson blinked. "Yes, that's it." He turned toward Cecilia, eager to end the vacuous exchange with Drake. "When will you finish your next book?"

Cecilia wagged a forefinger at him. "I would expect nothing less from you, Grayson. Always playing the businessman. We'll have plenty of time to chat about my writing career this weekend. Let's sit down so our friends don't have to wait on us."

An empty seat remained at our eight-person table. As if on cue, a single man appeared and inquired whether the seat next to me was available. I told him yes, and he sat down. Offering his hand, he introduced himself in a confident voice, "Professor James Mansfield."

Even if he hadn't included the title in his introduction, I would have guessed my dinner companion was a professor. Despite the springtime weather, he wore a tweed jacket with a matching vest. If he was roasting inside the wool, he didn't show it. Mansfield looked natural in tweed, almost as if he had been born wearing it. He completed his academic ensemble with a red handkerchief sticking out of his coat pocket. He reminded me of Professor Plum from *Clue*, except Mansfield was African-American and Plum's senior by a decade. After exchanging pleasantries, I asked Professor Mansfield what subject he taught and where.

Before he could reply, Doug broke in, "He teaches the most popular American history classes at Yale. Good to see you again, Professor Mansfield."

Mansfield gave a curt nod. "Professor Hollingsworth from Georgetown. I plan to read your latest book once the semester is over."

Not surprisingly, Frederick was listening from across the table. He asked teasingly, "Is there room for two history professors at this shindig?"

Mansfield didn't crack a smile. Perhaps Frederick had hit a nerve. "I'm sure we'll manage," said the professor.

Doug must have picked up on Mansfield's discomfort. "I'm not here as an expert or a member of the society. Kit and I are guests of my parents. We're using the occasion to visit with them."

I shifted my gaze to Professor Mansfield, who responded, "Thank you for the clarification. It is most appreciated."

Jeez, I hoped the wine steward would refill our glasses soon. We needed to lighten the mood. The springtime temperatures had done nothing to thaw the icy relationships within the Mayflower Society. This supposed group of longtime friends and their coldly formal ways could give the British royal family a run for its money.

Waiters began serving the first course, Maryland Crab Soup. Immediately after the soup was presented, the staff returned with a basket of rolls. They smelled heavenly. When I reached inside to select one, it was warm to the touch.

Cecilia must have noticed my fascination. "That's the famous Continental Club roll basket, dear. It's served at all our formal meals and functions. Quite delicious."

Her boy-toy husband aside, Cecilia seemed friendly enough. "Have you been to the Continental Club before?"

"I've been a member for almost a decade. After my first bestseller I was recruited."

Since my reading preferences were more along the lines of Laura Lippman than Ann Patchett, my Kindle library was notably light on literary fiction. Given this crowd, Cecilia might have won the Nobel or Pulitzer. Or worse yet, some other important award I'd never heard of.

Best to feign as much ignorance as possible, a trick I'd perfected as a Capitol Hill staffer. "I didn't catch your last name earlier. What type of books do you write?"

"My name is Cecilia Rose, and I write erotic romances. Perhaps you've heard of the Savannah's Sultry Nights series?"

Who hadn't? I'd assumed Cecilia penned novels filled with social commentary or criticism about the human condition. Instead, she was a woman after my own heart.

"Of course. I haven't read much romance, but I know your books. They're everywhere!" I wasn't exaggerating. Every bookstore, airport shop, and large retailer prominently featured the latest Cecilia Rose novel.

Grayson Bancroft interrupted. "Still behind Danielle Steel! Isn't that right, Cecilia? Can't seem to catch her."

Cecilia sighed. "Even Jackie Collins couldn't catch Danielle Steel, Grayson. Get over it."

Why did Grayson Bancroft care about Cecilia Rose novels? He didn't strike me as someone who liked to curl up with a racy story on a Saturday night.

Grayson satisfied my curiosity soon enough. "Now, now. That's not what I want to hear from my number one author."

Cecilia evidently noticed my puzzled look as I monitored the verbal volley between her and the Mayflower Society president. "Grayson owns my publisher," she explained. "That's why he's so interested in my career. He doesn't care a lick about what I write or what awards I win. He just wants to sell more books."

Cecilia's husband Drake had been listening to the conversation as he finished off his soup. Raising his hand to draw attention to himself, he said, "That's something Grayson and I have in common."

Cecilia rolled her eyes. "Typical."

"Drake is right. Nothing wrong with wanting to make money," said Grayson. "When did you say the next installment of Savannah would be ready?"

Cecilia picked up her refilled wine glass and drained half of it. "I didn't say."

The creases in Grayson's forehead deepened. "We can talk about the timing later. But there's going to be more books in that series."

Cecilia appeared unnerved by Grayson's insistence. "Fine. If you're so enamored with Savannah, maybe you should write it."

Frederick Valdez tittered. "It'll be a cold day in you-know-where when Grayson Bancroft writes a romance novel. Or anything more creative than a stock prospectus."

Lola laid her hand on top of her husband's. "There's no need for insults. We haven't even started our main course."

Grayson dismissed the jibe with a wave of his hand. "Water off a duck's back."

I'd been waiting for an opportunity to excuse myself to check in with Meg. She was responsible enough, but Clarence alternated between angel and devil. His bipolar nature plus his impressive doggie intelligence made him a worthy opponent. I hoped Meg hadn't gotten played.

Social clubs often didn't allow cellphone use in most public spaces within the building. After excusing myself, I headed downstairs one flight to the bar. After all, this was Washington

D.C. What respectable bar didn't allow a quick iPhone conversation?

The curved booth near the entrance was free so I ducked inside and whipped out my phone to text Meg.

How are you managing with Clarence?

Three dots indicated Meg was replying.

No comment.

Uh-oh. That didn't sound positive.

I wrote back immediately.

???

She responded with a photo instead of a text message. I clicked on the thumbnail to get a better look. A tan sandal that had been worked over by Clarence's teeth appeared.

What happened? I added a sad face emoticon to show Meg I felt her pain.

Likely writing a missive, Meg took a minute or two to answer. Sprinkled with a smattering of colorful expletives, her text explained that she'd taken Clarence out for a jog, just as we'd suggested. Clarence had waited until Meg jumped in the shower to carry out his clever canine caper. With shampoo in her hair, Meg felt as though someone was staring at her. She turned around, only to see that Clarence had peeked around the shower curtain with her sandal in his mouth. After brandishing his prize, he'd sprinted into the bedroom and proceeded to tear her shoe apart.

I rubbed my eyes.

I'll take you shopping soon. I added a smiley face.

Meg loved her fashion and had a quick temper. But she never stayed angry for long.

How's Buffy & Winston?

I typed back, *Surviving. Need to get back to dinner. Talk tomorrow.*

The bartender Charles appeared at the table. "Giving up this early on the conference?" He smirked playfully.

"No, I had to text my friend who's watching our dog this weekend. I'm headed back."

"Need a drink? I can fix you something that will make the rest of the night smooth sailing."

"A tempting offer, but I'd better keep my wits about me."

He gave me a polite salute, and I jogged back up the stairs. Hopefully no one had missed me. If I was really lucky, maybe the table conversation had turned in a more positive direction.

Edging unnoticed into my seat, I focused intently on my main course, which had just been served. The grilled Atlantic salmon smelled wonderful. While chomping away, I listened to the conversations around me. Drake had engaged in a passionate discussion with Buffy about tennis techniques. Mansfield was explaining his latest academic article to Winston Hollingsworth, who seemed to be in seventh heaven. Lola had monopolized Doug on the subject of politics, and my fiancé seemed in need of rescue.

I tapped him on his arm. "How's your steak?" Doug had opted for the more indulgent dinner choice.

"Excellent," he mumbled in between bites.

I lowered my voice. "What's the exit plan for this evening?"

"Exit plan?" he repeated.

"How long do we have to hang out? In case you haven't noticed, these people really don't like each other very much."

"What do you mean? Of course they do. The people at this table have been attending the annual Mayflower Society conference in cities across the country for the past two decades. They're old friends."

"With friends like that, who needs enemies?"

Doug shook his head. "It's nothing more than well-meaning competition. All these people are wildly successful and wealthy, Kit. Bragging is second nature to them."

It was an odd formula and certainly didn't resemble my friendships. Every once in a while Meg and I exchanged a barbed comment or two, but these people took sociable repartee to a new low.

I heard Buffy's voice. "Kit? Can you hear me across the table?"

"Yes, Mrs. Hollingsworth. I was just, um, enjoying my salmon." I shoved a big bite of fish inside my mouth.

"I'm glad you like it, dear. We need to go over the schedule. Grayson tells me a curator from Monticello is giving a lecture tomorrow morning after breakfast."

"That sounds wonderful." I tried to feign excitement. James Mansfield and Winston had stopped talking, and I felt the weight of the professor's stare. He could probably see right through me, just like those Yale undergrads he tortured on a daily basis.

Buffy clasped her hands together in excitement. "It's unfortunate we'll have to miss the talk."

"We will?" I looked quizzically at Doug. As far as I knew, the next two days were scheduled to the hilt—nonstop history overload. Maybe Doug's mother wanted to trade Monticello for shopping on M Street.

"Didn't Doug tell you? He was supposed to fill you in. The two of us," she motioned with her finger, "have an appointment with the events planner here at the Continental Club who specializes in weddings. It's the perfect opportunity to plan your once-in-a-lifetime event!"

Buffy could hardly contain her enthusiasm. She widened her eyes, already popping, thanks to expertly applied makeup.

Winston gave her a disapproving glance. "Really, Buffy. Did you ever think Kit might *want* to attend the lecture with Doug?"

From the look on Buffy's face, it was clear that notion hadn't crossed her mind. She huffed, "Of course, if Kit would rather attend the Mayflower event, I understand. However, it will be impossible to reschedule the appointment. Since we're not members, I had to rely on Cecilia for assistance."

I shot Cecilia a pleading glance. Surely she would empathize with the desperation I tried to silently convey.

No such luck. "You're right, Buffy. I'd keep the meeting. We had our wedding at the Continental Club and adored it, didn't we dear?"

Drake appeared more interested in his steak than reliving the details of his nuptials. His mouth full, he simply gave a thumbs-up with his left hand.

I could feel the weight of Doug's stare. There was no way out. "It can't hurt to talk to a professional planner," I said.

It was the best I could muster, but apparently it was enough. Buffy's face lit up like the White House Christmas tree. "Fabulous! Our meeting will take place after breakfast. Don't worry. We will join the rest of the group for the Mount Vernon tour in the afternoon."

Doug squeezed my knee in appreciation. I managed a tight smile in response before lifting my wine glass for a sizable chug.

Profiting from the lull in conversation, Grayson clinked his glass to attract everyone's undivided attention. "It gives me great pleasure to welcome my closest friends to another gathering of the Mayflower Society. Over the next several days, we will hear from historical experts and travel to several of our nation's most cherished landmarks and venues."

I stifled a yawn. The pre-dinner drinks and wine had begun to take their toll. Grayson's speech wasn't helping me stay awake, either.

"Before I say a few words to the entire society, I wanted to let you know that I plan to stand for another term in office as the Mayflower president."

A sideways glance at Winston Hollingsworth confirmed my suspicions. Doug's father didn't even bother to hide his annoyance. The rest of the table appeared indifferent. Drake fiddled with his phone, Cecilia checked her makeup with her pocket compact, Frederick asked the waiter for a wine refill,

Lola examined the printed program of scheduled events, and Professor Mansfield stared into space. Like me, Doug gazed at his father. He'd noticed Winston's grimace, too.

No pats on the back or congratulations followed Grayson's announcement. My future mother-in-law, who prided herself on her impeccable social graces, broke the uncomfortable silence. "The Mayflower Society is lucky to have you at the helm, Grayson." Her polite comment carried the weight of obligation.

"Thank you, Buffy. I'm sure the treasurer is especially happy to know my donation to the society will be secure for another year." He chuckled smugly at his own backhanded compliment.

Grayson's last remark must have been the last straw for Winston. "It's not required for the president of the Mayflower Society to donate more than the yearly dues, Grayson. And everyone at this table knows it."

Mansfield emerged from his daydream and perked up at Winston's comment. He rubbed his chin thoughtfully. "Winston has a point. Your generous support of Mayflower is appreciated, but it's not required for leadership."

Grayson's eyes narrowed. "Of course not. But my continued leadership and financial support keep these annual meetings affordable, especially for the less wealthy among us." He looked pointedly at Mansfield, who turned red with anger.

Lola Valdez chimed in, "I don't care about the money, but I do care about the direction of the Mayflower Society. This was never a politically conservative organization until you became its president, Grayson. You shouldn't be using it to further your own agenda."

This was getting interesting. Would anyone else register disapproval?

A hush fell over the table. Doug finally spoke. "Mr. Bancroft, can I ask where your wife is? Is she joining us for the meeting?"

Grayson looked grateful, as if Doug had thrown him a life

preserver. "Kiki returned last week from an extended trip to South America. She sends her regrets."

Cecilia piped up, "We'll miss her. Won't we, James?"

Professor Mansfield jerked his head upward when he heard his name. "Of course. Kiki always brightens up the Mayflower meetings."

Doug whispered, "Cecilia and Kiki have been lifelong friends. I'll tell you about Mansfield later."

I acknowledged Doug's private comment with a subtle smile.

Mansfield was the only other attendee at our table without a spouse. "Professor, will you be joined by a significant other?" I asked.

With a polite but irritated tenor to his voice, he replied, "No. I'm a bachelor." The terseness of his response implied he'd rather not entertain questions of a personal nature.

So much for raising a topic other than American history with the good professor. The wait staff began serving the dessert. Not a moment too soon. The sugar in the key lime cheesecake provided the only remnant of sweetness at our table.

After coffee arrived, Grayson Bancroft welcomed the entire room and promised an "intellectual feast of American history" during the conference. The dinner we'd enjoyed tonight had been none too shabby. As long as the food and drinks kept coming, the weekend held promise. Grayson also graciously accepted the society's nomination for another term. The actual election would take place at the end of the conference on Sunday. Doug's father remained silent throughout the whole affair, although if looks could kill, Winston Hollingsworth would be guilty as charged.

There was talk of after-dinner drinks at the bar. Cecilia and Drake led the charge, and others followed. Doug might have been enticed to have a port with his father, but I tugged at his sleeve, and he got the message. We excused ourselves after exchanging good night pleasantries.

"Where's our room?" I wondered.

Doug pulled out a key card. "Fourth floor."

An employee clearing the table must have overhead our conversation. "You are quite lucky."

Doug asked, "Why do you say that?"

She smiled kindly. "The mansion rooms on that floor are the most beautiful in the entire club."

"Let's go check it out," I said with enthusiasm.

We climbed the two floors and found our room, which was as impressive as promised. It included an antique king sized bed and a sitting room with sofa and high-backed chairs. The décor was old-fashioned, yet no amenity had been overlooked, including a self-service coffee machine, writing desk, and refinished modern bathroom.

"Your parents don't mess around," I said with a low whistle.

"They do not. Although I can't help but wonder if there's an ulterior motive at play."

I wrapped my arms around Doug. "Do you mean making me fall in love with the Continental Club so we'll have our wedding here?"

"I think so," Doug murmured before giving me a kiss.

"Let's play along for a few days."

Doug responded by turning off the lights.

Chapter Four

———

SUNLIGHT PEEKED THROUGH the decorative curtains inside our bedroom. It was that glorious time of the year when the days began earlier and stretched well into the evening. I pushed the button on my digital fitness band, which monitored steps walked, calories burned, stairs climbed, and hours slept. On my couch potato days, it scolded me. "GET MOVING KIT!" When virtue triumphed, it offered congratulations. "GOAL ACHIEVED KIT!" Quite frankly, its tone was a little bossy. But I couldn't toss it because it was also my wristwatch. I hit the main button and a bright "6:40" blinked back.

Drat. I'd slept longer than anticipated. Before drifting off, I'd had visions of squeezing in a jog before the day's scheduled events. Despite the exquisite accommodations and delicious food, spending the morning with a Continental Club wedding planner wasn't my idea of a jolly good time. A sweaty run would clear my mind and hopefully release much needed mood-enhancing endorphins. If I hurried, I could jog for thirty minutes and still have time to shower and dress for breakfast.

Doug was conked out. I dressed quickly in my exercise clothes and grabbed the room key card before quietly closing the door.

I skipped down two flights of stairs and arrived at the floor where we'd had dinner the night before. As I turned the corner past an antique grandfather clock, I spotted the portrait on the wall of Gertrude Harper, the granddaughter of the original mansion proprietors. I was no art historian, but I'd read that the Vermeer-influenced Frank Weston Benson had painted the comely twenty-four-year-old at the turn of the century. The National Gallery of Art owned the original oil painting, which had been on display in prominent places such as the vice-president's residence and the National Portrait Gallery. With no chance of acquiring the masterpiece, the Continental Club had commissioned an impressive reproduction.

I'd planned to examine the portrait last night. Impressionism, even the American version, was my favorite period of art. We hadn't lingered in the anteroom before or after dinner, so I'd given the painting no more than a passing glance.

Now I walked toward the mantelpiece to take a closer look. Gertrude really had been a beautiful young woman. The websites detailing the history of the building and the club hadn't exaggerated her enchanting smile and the long strokes used to depict her flowing white dress. She was the Continental Club's Mona Lisa.

My Fitbit buzzed, its annoying way of reminding me it was time to get moving. Somehow Gertrude Harper had managed to remain slim without jogging around Dupont Circle. I wasn't so fortunate.

I turned away from her portrait to head back toward the main staircase. In the far corner of the room near the entrance to the club's library, I spotted a man's dress shoe. *How odd.* The Continental Club wasn't the type of place where patrons had one too many glasses of wine and lost their footwear en route to bed. That went double for the Mayflower Society crowd who occupied the vast majority of suites inside the building.

Curiosity got the better of me. The library entrance was adjacent to another Continental Club treasure I'd wanted to check out, the bronze bust of Benjamin Franklin. During the Second World War, when the club met inside Dolley Madison's former house, the Franklin statue adorned the room where key discussions about nuclear fission and the atomic bomb took place. Now it resided on a perfectly engineered pedestal in front of a prominent arched window, inviting photographers strolling along the nearby street to take advantage of the striking profile it provided when the light was just right.

I didn't get much of a chance to admire Franklin or read the detailed inscription at the base of the statue. A guest who'd unwisely overindulged hadn't abandoned his shoe the night before. Instead, the shoe belonged to a man whose body lay flat on the floor of the library.

Chapter Five

———◆———

WITHOUT A MOMENT'S hesitation, I sprung to the man's side. The face was contorted, but I still recognized him. It was Grayson Bancroft, dressed in the same suit he'd worn to dinner. Obviously, Grayson never made it to bed last night. His skin was extremely pale. Not a good sign. Tentatively, I reached to feel for a pulse. After grasping his stone-cold hand for only a second, I recoiled. The president of the Mayflower Society was dead.

Now it was time to panic. The eerie silence consuming the entire building prevented me from letting out a scream. Instead, I scrambled around the corner and flew down the last flight of stairs to reach the main entrance. The concierge's desk sat empty. Didn't anyone start the day early in Washington, even at the Continental Club?

The delicious aroma of freshly baked rolls wafted in my direction. Of course, the Continental Club was a prime location for a Beltway power breakfast. I followed my nose, which led me to the entrance of the Garden Dining Room. Two well-dressed businessmen were waiting to be seated.

"Can someone help me?" I asked.

My black capri running pants, hoodie, and yellow tennis shoes didn't inspire confidence. The club's host took one look at me and wrinkled his nose.

"I'll be with you in a moment, ma'am. As soon as I seat these two gentlemen."

Given the circumstances, waiting was out of the question. "Sir, I'm sorry, but I need your assistance. NOW!" My voice was only a few decibels shy of a scream.

I'd gotten his attention. "Please, I have to ask you to wait your turn." The two men in suits shook their heads in disgust.

He'd left me no choice. I hadn't wanted to spoil breakfast for the eager diners. "There's a dead man upstairs. He's inside the library."

That did it. All three men stared at me, mouths agape. Given their reactions, I might as well have announced the arrival of Queen Elizabeth's corpse.

The host stammered, "What did you say?"

I cleared my throat and spoke in my clearest, most sophisticated voice. "His name is Grayson Bancroft. I don't know what happened to him, but someone might want to attend to the matter."

I turned on my heels and retreated. The club staffer followed behind, apparently deciding that the two guests were no longer a priority. When he caught up with me, he put his hand on my shoulder. "Can you show me …" his voice trailed off.

I turned to face him. "The body?"

He gulped. "Yes."

"Follow me." I motioned toward the stairs.

Once we reached the first floor landing, we continued past the portrait and reached Franklin's statue. I pointed in the direction of the library entrance. Fortunately, although not for Grayson, the body remained in exactly the same spot.

"He's the leader of the historical society group we're hosting for the next three days," the host stammered.

Despite my best efforts, I couldn't hide my exasperation. "That's what I was trying to tell you."

He knelt down beside Bancroft. "Are you sure he's dead?"

"I'm no medical examiner, but his hand is cold, and I can't detect a pulse. And he's not breathing."

"If you could, stay here. I'm going to call an ambulance and the police."

I nodded. If I'd had my phone, I could have texted Doug until the alerts on his device woke him. My best-laid plans for a jog had gone awry. I squatted next to the body for a closer look. The twisted features definitely belonged to the man I'd met the night before, enough to make a positive identification. Unfortunately, Bancroft didn't seem to be at peace.

Grayson had been in relatively good shape. His weight appeared average, and he was likely a few years shy of Medicare eligibility. If he'd suffered from an illness like cancer, the effects of such a serious disease certainly weren't apparent. Was it a heart attack? Perhaps he smoked. I got closer to his face and sniffed. I was particularly sensitive to the smell of cigarettes. Though I detected the lingering fragrance of men's cologne, perhaps Chanel, there was no hint of tobacco.

Something seemed odd about the placement of his body. If he'd been the victim of cardiac arrest, wouldn't he have fallen to the ground in a crumpled heap? Instead, Bancroft was lying perfectly flat on his back, arms and legs spread wide. It was as though he'd been in the middle of making a snow angel when he died.

I was tempted to close his wide-open eyes, which freaked me out. Common sense prevailed, and I kept my hands to myself. I got up and looked down the hallway past the portrait. No one was coming. Given the ashen hue of the dining room host after he saw Grayson's lifeless body, I assumed he'd opted to remain downstairs until the authorities arrived.

I returned to the library and bent down again. The expression on Bancroft's face seemed frozen, like something out of the ordinary had happened and he'd been unable to react. There was no way else to describe it. *Grayson Bancroft had been surprised to die.*

While staring at the expression of shock on Bancroft's face, I noticed a small red mark on the dead man's neck. It was on the left side, inches above the fitted collar of his button-down dress shirt. It was quite noticeable, and I was almost certain it hadn't been there the night before. Leaning over the body, I moved closer to his face for a better look. It wasn't a birthmark or mosquito bite. To my untrained eye, it appeared to be a puncture wound.

"Who are you and what are you doing?"

I drew back immediately at the sound of an authoritative female voice.

A petite woman whipped out a badge and flashed it. "Detective Maggie Glass. D.C. Metro Police."

I stood up and offered her my hand. "Kit Marshall. I discovered the body."

The detective was joined by several EMTs. Their visit would be brief because I was certain Grayson Bancroft was deceased. I moved away while the emergency medical personnel surrounded the body and confirmed the death. Glass motioned for me to exit the library.

The middle-aged detective was short in stature, but I could tell she meant business. Her brown hair was pulled back into a ponytail and she wore a fitted black suit that was professional yet also sporty in case a hot pursuit was called for. Silver button earrings provided a feminine touch. She pulled out a notebook and grabbed a pen from her jacket pocket.

"Ms. Marshall, you're a guest here at the Continental Club?"

I briefly described the reason for our visit and explained that I lived in the Washington D.C. metropolitan area.

"Where do you work?" Apparently even the District police asked this question as an opener. Maybe they also attended too many K Street cocktail parties.

"Capitol Hill. I work as the chief of staff for a member of the House of Representatives."

"A political type, I see. No surprises there. How did you come to discover the deceased?"

My workout attire corroborated my story, and Glass didn't question why I stumbled across Grayson.

She continued to write furiously in her notebook. Without looking up, she kept talking. "Only a few more questions, Ms. Marshall. This seems open and shut. The coroner will take it from here. It was most likely a heart attack or an aneurysm. We see these all the time in men of the deceased's age group."

Should I point out what I'd discovered? Detective Glass seemed like a woman who took her job seriously. She'd do a thorough job, but if Grayson got transported for an autopsy, who knew how long it would take for the medical examiner to alert the police to the possibility of foul play? At least twenty-four hours. At that point, the person responsible could have already escaped or covered any potentially incriminating tracks. Solving two other murders had taught me that time was of the essence. If Bancroft's death was a homicide, the investigation needed to start now.

I cleared my throat. That got Glass's attention. She glanced up from scribbling furiously into her notepad and asked, "Do you have something to add?"

"Detective, I'm sure you noticed the odd position of the body on the floor."

"Not really. I wanted to let our medical experts confirm the death. Let's take another look." She motioned with her pen that I should follow her inside the library.

Glass circled the body several times and paused to write in her notebook. She indicated that the medics should join us. "Fellas, does this look like a heart attack or an otherwise natural death to you?"

The younger guy shook his head. "Seems weird. It's like he hit the ground and froze."

The other EMT rubbed his chin. "Can't say I've seen anything exactly like this in real life. It reminds me of something I saw on cable TV."

"What do you mean?" I asked.

"You know, one of those channels with the historical documentaries. It's like that town in Italy where the volcano erupted thousands of years ago."

"Pompeii?" I offered.

He raised a triumphant forefinger. "You got it. Everyone was killed and then preserved instantly by ash. This guy looks like one of those unlucky people. Stopped dead in his tracks."

Glass stared at the paramedic for a long moment before speaking. "Well, one thing's for certain. There was no volcano in the middle of the Continental Club. So what killed him?"

The detective bent down to take a closer look. She immediately noticed the red mark on the dead man's neck and motioned for the History channel-watching medic to join her.

"What do you see here? Is it a wound? A bug bite?"

The paramedic hesitated, almost as if he wanted to tell Glass answering her question exceeded his pay grade. But he complied without protest, even whipping out a small penlight to shine on Bancroft's neck.

"I'm not a medical examiner, ma'am, but that's not from a mosquito," he concluded.

Glass grabbed the penlight and peered at the small blotch. "That's helpful. But what is it?"

"Maybe an injection site? You can see a dot in the center. There's a bit of blood around it."

Detective Glass must have agreed with the medic's conclusion. After examining Grayson's neck again, she leaned back and stood up. "Thank you for your help."

Everything had happened so fast, I hadn't had much time to think about the consequences of finding the mysterious mark on Bancroft's body. An odd and inauspicious start to my morning had suddenly turned into something more sinister.

Detective Glass jotted down more notes and tapped her pen to her forehead. To no one in particular, she stated the obvious. "I don't like how this is shaping up."

I drew nearer. "Detective, I'm clearly not going for a run this morning. Do you mind if I return to my room so I can speak with my fiancé and put on more appropriate clothes?"

With an absentminded sideways glance, Glass answered, "Of course." Then she quickly added, "Don't go anywhere else, Ms. Marshall. You may have just become a key witness to a murder."

I was no stranger to those fateful words.

Chapter Six

———

I RACED UP the two flights of stairs to the fourth floor. After fishing the key card out of my sports bra where I'd safely stowed it for my jog, I burst into the dark room. As I suspected, Doug hadn't budged an inch. The only sign of life was the sonorous wheezes emanating from the ornate four-poster. Considering the volume of Doug and Clarence's snoring, bedtime at home was like trying to fall asleep in the middle of Grand Central Station.

I hurried over to the bed. "Doug, wake up! I need to talk to you."

Doug rolled from his side onto his back, still in a deep fog. "Who are you?"

"Who else would I be? You need to wake up right now."

Doug flailed his arms in the direction of the nightstand. I grabbed his glasses and shoved them into his empty hand. "Put these on!" I ordered.

"Okay, I hear you. Just give me a second."

I turned on the bedside lamp. Doug raised his hands in protest as the room filled with bright light. He threw off the covers and got out of bed. "What's wrong with you, Kit?"

"Grayson Bancroft is dead."

Doug's eyes bulged. "He's what?"

"Dead. And it might be murder."

This revelation must have been too much for Doug at such an early hour. He sat down on the side of the bed. "Tell me what happened."

I recounted how I'd discovered the body and explained the unusual circumstances the detective and I had observed. I finished up with the supposition that a needle or fatal injection might have been the cause of death. Doug listened without comment. After I was done talking, my fiancé remained silent, a grave expression on his face.

"Aren't you going to say anything? What do you think?" Usually Doug wasn't shy about offering his opinion, especially when I got involved in a murder investigation. I braced myself for the lecture about the dangers of amateur sleuthing.

"What do you think the police will do next?" he asked.

"They'll probably establish a rough time of death. Then the detective will want to talk to other guests at the club to establish alibis or motives."

"That's what I thought. Come on, there's no time to lose. We need to get cleaned up and head downstairs so we can find out what's going on."

"Wait a second. I did promise Detective Glass I'd return for more questioning. But what's the rush?" I was confused by Doug's reaction. When it came to murder, he usually steered me in the opposite direction. My snooping gave him more heartburn than a spicy burrito.

"I have my reasons." Doug immediately headed for the bathroom and turned on the shower. Less than five minutes later, he emerged and dressed swiftly. As he left, he called over his shoulder, "I'll meet you downstairs."

The door closed behind him. I'd known Doug for many years before we'd decided to find jobs in the same city, move in together, and get engaged. His behavior was always measured, fiercely loyal, and unfailingly cautious. This strange and decisive reaction caught me off guard. Something was up, and it had to be connected to Grayson Bancroft's untimely death.

After getting ready, I decided to call Meg. I'd planned to touch base with her later today to make sure Clarence hadn't engaged in any more canine vandalism. Taking Meg shoe shopping to replace the ruined shoes wouldn't be a cheap enterprise. Hopefully, Clarence had kept his paws and jaws to himself for the remainder of the evening. The hint of a murder, however, meant that I couldn't wait to speak with my best friend and fellow gumshoe until the afternoon.

I punched the button on my iPhone to dial Meg and a photo of her with a glass of bubbly appeared. She would have appreciated last night's refreshments, for sure.

She answered after one ring. "Hey, what's up? I'm just leaving for work."

"I'm glad I caught you before you got on the Metro. We need to chat."

Meg's voice turned anxious. "Did you hear from the boss? Is something wrong in China?"

"Nothing like that. But I discovered a dead body this morning, and all signs point to foul play."

Meg's angst transformed to excitement as she squealed, "Who was it? Tell me everything!"

Once again, I recounted the details of this morning's escapade. After I was done, Meg exclaimed, "It's not fair!"

That was the second odd reaction to my story. "What isn't fair, Meg?"

"You're going to investigate another murder, and I'm stuck babysitting the office during a boring congressional recess." I could practically hear the pout in her voice.

Meg could be a little high maintenance at times, particularly when she thought she was missing out on an adventure. "Who said anything about investigating? I had good reasons to get involved in the two murders we encountered on Capitol Hill.

The detective on this one seems well equipped to figure out who did this."

"Give me a break, Kit. You're not the least bit interested in solving another homicide? It's practically your second job."

Sometimes Meg knew me better than I knew myself. "I'll admit that I'm curious. But Glass might have this wrapped up by the end of the day."

"We'll see. Do you think it was poison?"

"Could be. Or something that paralyzed him? His body reminded me of Han Solo frozen in carbonite."

Meg giggled. "Then it's easy to solve it, silly."

"Go ahead."

"Just find Jabba the Hutt." Then Meg provided her best imitation of the infamous chortle.

"In the entire galaxy, you are the least likely person to impersonate Jabba the Hutt." I was referring to Meg's slim shape, which she managed to retain even as she ate and drank whatever she pleased.

"I'd better leave for work so I'm not late. You know, I'm the boss today."

"You'll do great. Do you have plans tonight?"

"Nope. Capitol Hill is deader than a doornail, uh, maybe 'dead' is not an apt description, under the circumstances." During the two-week spring recess, Congress came to a standstill as lawmakers left town and lobbyists, journalists, and many staffers took a break from the daily grind.

"Maybe you can join us for dinner. Let me check the schedule." I grabbed the printed program we'd received last night outlining the Mayflower Society activities.

"I'll have to tend to Clarence before I can meet you."

"I almost forgot. How is my devil dog?"

"He behaved the rest of the night after we had a heart to heart discussion about the destruction of Nordstrom footwear."

"Don't worry. There's a new pair in Pentagon City Mall with your name on them."

"I'm not concerned. After our unfortunate incident, Clarence and I made up."

"Really?" Today was full of surprises. First, Doug sprinted to the scene of a murder. Now Meg had found a new four-legged friend.

"We shared a bag of popcorn while watching a Netflix rom-com. He even snuggled with me."

Meg was currently between paramours, so perhaps Clarence could provide her with precisely the TLC she needed. "Not to change the subject, but we are scheduled to have dinner on our own tonight. So feel free to join us."

With a discernible degree of suspicion, Meg asked, "With Doug's parents? Won't your future mother-in-law want to talk about the wedding?"

Meg was finding it difficult to adjust to my betrothed status. She'd come around in the past few months, but she was in no hurry for me to walk down the aisle.

"Yes, and you can provide the perfect antidote. Who knows? Maybe Bancroft's death will trump her fascination with making my wedding the premiere social event of the season."

"I'll drink to that," Meg replied sarcastically. "Now I seriously need to motor or all hell will break loose in the office. Junior congressional staff cannot be left unsupervised, even during recess."

Meg spoke the truth. "I'll text to let you know our plans."

"Okey-dokey. Don't worry about the office. Just focus on the wedding machinations and the murder."

"Thanks, Meg. See you later."

I clicked off my phone. I'd better return to the crime scene to determine why Doug was so motivated to find out what happened to poor Grayson Bancroft.

For the second time today, I raced down the stairs to the library. The crowd surrounding the deceased had grown considerably. Breakfast was scheduled for nine. Pretty soon, the august members of the Mayflower Society would discover their fearless leader was dead.

Doug was on the fringes of the police throng inside the library. He signaled me and walked toward the statue of Franklin. If someone strolling outside took a photo of the famous sculpture today, he'd likely catch the outline of a police officer next to it.

Doug sounded panicked. "What took you so long? This is a disaster. The evidence is mounting in the direction of murder."

"Did Detective Glass find something else?" I asked.

"When the medical examiner arrived, they went through his pockets for identification. They found a typewritten note asking Grayson to meet at midnight by the statue."

This was getting more interesting by the minute. "The killer passed him the note, luring Bancroft to his death. Is that what the police think?"

Doug nodded. "The detective talked for a while with the medical examiner. I overheard their whole conversation."

"Overheard?" I raised my eyebrows. Who was this man and what had he done with fiancé? Doug had many talents. Spying wasn't one of them.

"I eavesdropped. Nobody paid any attention to me, so I got all the important information. It's impossible to determine an exact time of death, but the medical examiner said midnight fits into his timetable. The body temperature and stage of rigor mortis supports the theory that whomever sent Grayson the note killed him."

"They agreed this was a murder?"

Doug wrung his hands. "That's their working hypothesis. I think it might be officially ruled a suspicious death for now. But the medical examiner believes the odd position of the body suggests something other than a natural death."

"Did they mention the small wound on his neck?"

"It's definitely the site of a puncture, but the medical examiner couldn't say for certain what caused it."

"The most obvious explanation is the killer stuck Grayson with a syringe filled with a poison," I said.

Doug pursed his lips and grabbed my arm, dragging me farther away from the library. "That's what I'm afraid of."

I'd had enough. It was time to find out why Doug felt the need to snoop. "Why are you so hell-bent on learning everything about this murder? You're the one who's always telling me I should mind my own business and not get involved in catching killers. Did you take a potion last night and wake up as Encyclopedia Brown?" My question wasn't far-fetched. Appearance-wise, Doug resembled an older, refined version of the famous boy detective.

"Lower your voice," he insisted.

"Why are you being secretive? Did you kill Grayson Bancroft?"

To my surprise, Doug remained silent for a long moment before answering. "No, I didn't. It's my father I'm trying to protect."

"Your father? Winston Hollingsworth?"

"The one and only."

"Your father resented Grayson because he wanted to become the president of the Mayflower Society. Surely that's not a reason to charge him with the murder."

"It's not. That's not the only problem, though."

This conversation had begun to remind me of a long, painful tooth extraction. "Doug, tell me why you think your father is going to be accused of the crime."

"The weapon. My father has access to syringes."

Now I was confused. The Hollingsworths were Boston lawyers, not medical doctors. "How? He doesn't have an illicit habit, does he?" Somehow I couldn't imagine Winston Hollingsworth removing his smoking jacket and Brooks Brothers button-down dress shirt to engage in intravenous drug use.

"Certainly not! He's a diabetic."

I narrowed my eyes. "You never told me."

"He doesn't like to tell people if he can avoid it. He tries to keep it under control through diet. His routine is one shot in the evening. He always travels with at least a dozen syringes," Doug explained.

I sighed deeply. My sleuthing had definitely rubbed off on Doug. "So you think your father is a likely suspect because he had a solid motive and a means to kill Grayson Bancroft."

Doug massaged his temples. "Don't you agree?"

I considered the facts. It wasn't an open-and-shut case, but we both knew from firsthand experience the police often focused on the most obvious suspect. It could prove difficult, if not impossible, to get law enforcement to reconsider new leads once they'd fixed on a likely collar.

Opening my purse, I found a small, round bottle. I plunked two blue pills into Doug's hand. "Take these. It will help with your headache."

Doug clasped them and scurried off, likely in search of a cup of water so he could ingest the medicine and prevent the onslaught of a full migraine. We'd need both brains operating at full capacity if Winston Hollingsworth became a credible suspect.

Detective Glass was deep in conversation with a uniformed police officer. When she finished with him, I approached. "Detective, thank you for allowing me a few minutes to freshen up. Do you need to ask me additional questions?"

Glass turned to face me. "Ms. Marshall, was that your fiancé I saw a few minutes ago? A man approximately your age with thick brown hair and glasses?"

Doug had been mistaken. He hadn't eluded detection. "Yes, it was. When I told him what happened, he came downstairs to monitor the situation."

A weak excuse, but better than telling Glass he was concerned his father would be fingered for the murder. Her chin jutted out, and she remained silent. In a noncommittal tone, she said, "Interesting. Most people run away from murders."

Perhaps Maggie Glass needed to know my background. "Most people, yes. I've been involved with two high-profile murders in the past year on Capitol Hill. I guess my inner gumshoe has rubbed off on Doug." I pasted a forced smile on my face.

"That sounds familiar. I try to keep up with all the big crimes in the city, even the ones outside D.C. Metro's jurisdiction. Do you have a contact with the Capitol Hill police?"

"Detective O'Halloran."

"Good to know. I do have a few more questions for you."

"Certainly, Detective."

"Can you account for your whereabouts last night after the dinner concluded?"

"Doug and I went to our room and didn't leave until I decided to head out for an early morning jog."

"You didn't leave the room? Not once? For a drink downstairs or to speak with another Mayflower Society attendee?"

"Nope. We really don't know many people here except Doug's parents. They invited us as their guests."

Glass wrote down my answers in her notebook. "Did you hear anything outside your room last night?"

"It was quiet. I didn't hear a peep."

"Are you sure, Ms. Marshall? Given your track record with the Capitol Hill murders, you must possess an impressive degree of observational skills. You can remember nothing out of the ordinary?"

"Well, we were um, busy, in the room, and then we both fell asleep." I felt my face flush.

An amused Glass gave me a knowing glance. "I suppose your fiancé will corroborate this story?"

"It takes two to tango."

My last remark was too much information for the detective. "Thank you, Ms. Marshall. The other guests are arriving for breakfast, and I need to assemble my team for interviews and room searches." Glass turned to walk away, and I suppressed a gasp.

"Detective, did you say room searches?"

"Yes, of course. There's no sign of forced entry from last night. The Continental Club maintains an excellent surveillance system, and we'll scour those cameras to make sure no one entered the building through an unlocked window or door. Assuming that didn't occur, we'll focus our efforts on the guests who were staying at the club last night."

"What are you looking for?"

Glass crossed her arms and countered, "Why do you want to know?"

"No particular reason. Do you have a working hypothesis to explain how Bancroft died?"

Glass moved closer. "You saw the body. There's a puncture wound on his neck but no other signs of physical violence. What would you conclude, Ms. Marshall?"

Our eyes locked before I answered, "Someone stuck him with a lethal dose of poison."

"That would be a reasonable deduction. Please excuse me. I don't want the other guests to learn too much before I have a chance to question them." Glass hustled off at a pace rivaling that of Speedy Gonzales.

Doug reappeared, and I shared the bad news about the room searches.

His face fell. "Any appetite I had for breakfast is lost, but perhaps we'd better head there so we can warn my parents?"

"Absolutely." My stomach rumbled at the mention of food. Sure, I was concerned about Doug's father and clearing him as a suspect. But no one can think clearly when hungry.

As we wandered into the foyer near the full-length portrait of Gertrude Harper, Bonnie appeared. "Can you tell us where breakfast is this morning? Was it cancelled?" Doug asked.

Bonnie was a bit the worse for wear. Her hair was a mess and her untucked blouse hung out over her pencil skirt. Slouching against the door leading to the ballroom, she seemed surprised by Doug's question. "Of course it's taking place as planned, Dr. Hollingsworth. The Continental Club apologizes for this inconvenience."

I couldn't bite my tongue. "Little more than an 'inconvenience,' isn't it? Someone has been murdered."

Bonnie shifted her feet and stumbled. "Don't say that! It may be suspicious circumstances, but surely not murder."

"Sorry, Bonnie. Kit is right. The police think someone killed Grayson Bancroft last night. Most likely a guest of the club," said Doug.

At this pronouncement, Bonnie backed away into the ballroom. "That's not possible. No one has ever been murdered at the Continental Club."

"There's a first time for everything. We'd better catch up with Doug's parents at breakfast. Where is it?" I asked.

"We had to move it downstairs to the Green Dining Room. It's between the larger dining room and the bar."

We thanked Bonnie and headed downstairs. Following the sound of voices, we found the relocated Mayflower Society breakfast in a small enclave that had been walled off from the area where club members and their guests were assembling for Washington D.C. power breakfasts. How many Pulitzer Prize ideas had been exchanged over coffee and freshly baked rolls?

The sequestration of our morning meal was no accident. Had the police insisted on privacy while they interrogated the Mayflower Society attendees? Or had the Continental Club thought it best to separate murder suspects from the rest of the well-heeled crowd?

The delicious smell of eggs and bacon lured us in the direction of the dining room. Before we could open the door, I heard familiar voices. Cecilia Rose and her husband Drake were inside the bar, chatting with the chummy bartender from last night, Charles.

I whispered to Doug. "I'll join you at breakfast in a few minutes." He followed my gaze and nodded.

Cecilia and Drake were sitting on high-backed stools, their elbows resting on the bar while they sipped their drinks. Charles leaned over the countertop, deep in conversation with the couple. I walked over to the trio and announced my presence. "I'd say good morning to everyone, but that doesn't quite seem appropriate, given the circumstances."

"I'll drink to that." Cecilia raised her glass, and Drake joined her.

"Would you like a Bloody Mary, Kit? These two are getting ahead of the day by indulging in my favorite recipe, even though the bar isn't officially open." Charles winked playfully.

I was no stranger to libations. Sometimes I thought Doug and I singlehandedly supported the entire Northern and Shenandoah wine regions of Virginia. That said, I refrained from drinking in the morning, particularly Bloody Marys. My palate didn't favor the combination of vodka, tomato juice, and spices.

"No, thank you. I'll take something with caffeine."

"My Bloody Mary recipe is as good as it gets."

"Sorry, Charles. I'll have a cup of that coffee brewing behind you."

The eager bartender barely masked his disappointment. Nonetheless, he poured me a steaming cup of java and pushed the cream and sugar packets my way.

I turned toward Cecilia and stated the obvious, "You must be very upset about Grayson's death."

Cecilia stared at her drink before answering. "I'm not sure I can articulate my feelings. I'm in shock. I've known Grayson for decades."

"From the Mayflower Society?" I asked.

"No, much further back than that. Grayson and I met when we were both trying to make our respective fortunes. Grayson was climbing the corporate ladder, and I was desperately trying to establish myself as a fiction writer." She smoothed her shiny brown hair, showing off her perfectly manicured nails.

"You've been friends for a long time, then."

"Friends, lovers, business associates. You name it, we've done it."

I was taken aback by Cecilia's matter-of-fact tone. I snuck a peek at Drake, who seemed preoccupied with his drink.

"You had a romantic relationship with Grayson."

"Of course, darling. Everyone knows that. Savannah's main romantic interest in my series was inspired by Grayson Bancroft." She smiled devilishly.

"Fascinating," I murmured.

Drake appeared completely uninterested in Cecilia's stroll down memory lane, even if it included a revealing description of a significant notch on her bedpost. Cecilia might as well have been talking about the weather or what she ate for breakfast.

"Drake, did you know Grayson Bancroft?" I asked.

His eyes, already glassy from the morning's indulgence, shifted from his almost empty Bloody Mary glass to the two of us. Perhaps he wasn't used to being included in the conversation. "Until last night I'd only met him in passing."

I sipped my steaming cup of coffee, thankful that caffeine was now coursing through my veins and clearing the morning fog. I never scheduled early morning meetings on Capitol Hill without making sure coffee was available or easily obtainable. Some chemical dependencies were perfectly acceptable, and coffee was fortunately in that category.

"What did you think of him?" The question was slightly inappropriate, but without it, I'd learn nothing from Drake, who seemed to struggle with adult conversation.

Drake ran his hands through his golden hair. "Cecilia has a past with him. Then he owned her publisher, so that complicated matters."

So Drake wasn't totally clueless. I turned to Cecilia. "Grayson wanted to talk with you about the next Savannah book. Were you able to speak with him last night?"

Cecilia motioned to Charles for another drink. Knowing refills would be welcome, he had prepared a large pitcher and poured her another glass.

After taking a sip of the refresh, Cecilia replied, "No, we didn't. After the dinner ended, Drake and I came down to the bar for a nightcap. Then we headed upstairs and went directly to bed. Right, darling?"

"That's what happened. I must have been tired because I slept really well last night. Didn't hear a peep until the wakeup call from the front desk woke us at eight."

"We're both incredibly sound sleepers, aren't we? Completely dead to the world, no disrespect intended. It's the busy lifestyle, amongst other nighttime activities. Right, darling?" Cecilia gave me a knowing glance.

Asking a romance writer about her sex life was like asking Donald Trump how he felt about his hair. You just didn't go there.

"Your writing career must be demanding," I commented.

"You don't know the half of it. Between appearances, signings, blogs, fan conventions, and writing the next book, it's absolutely *craaaaazy*." She drew out the last word for emphasis. The second Bloody Mary was talking.

Drake chimed in. "Sometimes she misses our couples' tennis lessons."

Cecilia sighed. "Someone has to pay for all this." She gave a broad sweep of her hand.

Charles had remained silent in the background until now. "And we're glad you frequently patronize the Continental Club, Ms. Rose."

"Thank you. It's nice to be appreciated." Cecilia delivered this last line with dramatic flair worthy of a Tony Award.

Breakfast couldn't be delayed too much longer. First, there was my rumbling tummy. Second, I needed to check on Doug to make sure he'd apprised his parents, particularly his father, of the delicate situation brewing. On the other hand, this was a fortuitous situation, especially since Cecilia and Drake had both proven to have loose lips. One or two more questions should do it.

I wondered out loud. "Do you think someone notified Grayson's wife?"

Cecilia perked up. "Kiki? James Mansfield probably beat the police to the punch."

I sipped the last of my coffee and indicated with a hand on top of the mug I didn't want a refill. "What do you mean?"

"Not to put too fine a point on it, but everyone knows about the longstanding affair of the heart between Professor Mansfield and Kiki Bancroft."

"Not me," I offered.

"Me either," said Drake.

Cecilia dismissed our ignorance with wave of her hand. "I mean everyone who is anyone, darlings."

Cecilia certainly had a winning personality. Still, this was getting more interesting by the minute. "Kiki was committing adultery?" I asked.

Cecilia wavered. "That's the popular way of describing it. Despite our friendship, I never asked for the sordid details." Cecilia leaned closer. "But most people viewed it as more of an emotional love affair."

I rubbed my temple. "An emotional love affair?"

Cecilia's lip curled. "Yes. I wouldn't expect someone at your stage of life to understand."

Thank goodness, Drake saved the day. "I don't know what you mean, either."

"Let the best-selling romance novelist explain love to two naïfs. It's a complicated business. James and Kiki have a deep connection that transcends physical expression. They're soul mates."

"So they weren't sleeping together?" I clarified.

Cecilia looked sharply at me. "I have no idea what they do in the bedroom. That's beside the point. The focus of their relationship is on emotional intimacy and attachment."

After taking another swig, Drake spoke. "So they talked a lot but didn't have sex."

Cecilia pounded her fist on the bar. "Neither of you understand. You should both hole up in your rooms with my books so you'd learn something about *affaires de coeur*."

I'd never been taken to task by a romance novelist before, but there was a first time for everything. A graceful exit was in order. "I'm clearly lacking experience in this department. Thank you, Cecilia and Drake. It has been a pleasure chatting with you this morning. You have my condolences about Grayson."

They raised their glasses in polite acknowledgment. The police needed to speak with them, but Detective Glass had better hurry. One more round of Blood Marys and she'd likely lose the opportunity to conduct a coherent interview with either of my drinking companions.

Chapter Seven

————

I SAUNTERED ACROSS the hallway to rejoin the Mayflower Society. A beautiful spread of breakfast foods had been arranged as a buffet. Fruits, eggs, pancakes, bakery items, and oatmeal called my name. I spotted Doug in the center of the room, deep in conversation with his parents. Best to fill my plate first and then head over for a potentially riveting convo with my future in-laws. Wedding chatter annoyed me, and I was no fan of high society protocol. However, while stacking my plate with a delectable array of smoked salmon, cream cheese, and a bulky New York bagel, I silently hoped that my father-in-law wouldn't be clad in a prison jumpsuit when Doug and I eventually said our 'I dos.'

Judging by the hardly touched food on the plates of the Hollingsworths, they'd lost their appetites. Etiquette dictated that I restrain myself since they weren't eating. But then the salty salmon aroma wafted up to my nose. No point in resisting. Besides, leaving so much tasty food on my plate would be wasteful. My parents would not approve.

The volume of their voices barely exceeded a whisper. I leaned in closer so I could follow the conversation. Buffy was saying, "Are you sure we shouldn't just throw the syringes out? We can put them in the Dumpster behind the club."

Doug shook his head vehemently. "That won't work, Mother. The police will search this entire city block."

Winston agreed. "Remember how I make my living, dear. I'm a member of the Massachusetts state bar. If I tamper with evidence, I'll be tossed out immediately."

Buffy wasn't convinced. "Better to be disbarred than in prison."

After swallowing a piece of bagel and clearing my throat, I interjected, "Sorry I wasn't here for the whole conversation, but why are you talking about throwing out the syringes? You have a perfectly good reason to have them. There's no need to contemplate discarding them," I took a sip of my coffee, "unless, of course, you killed Grayson Bancroft."

I'd meant the last sentence as a wry joke. Three pairs of eyes stared at me in stony silence. Obviously, my attempt to lighten the mood had failed. I should have known. Joviality wasn't high on the list for Buffy and Winston.

Doug broke the hush. "You're going to have to comply with the police's requests. Kit's right. Doing something rash will only make them suspect you more."

At that moment, Detective Glass introduced herself to the Mayflower Society attendees and explained that everyone was now part of an ongoing suspicious death investigation.

Lola Valdez raised her hand and Glass acknowledged her. "We are heartbroken over Grayson's death. However, many attendees want to know if today's events will be allowed to continue as planned."

The detective's lips twitched. She'd been expecting this question. "This morning's lecture has been cancelled since we will be conducting room searches and interviews with each of you about your whereabouts last night. However, barring any big breaks in the case, the afternoon trip to Mount Vernon will proceed as scheduled."

A murmur broke out within the room. The chatter indicated people were annoyed, but most seemed satisfied that the excursion to George Washington's mansion was still on.

Buffy Hollingsworth raised her hand. "Excuse me, Detective. But my future daughter-in-law and I have an important appointment with a wedding planner this morning at the Continental Club. We will need to keep that commitment."

Had Buffy lost her mind? Her husband was about to become the prime suspect in the murder of one of the wealthiest men in the United States, and she was concerned about sealing the deal for our wedding? I clenched my fists underneath the table and shot Doug an incredulous glare.

He shook his head slowly but said nothing. Glass raised her eyebrows but kept her voice even. "I understand, ma'am. Talk to one of our officers, and we'll see what we can do."

Buffy made an immediate beeline for the cop standing closest to the detective. Her gesticulations indicated she was intent on keeping our appointment.

"Doug," I hissed, "wouldn't it make more sense if I could listen to the questions the detective asked your parents? Particularly your father."

His features tight with resignation, Doug said, "I agree with you, but it's best not to agitate Mother now. She's already annoyed with the whole situation."

"I can't wait to see her at the murder trial," I mumbled.

Buffy rejoined us, sporting a confident smile. "We're all set. Let's go, Kit. We don't want to be late." She pointed toward the door.

"Wait a second. Don't you need to talk to the police?" I asked.

"Of course. Despite our station in life, I can't expect different treatment. I'll talk with them after our meeting."

Clearly Buffy Hollingsworth believed the concept of 'equality' offered a little wiggle room. Doug pursed his lips but said nothing. In a forced voice, Winston said, "You and Kit should enjoy yourselves. I'll be fine."

At least Doug could provide moral support. "Be sure to stay with your father when the police search the room and ask him questions," I said.

"I'll keep my eyes and ears open," Doug promised.

Buffy gently put her hand under my elbow and steered me toward the door. It took considerable inner fortitude to resist jerking my arm back and telling Buffy to stuff her wedding meeting where the sun doesn't shine. Instead, I willed my fists to unclench as we headed down the hallway. Hopefully, Doug had picked up a few of my sleuthing tricks, and he'd figure out if the police considered Winston a credible suspect.

We ended up in a small business office. No surprise, Bonnie greeted us. I'd already figured this whole Mayflower Society sojourn had been one big setup to facilitate a firm plan for our wedding. I remembered my "play nice" pledge to Doug yesterday evening, although now that a murder was in the mix, I had my doubts about its lasting wisdom.

Bonnie soon passed us off to a middle-aged woman dressed in a spring crepe pantsuit. A designer scarf, which she'd twisted into a fancy knot, complemented her outfit. How did women manage to contort scarves into elaborate masterpieces? She looked like someone who had perfected at least thirty specialty knots on her vast neckwear collection. *French knot, double-sided twist? Not a problem.*

Our host spoke first. "My name is Tammy, and I'm an event planner at the Continental Club." Turning to me, she added, "Congratulations on your engagement, Kit. What an exciting time."

Almost as exciting as a dead body showing up in the upstairs library. But I stifled my inner snark and kept it simple. "Thanks, Tammy."

She pulled out a folder with several brochures inside. "The Continental Club is one of the premiere venues for a Washington D.C. wedding. Do you have a date in mind?"

Before I could speak, Buffy answered, "A fall wedding is

ideal, isn't it? Especially with the weather around here."

Tammy perked up. "Absolutely. Autumn is the perfect choice. It gives you all the advantages of a shoulder season but it's not as demanding as the springtime."

Buffy added, "Plus, the fall colors are lovely." She turned her head in my direction. "Kit's brown hair and coloring might look best with those hues. Blondes have the advantage in the springtime."

Tammy listened intently. "I like your thinking, Mrs. Hollingsworth. After all, this is the bride's day."

I slumped in my chair, at a loss for words. Where was Meg when I needed her? Thank goodness I'd invited her along for dinner tonight.

Tammy and Buffy embarked on an extended discussion covering food and drink options, overnight accommodations for guests, string quartets, seating arrangements, chefs, and cakes. I listened halfheartedly. No one directly asked my opinion, which was fortunate, since I had none to offer. My mind wandered to other topics, namely Grayson Bancroft's murder. The trip to Mount Vernon would be a good opportunity to talk to others who knew Grayson and could be considered suspects. The police would need to pursue top leads, but that didn't mean Doug and I couldn't spring into action and develop our own theories.

Buffy interrupted my contemplation. "Kit, Kit. Are you listening? Do you plan to buy a dress with a long train? That will affect the setup of the aisle for the ceremony."

Enough was enough. I'd held my tongue and played along with the charade of a high society wedding. It wasn't fair to Tammy, or Buffy for that matter, to believe I was interested in all the fancy trappings they were debating.

I took a deep breath. "I have no idea what type of dress I'll wear on my wedding day. In fact, the only thing I'm certain about is marrying Doug. Nothing else matters, quite frankly."

Two faces slack with utter astonishment stared back at me.

I'd managed to silence both Tammy and Buffy, an almost impossible feat. Our most skilled CIA interrogators would have failed where I'd succeeded. They didn't know the right pressure point.

Tammy straightened in her chair. "It's quite normal to feel overwhelmed as a bride." She whispered to Buffy, "I see this all the time."

"I do feel overwhelmed, Tammy. As you must know, a man was found murdered this morning. I discovered the body."

Tammy gasped. "I had no idea! You poor girl!" She reached across the table and gave me a shoulder hug.

I felt the tide changing in my favor. "It's very hard to focus." For dramatic effect, I fished a Kleenex out of my purse and dabbed my eyes. I sneaked a peek at Buffy. She was fuming.

"Perhaps we should postpone this meeting until our bride is in a more festive mood." Tammy closed her numerous binders filled with sample menus, table decorations, and floral arrangements.

"Thank you for being so considerate." I clasped Tammy's hand and shook it politely.

Buffy glared. "We appreciate your time. The Continental Club remains a top choice for this wedding." Buffy pronounced the last sentence with defiance comparable to Martin Luther nailing the Ninety-Five Theses to the church door in Wittenberg.

Buffy didn't speak until we entered the Continental Club lobby. Then she unleashed. "Kit, I need to ask you an important question. Do you want to marry my son?"

A direct question deserved a direct answer. "I do, Mrs. Hollingsworth."

"Then why aren't you showing more enthusiasm about planning this wedding?" Buffy sounded more hurt than angry.

"You're confusing the wedding planning with my excitement about marrying Doug."

"Why aren't you interested in both, Kit?"

"I wasn't lying to Tammy. I'm overwhelmed." I lowered my eyes. Surely I'd made my point of view clear.

Buffy studied me carefully. "Well, my dear, you'd better get over it."

I leveled my gaze. "What do you mean?"

"You're marrying a Hollingsworth. We're in our fifth century of residence in North America. That lineage brings with it a certain station in life and participation in societal events."

I pursed my lips. "Doug usually runs away from those types of functions. He doesn't even like going to his department's holiday party."

"We all know Doug's proclivities. But one day, he and his brothers will be expected to lead this family and uphold the Hollingsworth name."

"What does that have to do with my wedding?"

Buffy sighed. She was the dame of the American gentry, and I was her lost cause. "It will introduce you and Doug as a couple to the people who matter, Kit."

Buffy's choice of words stung. I doubted we agreed on who belonged in the group of "people who matter." I'd said enough already. It was best to end the conversation. "Mrs. Hollingsworth, I need to use my phone, so please excuse me."

As I darted inside the adjacent room, I heard her voice behind me, "Call me Buffy, darling. We'll chat more later!"

I had to credit Buffy with persistence. The woman didn't take no for an answer. Thank goodness cell use was restricted inside the club. It had been a convenient excuse for escape. I whipped out my phone to text Doug.

Where are you?

My parents' room

Which is?

401

On my way

I ran up three flights of stairs, taking two at a time. Missing my morning jog wouldn't matter if this mystery forced me to run between floors all day long.

Located at the end of the hallway, Room 401 was right next to the stairwell. The door was wide open so I walked inside. Apparently, my timing could not have been better. Wearing gloves, a police officer held a package of Winston's diabetic syringes. Detective Glass leaned in to inspect her colleague's discovery.

Indulging in an old habit he couldn't quite break, Doug was chewing on one of his fingernails. Winston stood next to him, sporting a surprisingly placid expression for a man who had just moved to the top of the suspect list for murder.

Glass pointed to the box. "Bag it. Continue to search the room for other pieces of evidence."

Over her shoulder, she spotted me. "Well, well. The whole family is here now." In a voice dripping with sarcasm, she asked, "How was the wedding planning?"

"We decided to table it, given the circumstances."

Doug perked up. "My mother agreed to a postponement?"

"It was best for all involved," I said wryly.

Winston guffawed and slapped a hand on his leg. "I would have paid a thousand dollars to be a fly on the wall."

Doug glared at his father's incongruous comment. Didn't Winston care that the police had discovered what they believed was the murder weapon?

"I hate to break up this party, but I'd like to question Mr. Hollingsworth again," said Detective Glass. She pointed to the syringes. "In light of our discovery."

"Father, perhaps you should call an attorney?" Doug's face had turned red faster than a traffic light on Pennsylvania Avenue.

"Hogwash. I've done nothing wrong." Winston directed his response to Detective Glass. "I'd be happy to answer your questions."

"This room is getting a little crowded. Do you mind coming downstairs with me?" she asked.

"Certainly, Detective." Winston grabbed a pen and the pad of paper provided by the Continental Club and inserted it inside his coat pocket. At least he was smart enough to know he should take notes about the questions she asked.

"Perhaps I should join you," said Doug.

Detective Glass replied quickly. "No need. This won't take long."

Winston motioned for Doug to stay put. Without protest, Doug sat in an overstuffed armchair. I went over to join him.

In a low voice, I said, "Don't worry. The evidence is circumstantial."

"I'm not worried about what Father will say. He's smart. But Detective Glass has been talking to the other Mayflower Society members."

"And …?" I pressed.

"No one despised Grayson Bancroft more than my father. He made no bones about it, Kit."

I sat on the side of the chair and put my arm around Doug's shoulder. "You're wrong, Doug. Someone hated him more than your father. When we figure out who that person is, we'll know who killed Grayson Bancroft."

Chapter Eight

———❦———

W E STILL HAD an hour to kill before the Mayflower Society tour of Mount Vernon departed. Doug reported that his headache had been reduced to a dull throb. Nonetheless, he opted to rest in our room and regain his strength before our afternoon sojourn. I, on the other hand, was antsy and missing my exercise regimen. If I stayed in the room with Doug, he would find solace in a book, and I'd have nothing to do but play Candy Crush on my iPhone.

Why not explore? After all, we were staying in a building on the National Register of Historic Places. I loved our Arlington condo for its amenities and convenience but there was zero chance that modern monstrosity would ever qualify as a historic dwelling of note.

I didn't have to go far. Catty-corner from our guest chamber was a small enclave labeled the "Poets' Room," filled with shelves of books and cozy nooks with windows. Apparently the room wasn't limited to bards. A variety of framed literary mementos decorated the walls. I was examining a mounted book cover of Betty Friedan's *The Feminine Mystique* when a whiny voice broke the blessed silence.

"What do we have here? The problem that has no name."

One person, and one person only, would find it amusing to quote Friedan in a blatant attempt to insult me. I turned to face the interloper. "You damn well know my name, Trevor."

The youthful face of my former congressional colleague peered around his MacBook. Trevor was in his thirties like Doug and me, yet his impish demeanor belonged to someone a decade younger. We had worked together in the Senate for several years until our boss was murdered. Circumstances led us to join forces and find his killer. A few months ago, Trevor had interjected himself into yet another homicide investigation, this time in the House of Representatives. No longer a staffer, Trevor had shown acute interest. Cunning, smart, and quick-witted, Trevor was a Washington D.C. personality for the ages.

My colleague-turned-conspirator peered at me from beneath his rimmed glasses. "Kit Marshall, you have a habit of turning up in the most unusual places."

"I could say the same about you. Why are you hiding on the fourth floor of the Continental Club?"

Trevor shut his laptop. "As a matter of fact, I'm a member." He reached into his pocket, opened his wallet, and showed me his ID card.

"Since when?"

"A few months ago. After my blogging days came to an end."

I scratched my temple. "I don't understand the connection, Trevor."

"It hasn't been publicized, but I signed a lucrative publishing deal after *Hill Rat*."

"You're writing a book?"

"Your deductive skills are as sharp as ever. We are sitting in the Poets' Room, the haven for writers at the club."

He had me there. "What are you writing? A novel?"

"No, more of a Washington D.C. tell-all."

"That will certainly boost your popularity."

"It is risky," Trevor admitted. "But the publisher's advance made the risk worthwhile."

"Just keep me out of it. I still work on Capitol Hill, and the last thing I need is more controversy."

Trevor chuckled. "Don't worry. You're not in my book. I'm going after bigger fish."

Ignoring his not-so-subtle jab, I said, "I'm glad to hear it. We're keeping our heads down in our congressional office until after the election this fall."

Trevor raised his eyebrows. "You're not doing a good enough job."

"What do you mean?"

"When I arrived a few hours earlier, I noticed a police presence inside the building. The second floor library is completely sealed off. An officer told me a man died under suspicious circumstances last night."

"I'm here with Doug and my future in-laws for the Mayflower Society gathering. The victim was the president of the organization, Grayson Bancroft."

Trevor did a double take. He didn't surprise easily, and my revelation had apparently thrown him for a loop. "Grayson Bancroft, the conservative multimedia tycoon?"

"The one and only."

He whistled softly. "Now that's something. Doug's parents knew him?"

"You could say that." I filled him in on the details of the case, including the evidence mounting against Winston Hollingsworth.

"I was joking earlier, but you really have found yourself in another predicament," Trevor said.

"I don't go looking for trouble."

"No, but trouble finds you, Kit." Trevor leaned back in his chair. "What's your next move?"

"We're headed to Mount Vernon this afternoon as part of the Mayflower Society program. I'll talk to the people who knew

Grayson to see if anyone else had a motive or the opportunity to kill him."

Trevor rubbed his chin. "Unlike the other cases you've investigated, the details of this homicide indicate the killer planned the crime methodically, perhaps for months. Poison requires careful research."

"There's no doubt the murderer carefully selected the time, manner, and place," I said. "Unfortunately, the Mayflower Society attendees are uniformly well-heeled and intelligent. Each of them has the resources and brain power to pull this off." I paused, and then added. "With the exception of one."

"Who is?"

"Cecilia Rose's husband, Drake. She's a popular author of erotic romances. Her spouse is a lot younger and short on smarts." I tapped my forehead.

After a pause, Trevor said, "I'd have to speak with Drake myself, but I wouldn't dismiss him too quickly. Perhaps he had an accomplice."

He had a point. It was way too early to eliminate anyone, particularly when identifying credible suspects could take the heat off Doug's father.

"I'll get the lay of the land. A man like Grayson Bancroft must have several enemies," I said.

"I hope so, for your future father-in-law's sake. Let me know if I can help. These walls have ears, you know," Trevor added with a sweeping gesture.

"I've heard. Thanks for the offer. I may take you up on it. In the meantime, let me know if you stumble across anything that might be important."

"Like a syringe with poison in it?" he asked.

I ignored Trevor's sarcasm, which I could barely stomach. Thank goodness Meg wasn't here. She had a zero tolerance policy when it came to Trevor. "See you later. Good luck with your book."

I wandered farther down the corridor. The rest of the floor

was unremarkable. A cramped fitness center was the only other discovery of note. There wasn't enough time to squeeze in a workout before Mount Vernon. At least George Washington's grounds would provide ample opportunity for walking and burning calories.

Just as I suspected, Doug was ensconced in a book about the history of Washington D.C. when I returned to the room. "Did you know that when the Harper family rebuilt this house in the late 1800s, it was on the outer edges of the city?"

"Doug, why do you even ask me? You know damn well I have no idea." I sat on the corner of the bed and smiled.

"Look at this 1894 map showing water mains and pipes." He pointed to the edge of the drawing. "That's where we are now."

I leaned over his shoulder and noted that the streets continued to the north and east, but at that time, no residences or water service existed beyond the current site of the Continental Club.

"This was the boondocks," I concluded. It was hard to believe, given the volume of traffic on nearby Massachusetts Avenue today.

"Pretty much. Isn't history fascinating?"

Doug returned to his book, and I let his comment slide. History in small doses was charming. I had a feeling the next couple of days might exceed my limits.

After I freshened my makeup and checked office emails, it was time to head downstairs. According to the schedule, a bus would pick us up behind the building in the valet parking lot.

"I hope this trip hasn't been canceled," Doug said.

"Me, too."

Then we added, in unison, "We need to interview suspects." I laughed. "You're coming along nicely as a detective."

His face remained somber. "Not really. But I am concerned about my father."

I squeezed his hand. "We always figure it out, don't we?"

He squeezed back. "You're right. I should have more faith."

Outside, a smaller coach bus awaited us. "Doesn't the Mayflower Society need a bigger vehicle?"

Professor Mansfield overheard my question. "We do, but most attendees decided to cut their trip short after what happened to Grayson."

"The police allowed people to leave?" I asked.

"Apparently so. As long as they completed an interview with the detective and her team and provided them with local contact information. Not many wanted to stay in the mansion another night."

Had Detective Glass permitted others to leave the scene because she felt she already had the likely murderer in her sights? I climbed on board the bus. No sign of Doug's parents.

I whispered to Doug, "I hope your father didn't get escorted downtown to police headquarters."

Doug pulled out his phone and unlocked it. "He didn't call me."

We sat on the bus in silence for several minutes. Not everyone had decided to abandon ship. Beside Professor Mansfield, Frederick and Lola Valdez appeared, along with Cecilia Rose and Drake. The latter didn't look too much the worse for the wear. Maybe early morning drinking was par for the course for them.

I could tell Doug was growing more nervous as the departure time drew nigh and his parents hadn't appeared. We both breathed a huge sigh of relief when we heard a booming voice say, "Don't leave without us. We can't miss Mount Vernon." Doug's father appeared, with Buffy in tow. They took the empty seats directly in front of us.

Doug whispered, "I need to find out how the rest of the interrogation went."

Even though I'd surely regret it, I said, "Don't let everyone else hear. Switch seats with your mother so you can talk quietly to him."

A moment later, Buffy Hollingsworth settled in next to me.

Our meeting earlier this morning hadn't ended on a friendly note. Since then, the police had focused even more attention on Winston. Certainly that would change Buffy's perspective, right? *Au contraire.*

The conversation during the entire fifteen-mile trip along the picturesque George Washington Memorial Parkway was peppered with wedding talk. Buffy had willfully chosen to forget my paucity of interest in the morning's planning session. At least her main focus wasn't on the Continental Club as the venue. Instead, she talked nonstop about color schemes, wedding favors, photographers, videographers, cake designers, rehearsals, custom cocktails, and the latest trends in bridal couture. I'd never been so happy to see the traffic circle outside the Mount Vernon entrance. Buffy didn't seem to notice I'd said next to nothing on the bus ride. During the tour, I would have to shake her. My sanity was at stake.

On the long path leading toward Washington's beloved mansion, I fell in step with Doug. "What did your father say about the police?"

"Standard questions. They asked him over and over about his whereabouts last night. There's not much to say. After dinner, he and my mother joined everyone in the bar for a cocktail. Then they headed upstairs to their room and remained there until morning."

"We can corroborate their story. We didn't hear them leave their room last night," I said.

Doug pursed his lips. "I agree, but I don't think it will matter. My parents' room is in the corner of the hallway, immediately next to the stairwell. If my father had headed downstairs, he wouldn't have passed in front of our room first."

I thought about Doug's comment. "Unfortunately, their room would have been perfectly situated for the murderer."

"Even worse, my father requested that room. It's his favorite at the Continental Club."

"Terrific. Detective Glass will claim that's evidence of premeditation." I sighed.

We'd emerged from the sheltered walkway to the main lawn in front of the house. Doug's work as a professor of American history meant we visited important historical sites on a regular basis. We'd been to Mount Vernon several times, both for fun and work-related events. The annual fall Virginia wine celebration was legendary, as well as the festive Fourth of July daytime fireworks display. The Mount Vernon grounds were vast and included farm demonstrations, gardens, slave quarters, and a museum. According to the Mayflower Society schedule, we'd focus on the mansion itself during our tour.

Dressed in eighteenth-century garb, an older woman presented herself to our group. "My name is Sandra, and I'll be your Mount Vernon guide. I understand this group knows a lot about American history already." Sandra was beaming with enthusiasm.

Lola Valdez spoke up. "We don't need the basics. Give us the advanced version."

Her husband Frederick rolled his eyes and said, "Give the woman a chance, Lola. She's trying to do her job."

Sandra seemed unfazed. "I'll spare no details and provide you with as many interesting facts about the mansion and the Washington family as possible. Follow me."

We bypassed hundreds of tourists waiting in line for a standard house tour. As we marched in front of them, I felt the sting of the jealous stares. At least the Mayflower Society offered some tangible benefits.

From my previous visits, I knew that George Washington built the mansion in stages. The wooden construction was Palladian style European architecture featuring porticos along the front and rear. The signature red shingled roof provided a striking contrast to the farmhouse's pristine white. Washington built the original two-story structure in the late 1750s after he inherited the estate from his brother. Secondary northern and southern wings enlarged the manse during the Revolutionary War to its twenty-one-room final configuration, complete with an octagonal cupola tower topped with a dove of peace weathervane selected by Washington himself.

After watching a short video outlining the mansion's history, we strolled inside the house. Sandra announced, "Ladies and gentlemen, may I present the New Room."

Buffy swiveled her head around, surveying the grand salon. "I could have sworn this was a dining room."

Now it was a large, open room with chairs lining the edges. It was painted an unusually bright bluish green, with numerous grand paintings on the wall. There was no serving table or indication the room had been used for dining.

Sandra clasped her hands in apparent delight at Buffy's comment. "You are correct! Mount Vernon previously identified this room as a place in which the Washingtons served impressive luncheons and dinners. However, further research proved it was designed as a European saloon."

Frederick Valdez chortled. "Saloon? I don't see any booze. If you're serving some of Washington's whiskey, be sure to let me know."

Sandra smiled tightly. "Not a 'saloon' in the American sense of the word. In European architecture, saloons showcased great wealth. They had little practical purpose, except to advertise the prosperity of the home's owners by displaying impressive collections of artwork. We like to call it Washington's 'statement' room."

"What statement was he trying to make?" asked Drake.

Sandra didn't miss a beat. "At eleven thousand square feet, Mount Vernon was ten times the size of the average colonial home in Virginia. This house was the foremost residence in the New World. That is precisely the statement Washington wanted to make."

The buzz of conversation that immediately erupted indicated Mayflower Society attendees were impressed by Washington's grandiose statement. The tour continued through several parlors and into the main entryway. Sandra pointed out an iron key hanging on the wall inside a glass enclosure. "This was one of Washington's most prized possessions. It is the key to the Bastille given to him in 1790 by the Marquis de Lafayette after that prison's destruction in Paris."

I heard Drake mutter to Cecilia, "That name sounds familiar."

I interjected myself into their conversation. "There's a portrait of Lafayette on the floor of the House of Representatives. He was the first foreign dignitary to address a joint session of Congress."

"Drake's really becoming a history buff," said Cecilia proudly. "All of our time spent at the Continental Club is having a real effect on him."

Drake nodded. Perhaps Cecilia was telling the truth and Drake was smarter than he seemed. However, something told me Drake was more familiar with the first floor bar than the second floor library.

The last stop on the ground floor was Washington's study. "George Washington got up at four in the morning, dressed inside this room, and reviewed paperwork until breakfast. He often read in this room until going to bed at nine."

I heard Drake's voice yet again. "Not exactly my schedule."

There was no doubt I was eavesdropping, but Drake had provided me with another tidbit. "Are you a night owl?" I asked innocently.

Before Cecilia could interrupt, Drake replied, "The party usually gets started around midnight." With a chuckle, he added. "But not last night."

"Really? I heard there was quite a party at the bar after dinner."

"Nope, at least not for me. I had one drink and headed upstairs to bed."

Cecilia linked her arm with Drake's. "We were tired from our trip to D.C. from South Carolina."

Drake had been quick to mention he retired early last night. Was he intelligent enough to realize the importance of a tight alibi? Or was he simply telling the truth? Was Cecilia covering for him because he was guilty or just plain dumb?

We walked upstairs to the second floor, which consisted entirely of bedchambers. Sandra regaled her attentive audience with various details about each room, including who had slept there and why specific colors and decorations were chosen. Finally we arrived at the last room on the floor. Sandra motioned for our group to gather around her so everyone could hear her spiel.

"This is one of the most important rooms in the entire house, the chamber of George and Martha Washington." She stepped aside so we could get a good look. The bedroom was the largest of the lot, located directly above the study.

Sandra continued, "Notice the bed and its size. It's much longer than the conventional bed of the time period. Washington was over six feet tall, so he needed a bigger frame to prevent his feet from hanging over the edge."

Although grander in scale than the other bedchambers, the room had an elegant simplicity about it. The Washingtons had apparently reserved their regal statements for the downstairs entertainment salons. Their own private sanctuary conveyed more of a minimalist austerity than grandiose wealth or power.

"This was also the room in which Washington died. His illness was very short. He contracted a throat infection after riding his horse during inclement December weather. Two days later, he was dead."

"Did Washington die in that bed?" Lola asked.

"Yes, he did. After his death, Mrs. Washington closed up the room and moved upstairs to the third floor. She couldn't bear to set foot inside their bedroom again."

Every time I heard the story of Washington's death, I was surprised all over again by the rapidity of his demise. Of course, eighteenth-century medicine left a lot to be desired.

Washington's doctors likely did more harm than good, hastening his passing instead of preventing it.

Since the upper floor was rarely open to visitors and not part of the mansion tour, we headed back downstairs. We walked outside onto the piazza, which ran the entire length of the house and provided a memorable view of the Potomac River. Thanks to First Lady Jackie Kennedy's intervention, commercial development within sight of Mount Vernon was not allowed, thus preserving the pristine landscape George and Martha enjoyed on the east side of the house.

Something was nagging at me, but I couldn't quite put my finger on it. Maybe a minute to clear my head would help. After all, it had been a trying day. I sat in one of numerous wooden chairs lining the piazza, rested my head on the high back, and closed my eyes.

Less than a minute later, a familiar voice interrupted my reverie. "Penny for your thoughts?" Doug asked.

"We're at Mount Vernon. Don't you mean a quarter?"

Doug chuckled. "Yes, a quarter. Your thoughts are certainly worth more than a penny."

"I hope so," I said, "but I was referring to Washington's handsome profile." I sat up straight. "I've got one of those notions inside my brain I can't quite shake."

Doug tilted his head to the side. "It usually means you're on to something."

"Correct. But it's no good unless I can figure out what that is."

Doug leaned closer. "When did the feeling appear?"

"A few minutes ago. At the end of the mansion tour."

After replaying the tour in my mind, I snapped my fingers. "Got it!"

"Tell me." Doug's voice had gotten too loud. The killer could be sitting next to us.

I motioned with my hand for him to take it down a notch.

"Relax, Doug. I haven't solved the case. But Washington's death gave me an idea."

"George Washington? He died because he didn't take off his damp clothes after prolonged exposure to a cold winter rain. He wasn't poisoned."

"I'm well aware of the details. The relevant part of the story is the speed of his passing. Before anyone could chop down a cherry tree, he was dead."

"Why does that matter?" The glimmer of hope on Doug's face was gone.

"We haven't considered how Grayson Bancroft died."

"He was poisoned, Kit. Try to keep up."

I ignored his sarcasm. "I meant the type of poison. Whatever the concoction, it was extremely fast acting. Think about the timing for a moment. Grayson was dead in less than seven hours."

"Aren't all poisons instantaneous? That's what happens in the movies." Doug grinned.

Here's where my penchant for reading mystery novels came in handy. "Not especially. I'll have to research it, but I don't think this fits the profile of the big three."

"You've got me. 'The big three'?"

"You don't have to look any further than Dame Agatha. Arsenic, cyanide, and strychnine. Remember, Grayson died so quickly, he wasn't able to scream for help or stagger downstairs. It's unusual."

Doug rubbed his chin. "I suppose you're right."

I grabbed his hand in excitement as another thought surfaced. "The method of delivery could be important, too."

"The needle?"

"I'd call it an injection for now. If the murderer invited Grayson for a drink, why not put the poison in a libation when his back was turned? Why risk the violent act of sticking our victim in the neck?"

"I like where you're going with this."

"Don't get too excited. Right now, we have more questions than answers."

Doug's eyes sparkled. "As long as those questions point toward my father's innocence, I'm grateful."

I shifted in my chair and drew back. For Doug and me, the stakes in a murder case had never been higher. Surrounded by the spring beauty of bucolic Mount Vernon, I should have felt sprightly and hopeful. Here the father of our country had shouldered all the problems of a young country. At this moment my burden felt no lighter. I had to clear Winston's name. Our future happiness depended on it.

Chapter Nine

———— ∿ ————

"You have one hour to explore Mount Vernon before your bus leaves." Our guide Sandra's voice interrupted my solemn musings about our current predicament. Doug and I reluctantly rose to our feet.

Having visited Mount Vernon on numerous occasions, we could skip the stroll around the grounds. With my back to the Potomac, I scanned the portico. Out of my left eye, I spied a couple walking across the lawn toward several of the outbuildings flanking the southern edge of the mansion. The woman's distinctive long, flowing dress identified her as Lola Valdez. Her husband Frederick accompanied her.

I gave Doug a gentle nudge. "Let's follow them."

We took off in quiet pursuit. Frederick and Lola headed inside the storehouse and smokehouse. Doug and I finally caught up with them inside the washhouse.

Spotting us, Frederick extended his hand to Doug. "Too nice of a day to spend inside at the museum."

I admired the way Lola's blue, feathery earrings framed her face. "Every time I see this building," she said, "I'm in awe.

Imagine dealing with the laundry for the entire estate without a washer and dryer."

I was in awe, too. The large copper tubs of water sat near the hearth. The elbow grease of slave women had powered the washers, not electricity. After cleaning, they hauled the wet clothes and linens outside to dry and then carried them inside again for ironing and folding.

As we milled around the structure, I asked, "Where are you walking next?"

"The pioneer farm. Care to join us?" said Frederick.

We nodded eagerly and followed. "That wasn't difficult," Doug whispered.

"Let's see if they know anything about the murder," I whispered back. "I'll take the lead." Doug's anxiety about his father's status as a suspect was obvious. Frederick and Lola seemed intelligent. A direct approach might scare them off, particularly if either one was responsible for Grayson's death.

Frederick pointed ahead to the educational center. "We need to catch this shuttle or we won't make it back in time for our departure."

The four of us hustled and climbed inside the vehicle. Our bus driver informed us it would take five minutes to reach our destination in the southwestern corner of the estate. Lola beamed. "We haven't visited the sixteen-sided barn in ages."

"We've never seen it," I said.

Lola gasped and squealed in delight. "You're in for a real treat."

Frederick rolled his eyes and checked his cellphone. I edged closer to Lola. "Are you staying at the Continental Club tonight, despite Grayson's death?"

Lola readjusted the headband restraining her lightly tousled tresses. "We're not leaving," she answered firmly.

"You and Frederick knew Grayson well, right?"

"For decades, just like the Hollingsworths. As Frederick

may have told you, I'm the history buff in the family. We never missed a Mayflower Society meeting."

"What did you think of Grayson?" I softened my voice so the interrogation wouldn't seem too obvious.

Lola blinked rapidly. "Everyone had an opinion about Grayson Bancroft."

"I can only imagine. Did you like him?"

"There's no easy way to answer that question. He was a complicated man. I appreciated his support of the Mayflower Society. But I didn't like how he ran it."

"Really? This is my first meeting, but everything appears in order."

"Grayson threw a lot of money around as a bigwig donor. That's why we receive such first-class treatment at places like this." She swept her arm around in a circle. "But he had an agenda, like everyone in Washington."

"An agenda for a historical society?" I suppressed my frustration. Lola seemed credible, but she was losing me.

The bus stopped at our destination. As we exited, the driver reminded us we had half an hour to explore the pioneer farm before the next shuttle back to the mansion grounds departed.

Before I could follow up with Lola, she pointed in the distance. "There's the barn. Let's go! We don't have much time."

Frederick fell in step with me. "Best to do what she says. Once Lola gets fixated on something historical, no one gets in her way." Although Frederick hadn't meant his comment as incriminating, it made me wonder if Grayson's so-called agenda provided Lola with a credible motive for murder. It seemed that she might be the only person who took the Mayflower Society as seriously as Doug's father did. Her enthusiasm might even exceed Winston's.

"Why is this barn so impressive?" Doug seemed puzzled. Focusing as he did on political history, he must have missed the lecture on American agrarian practices.

Lola grinned, ecstatic to have at least one eager pupil. "It's not really the sixteen-sided shape of the barn, but the two levels of the building." We followed her inside.

"Horses were led inside the barn after wheat was placed on the ground. After the horses treaded the crop for less than an hour, the grain fell through the spaces between the floorboards to the first floor. The wheat stalks could be discarded and the valuable seeds collected from underneath. Ingenious!"

Lola and Frederick left us to read a plaque detailing the architectural design of the barn. I caught up with Doug as he gazed around the polygon structure. "Don't get too caught up in the excitement, Mr. History. Remember, we followed the Valdezes so we could find out if they're credible suspects."

"You don't need to remind me. I chatted up Frederick during the shuttle ride."

"And …?" I asked, hands on my hips.

"There was a longstanding, competitive rivalry between Frederick and Grayson. Sort of like a battle of the modern-day robber barons. Frederick has made a ton of money on cellphones, yet I got the sense his wealth never came close to Bancroft's. That disparity clearly bothered Frederick."

"Enough to kill Grayson?"

Doug shrugged. "Hard to say. I had a feeling he would have told me more, but just as we were getting to the good stuff, we arrived at our stop."

"Same with Lola. She mentioned something about Grayson having an agenda attached to his leadership of the Mayflower Society. I ran out of time before I could probe deeper."

"We'd better head back to catch that bus or we'll miss our ride back to the Continental Club," said Doug.

Frederick and Lola must have had the same concern. They were waiting for us outside the barn, and we walked together to the shuttle stop. A minute later, we were on our way.

Doug and I both wanted to continue our conversations, but as soon as we boarded the shuttle, both Valdezes closed their eyes. Rather than risk annoying them, I stared outside at the bucolic farmland. No wonder Washington returned to Mount Vernon every chance he had.

The day must have been exhausting for everyone. The ride back to D.C. was quiet and uneventful. I caught up on email and Doug listened to music using his trusty Bose In-ear Headphones. When we exited the bus at the Continental Club, Buffy stopped us.

"Let's have a drink in the bar in a half hour. I need to drop my packages in the room and freshen up." It was a command more than an invitation.

Buffy was hauling three large bags. "Did you go shopping during our hour of free time?" I asked curiously.

"Of course, darling. The shops at Mount Vernon are not to be missed." She showed me an abundance of items, including Christmas tree ornaments, garden accessories, and even a *Dining with the Washingtons* cookbook.

The latter intrigued me. I didn't know Buffy enjoyed the culinary arts. "Are you going to try your hand at eighteenth-century cooking?"

Buffy narrowed her eyes. "Of course not. It's a gift for our housekeeper, Marta."

I should have kept my big mouth shut. Doug broke in, "We'll see you downstairs shortly, Mother."

Back in our room, we collapsed onto the bed. "What a day," I murmured.

For a while we rested quietly with our thoughts. Doug broke the silence. "Do you have an idea who did it? Other than my father, of course."

I propped myself up on my side to face him. "Doug, I'll be honest with you. I have no idea. Quite frankly, it's pretty complicated. We think Grayson died of poisoning, but we have no specifics. On television shows, toxicology reports arrive before the autopsy is completed. That's not the case in real life, especially in Washington."

City services in the District were notoriously underfunded.

The constant tug of war with Congress on D.C. funding rivaled the *Hunger Games'* fight to the death. Few survived without suffering serious wounds. I doubted the Medical Examiner's office had emerged unscathed.

"We don't need to know which poison killed Bancroft, do we?" Doug fidgeted on his side of the bed.

"Not necessarily, but it would help. We also don't have any eyewitnesses, unless Detective Glass uncovered information in her interviews today that we don't know about."

Doug stared at the ceiling. "What should we do, Kit?"

I reached for his hand. "We work the motive angles, like we've been doing. We need to figure out who wanted Grayson dead. So far, we know Frederick Valdez was jealous of his success. Lola was angry about the direction of the Mayflower Society under Grayson's watchful leadership."

"Anyone else?" asked Doug, ever hopeful.

"Cecilia Rose wanted to talk to Grayson about her next novel. He owned her publisher, and I get the sense Savannah's sultry liaisons were about to cool down."

"What about her husband? What's his name?"

"Drake isn't the sharpest tool in the shed. But Trevor warned me not to write anyone off at this point."

Doug sat up. "Trevor? When did you talk to him?"

"I forgot to tell you. I ran into him before we left for Mount Vernon. He's writing an insider book on Washington, D.C. and he's a member of the Continental Club."

Doug shook his head slowly. "That guy really gets around."

"You could say that. In this case, he might be helpful. Trevor has an uncanny knack for picking up all kinds of details when people don't think anyone is listening."

"It can't hurt. It's almost time to head downstairs for a drink and then dinner."

I'd almost forgotten about Meg. Hopefully Doug wouldn't mind that she was joining us. "By the way, I invited Meg to dinner tonight. Do you know where we're eating?"

"Why did you invite Meg?" I noted the barely concealed whine in Doug's voice.

Initially, I'd needed Meg to help resist the forces compelling me toward a society wedding. But Grayson's death provided another reason to include her. "How am I supposed to solve a murder without Meg?"

Doug seemed to weigh my argument. Meg annoyed him on a regular basis. However, she'd proven instrumental in my previous crime-solving ventures. I could almost see him tallying up the pros and cons.

"You have a point," he said slowly.

"Yes, I do. She's resourceful, observant, and quick on her feet."

"Of course. When I think of Meg, Lisbeth Salander comes to mind."

I ignored his sarcasm. "Where should I tell her to meet us?"

"A historic restaurant called the Iron Gate in Dupont Circle. Father has already made the reservation." Doug grabbed a light jacket. "We'll be dining outside. You'll need a sweater."

"Outside?"

"The Iron Gate is a treat. You'll both enjoy it."

"Head downstairs without me. I'm going to call Meg to catch up. I'll join you in a few minutes."

Doug peered around the door before closing it. "Hendrick's with tonic?"

"Tell Charles it's for me."

Doug nodded absently and closed the door. I pulled out my iPhone and punched in Meg's number. By now, she should be home with Clarence and available to talk.

"Hey, girlfriend."

The wonders of caller ID never ceased to amaze me. I was old enough to remember a time when answering the phone had an element of mystery to it.

"Good evening, Meg. Time to chat?"

"Sure. Clarence and I got back from our walk a few minutes ago."

"He's being a good boy?"

Meg hesitated. "Yes, but he seems antsy. You're still coming home tomorrow, right?"

As long as Doug's father was a suspect, it might be tough to dislodge him from the Continental Club. Even so, two nights away was enough for me. "I plan to be home Friday evening."

I heard a sigh of relief. "He's not done anything *bad*. But he's looking at me with those puppy dog eyes. He wants you, Kit. I'm a poor substitute."

My heart warmed. Clarence missed me. Anderson Cooper had famously been asked on *60 Minutes* whether his dog loved him. He thought she might be scamming him for food or attention. Clarence's behavior was proof he was genuinely besotted. After all, he'd been getting his fill of treats with Meg. With her healthy appetite, she hadn't stopped with the rom-com and popcorn.

"He'll survive. How was work?"

Meg dove into a laundry list of details about our congressional office staff. House members could only employ a small number of people in Washington. The budget we received from the federal government had to cover our D.C. and North Carolina office expenses. The law prevented our boss from raising more money to supplement the budget. It wasn't like the Senate. With only one hundred elected members, staff sizes were triple the size of House offices. Due to our restricted numbers, everyone had to answer the phones, make photocopies, and answer mail. Making sure our staff remembered the "team first" attitude often presented a management challenge of epic proportions. After Meg related her final tale of woe, she took a breath.

"Finished? Or is there more intrigue you'd like to share?"

"That's all for now. Don't worry, Kit. I can handle it."

Meg vacillated between complaining about our colleagues'

behavior and asserting her authority as my second in command. A competent and experienced congressional staffer, she deserved the chance to steer the ship, at least during my absence. She'd take care of business.

"I have updates on Buffy's wedding obsession and the murder. Which one do you want to hear about first?"

"Murder, please." That was no surprise. A free spirit enjoying the life of a singleton, Meg saw little benefit, for either of us, in my transition to marital bliss.

I caught Meg up on the details of the case, recounting my conversations with Cecilia and Drake in the morning and Frederick and Lola at Mount Vernon.

"Are they going to arrest Doug's father?"

"He's a person of interest right now. But the longer this goes unsolved, the better he looks as the culprit. You know how this works."

"Are you sure you still want me to come to dinner tonight?" Meg asked hesitantly.

"Absolutely. Besides the murder, I need a buffer to help me fend off the wedding shenanigans."

Meg giggled and couldn't stop.

"What's so funny?"

"You need a buffer to handle Buffy! It's hilarious."

My best friend had a way with words. "Save your wit, Meg. With this crowd, you'll need it."

Chapter Ten

W HEN I ARRIVED at the bar, Doug had my drink waiting.
Winston wore the same suit from earlier in the day.
Buffy had changed into a simple but elegant long-sleeved
crinkly georgette dress with a daisy vermilion print. Her ever-
present classic string of white pearls and matching earrings
completed the look.

A long sip of Hendrick's loosened me up, and I leaned closer
to Buffy. "Your dress is beautiful."

She responded with a knowing smile. "Thank Oscar de la
Renta." Knocking back what remained in her martini glass, she
asked, "Where do you shop, Kit?"

This exchange was heading south fast. I should have kept
quiet about the dress. "I'm not really that into fashion. My
work clothes need to be functional." Down went another gulp
of my gin and tonic.

Buffy motioned to Charles for a refill. She must be planning
to drink quickly if we were going to keep our reservations for
seven.

Apparently, she wasn't finished with the conversation. "We
should talk more about your wardrobe. I'd be happy to take

you on a shopping spree as an engagement present. Perhaps tomorrow we could go to a few stores. I remember seeing several suitable boutiques in Georgetown when we visited Doug at the university."

I winced. "Don't you think we should attend the Mayflower Society events?"

"I marched from one end of Mount Vernon to the other today. I don't need to repeat that exercise in futility tomorrow."

Hearing a lull in the chatter between Doug and his father, I jumped in, "I hope Doug told you I've invited a friend to dinner. Her name is Meg Peters, and we've worked together on Capitol Hill for many years."

Winston's eyes lit up. "We love surprise dinner guests, don't we, dear?"

Buffy polished off her second drink and said in a tight voice, "Delightful."

Doug grabbed my hand and pulled me to my feet. "We'd better head out to the restaurant."

Out of habit, I grabbed my phone. "Do you need me to request an Uber?"

Doug chuckled and pulled me closer. "Father has a driver on call when he travels."

"Oh." I felt a flush creeping across my neck and returned the phone to my purse. Thank goodness Meg was joining us to take some of the pressure off.

Once we were on our way, Winston asked whether I'd ever dined at the Iron Gate.

"No, but Doug said it's a real treat."

Winston addressed his son in a scolding tone. "Shame on you, Doug. All these years in Washington with Kit, and you never took her to the Iron Gate?"

Doug wore a sheepish expression, a little like Clarence after chomping the remote control for the umpteenth time. "Must have slipped my mind."

Winston shook his head in benign disapproval. "Not to

worry. You'll enjoy it tonight. Until recently, it was the oldest continuously running restaurant in the District."

"How long was it open?"

"Eighty-seven years. The building was constructed after the Civil War and then the National Federation of Women's Clubs bought it in the early twentieth century. They ran a tea room in the space during the Prohibition years."

Buffy interrupted. "In the seventies, when Winston and I were newly married and he was building the firm, he traveled frequently to Washington on business. I accompanied him, and we often dined at the Iron Gate."

"Along with notable diplomats and journalists. That was its heyday," Winston added, almost wistfully.

"Did it close down? You said until recently it was the oldest restaurant in the city?"

"Unfortunately, it was shuttered in 2010. But it reopened a few years ago under the direction of an exciting new chef. The reviews have been quite promising."

We pulled up to a carriage house set apart from the bustling N Street corridor. No surprise, an iron gate guarded a long pathway, framed by a row of picturesque lanterns blazing the otherwise dark path to the restaurant's entrance.

Meg had already arrived. Spotting us, she waved enthusiastically. Buffy couldn't fault Meg's attire. She was clad to the nines in an off-the-shoulder black dress with ruffles. A bolero sweater made it appropriate for springtime outdoor dining.

My best pal gave me a quick hug and didn't wait for introductions. "I'm Meg Peters. I'm so happy to meet you. I've heard a lot about you!"

Buffy offered her hand and Meg blew past it, instead enveloping my future mother-in-law in an embrace. Winston burst into a belly laugh as Buffy stiffly received Meg's exuberant welcome. He opened his arms, and Meg gladly hugged him as well.

"We're happy to meet you, Meg," said Winston.

"We are charmed." Buffy's rigid posture had relaxed, but she was still recovering from Meg's unanticipated welcome.

Doug watched the unfolding scene with amusement. "Let's check in with the host."

Meg sidled up next to us as Winston dealt with our reservation. "I hear there's a murder that needs solving," she said.

"Did Kit tell you the details?" asked Doug.

"She filled me in over the phone. I bet you're not opposed to our sleuthing on this one, are you?" Meg put her a hand on her hip and twirled her designer handbag with the other.

Doug kept his cool. "The more eyes we have on this, the better. That doesn't mean I want either of you to do anything risky."

"You always say that. Has anything bad ever happened?"

Doug pressed his finger to his temple as he pretended to contemplate Meg's question. "Let's see. I seem to recall two recent life-threatening encounters with murderers. Do either of those count?"

Doug's question went unanswered when Winston motioned for us to follow. We entered a beautiful outdoor patio surrounded by a lush garden. A wisteria vine dotted with white lights served as a makeshift ceiling.

"What a gorgeous space," said Meg.

Buffy concurred. "It's enchanting."

"Just as you remembered it, dear?" asked Winston.

Doug remarked, "According to the popular dining blogs, it's consistently named one of the most romantic restaurants in Washington D.C."

That captured Buffy's attention. "You've given me the most marvelous idea!"

We took our seats and waited for Buffy to explain. I could only guess where this was headed.

She was glowing. "We should have the wedding here! I'm

sure the owner and chef would be amenable to hosting a private event."

Meg and I exchanged knowing glances. She reached insider her purse for her phone. Sure enough, my phone buzzed a moment later. I discreetly peeked at the text Meg had sent: *4 minutes to mention wedding*

I typed back, *New world record*

Our clandestine convo over, we rejoined the table's conversation. Doug had apparently said something to dampen Buffy's enthusiasm because her cheerful countenance had turned gloomy.

"Douglas, someone needs to make a decision about the venue and the date." *Wow*. I'd never heard either Hollingsworth parental pull out *Douglas*. Her patience had run out.

Meg, a neophyte in dealing with the parents of significant others, thrust herself into the debate. "Kit is still exploring her options. We've been tied up at work. No time for wedding planning when the nation's political woes require our full attention!" She grabbed my hand and squeezed it.

Buffy wasn't persuaded. "This is why I don't visit Washington D.C. regularly. Everyone around here is obsessed with work. Doesn't anyone care about life's other priorities?"

Meg certainly did, and it began with the letter L. Not love, but libations. She took Buffy's hissy fit as a perfect opportunity to signal our waiter she was ready to order a drink. "I'll have an Across the Aegean." Iron Gate was known for its Greek and Italian cuisine, which extended to its menu of original cocktails.

Since we'd already enjoyed strong spirits at the Continental Club, the rest of us ordered a glass of wine. The break offered an opportunity to shift the subject of our table conversation away from the wedding and toward more important matters, such as murder.

"Meg helped me solve two murders on Capitol Hill in the past year," I explained.

Buffy smoothed her hair. "I thought your jobs were so demanding, you had no time for anything else."

"In each case, Kit's job depended on solving the murder. So it became the top priority," Meg said.

"How thrilling!" Winston said. "We've kept up with the headlines from afar. Has Kit told you about the unfortunate death of Grayson Bancroft?"

Meg nodded. "She filled me in earlier today."

Winston leaned in. "And what do you think happened to poor Grayson?"

Without blinking, Meg answered, "As I understand it, you're the prime suspect, Mr. Hollingsworth."

The waiter served our drinks and took our dinner order. Doug squirmed in his chair. Not many people asserted themselves with Winston, but Meg hadn't flinched.

I couldn't leave my BFF hanging. "What Meg is trying to say is we may have to point to other suspects if the police are going to stop focusing on you. The best way to clear you of all wrongdoing is to find the person who really killed Grayson."

Buffy swirled her Sancerre. "The police will figure it out. If they don't, we'll simply bring in the best defense attorney in Washington. You don't need to concern yourself."

Doug's face turned a deep shade of red. "I disagree, Mother. If we need to hire a lawyer, it means Father has already been arrested or has been brought in again for formal questioning. This is the nation's capital. There are enterprising reporters in every nook and cranny. Don't you think one of them will get wind of it and write an article about the intrigue of a high society murder, fingering Winston Hollingsworth as the guilty party?" He took a sip of his wine and slammed the glass on the table, almost causing his California blend to spill.

Buffy remained silent, but the sudden pallor of her skin implied she'd received Doug's message loud and clear.

Winston rubbed his chin thoughtfully as he said, "Perhaps

it's not a bad idea to explore alternative explanations of Grayson's death."

Doug breathed a sigh of relief. "Thank you."

"I have a few questions about the other Mayflower Society members who knew Grayson well," I said.

Winston glanced at Buffy, who nodded. He replied, "Ask away, Kit."

"Lola and I spent time together this afternoon. She didn't particularly like Grayson's leadership of the Mayflower Society. Can you tell me about her difficulties with him? Did you have the same issues with Grayson?"

Winston sighed and took a sip of his wine before answering. "You've definitely hit a nerve. Lola Valdez hated the direction the Mayflower Society was going in under Bancroft. As you may have ascertained, I was no fan of Grayson, either. But for a different reason."

Buffy touched his sleeve and added, "Lola can't keep her politics separate from her passion for history. Winston just wanted Grayson to step aside so he could serve as president of Mayflower."

"My wife is mostly correct. I didn't care for Grayson's ideological bent, either. But I really detested the man because he used his money to maintain a stranglehold on Mayflower."

Meg listened intently. "Can you tell us more about Lola's problem with Grayson? I still don't understand her intense dislike of the man."

"Lola got a doctorate in history decades ago at Berkeley. Doug, do you remember the subject of her thesis?"

Doug replied, "Radical and Reconstructive Views of Early Puritan leaders. Her research was avant-garde, to say the least."

"That's Lola," Winston said. "Always pushing the boundaries. Her liberal politics never meshed with Grayson's conservatism."

Meg put down her glass for a brief moment. "We understand political disagreements and how they can result in murder. But Lola and Grayson weren't fighting over health care or immigration policy. Historical societies don't exactly raise hackles, right?"

Buffy snickered. "You haven't seen the Mayflower Society in action."

I looked to my future father-in-law for an explanation.

"Grayson believed strongly that conservatives were the true disciples of American history. He advocated for strict and traditional interpretations of the past. He abhorred revisionism of any kind."

The argument was becoming clearer. "Lola was the other extreme of the spectrum," I said.

Doug nodded. "She was part of the New Left movement in the seventies, and her beliefs stayed with her. She detested the Republicans claiming they are the true protectors of American history."

I glanced at Meg, who was clearly on the same wavelength. "Go ahead, Meg. Ask the question."

"Could Lola's disagreement with Grayson be a motive for murder?"

Winston hesitated, but Buffy did not. "Of course," she said. "Lola's passion for history played second fiddle to Frederick's success as a cellphone magnate. She never pursued the academic career she wanted. The Mayflower Society is the outlet for her true passion."

Buffy was certainly familiar with the latest output of the rumor mill. Still, I wanted to hear Winston's opinion.

At my pointed look, he obliged. "A few years ago, Grayson started inviting right-wing speakers to the annual meetings. He also recruited more members who shared his view so that the old guard, which included Lola, would eventually be in the minority and silenced within the society."

"Sounds downright nasty," murmured Meg.

"The study of history can be deadly," Doug said, taking my hand.

Visions of academics slaughtering each other at the

American Historical Association annual conference flashed before my eyes. Somehow the sight of intellectual post-modernists eviscerating the ancient-history specialists didn't exactly ring true, but I didn't want to burst Doug's bubble.

"Point taken. How does Grayson's death change the direction of the Mayflower Society? What will be different without him around?" I asked.

Our waiter's arrival interrupted our conversation. He placed a generous portion of rotisserie chicken and fennel sausage cannelloni stuffed with baby spinach and ricotta before me. The fragrance of Italian spices made my mouth water. Murder was important, but so was savoring an excellent meal. Our table fell silent except for the clink of silverware.

We all praised our meals, and I gently prodded Winston to answer my earlier question. After careful consideration, he finally spoke. "It's hard to say. We should know more after Sunday's business meeting. The society will have to elect a new president. Lola should have the votes to make sure Grayson's successor doesn't follow in his conservative footsteps. I'm quite certain she would support my candidacy."

Doug raised his eyebrows. "Father, given the circumstances and the suspicion directed at you, putting your hat in the ring is a risky move."

Buffy waved her hand. "Forget it, Doug. Your father has waited years for this moment. He's not going to forego an opportunity to serve as president of Mayflower."

Meg paused from inhaling her mixed grille platter. "You'll be playing right into the hands of the police, confirming the motive they want to pin on you."

Winston refused to back down. "We'll see what develops. Perhaps the murderer will be apprehended, by the police or someone else." He winked at me.

"What about Frederick?" I said. "Doug chatted with him earlier today, and there's no love lost between the two of them."

"That's easy," Buffy said. "I need only one word to describe the relationship between Frederick and Grayson."

We all waited with bated breath as Buffy tilted back her glass to savor the last drops of her wine. "Jealousy."

"From what Kit told me, Frederick was wildly successful in business. Why was he jealous of Grayson?" Meg inquired.

"It's all a matter of degree," Winston said. "Bancroft was untouchable, particularly in Washington circles. Frederick could never unseat him." He ticked off the reasons on the fingers on his right hand. "In philanthropy, business, Republican intellectual circles, Bancroft had the edge, and Frederick couldn't keep up. The *Capital Observer* was the last straw."

"The conservative Washington newspaper?" Doug asked.

"You got it. Despite the economic futility of traditional journalism these days, Frederick tried to buy it last year. He wanted to use his knowledge of the mobile phone industry to revolutionize the paper's online presence. Just between us, he also wanted to buy the paper before the upcoming elections."

Meg finished the last remaining morsels on her plate. "Something tells me Frederick didn't get to buy his right-wing mouthpiece."

The waiter cleared our empty plates and placed after-dinner menus before us. A firm believer in never foregoing dessert, Meg avidly scanned the options.

"He never had the chance," Buffy explained. "The scuttlebutt inside Mayflower Society is Grayson heard about the offer Frederick was putting together and doubled it."

"Did Grayson really want to own the *Observer* that badly? It doesn't exactly enjoy the distribution of the *New York Times*," I said.

Buffy leaned in and lowered her voice. "There's the rub. He only bought it to prevent Frederick from owning it."

Meg muttered, "No shortage of motives."

Doug must have heard Meg's muted comment. "We shouldn't

have a problem casting suspicion in another direction."

"The question is whether the police will take these motives seriously. How can we get Detective Glass to investigate suspects other than your father?" I wondered aloud.

Meg dove into a plate of crispy Greek doughnuts. A small drop of syrup on her chin emphasized her otherwise flawless appearance. Between bites, she pointed to her dessert. "That's easy. Sweeten the pot."

I gazed skeptically at my best friend. "How do you propose we do that, Meg?"

"With poison, of course."

Chapter Eleven

———✦———

WHETHER WE WERE exhausted from heady conversation about murder or sinking into a food stupor, our return to the Continental Club transpired in silence. Meg's parting words of wisdom weighed heavily. A titan of business, politics, and philanthropy, Grayson Bancroft had earned his fair share of enemies. Any number of power players would benefit from his death. But only one person administered the lethal dose. If we wanted to clear Doug's father, we'd needed to figure out how Grayson died and who could have poisoned him.

At the club, the four of us stood at the foot of the grand staircase that led to the ill-fated library and the guest rooms above it. Long days were my strong suit. Capitol Hill staffers often began their morning with no idea of how many hours of work remained ahead of them. Even with that vigorous training, I could admit that today had been quite a marathon.

As I moved toward the stairs, Buffy placed her hand on my arm. "Kit, would you care to join me for a nightcap?"

I looked warily at Doug.

"Mother, can she take a rain check?" he asked.

"Of course, if she's too tired." She sighed. "But I did want to speak to her about something important."

The expression on Buffy's face was inscrutable. It wasn't a glare of condescension or a scowl of superiority. What was it? After a moment, I figured it out. Buffy Hollingsworth looked desperate.

"It's all right, Doug. I'll meet you in the room shortly," I said.

Doug followed his father upstairs, and I trailed behind Buffy to the bar, which was rapidly becoming familiar turf. I scanned the room, and my worst fears were confirmed. Charles the bartender had abandoned me. Not that it mattered, because Buffy ordered for both of us. "Two glasses of sherry. Amontillado Napoleon, please."

Our bartender arrived with our order. I tentatively took a tiny sip. Not as bad as I expected. Rather than a sickly sweet taste, it was creamy and nutty.

It didn't take Sherlock Holmes to figure out sherry wasn't my thing. I'd never been talented in concealing my true feelings. My hesitation caught Buffy's attention. She tapped her glass. "You don't like sherry."

My smile was apologetic. "Given my unpredictable work schedule, I'm often too tired to enjoy after-dinner drinks. But when I do burn the midnight oil, I prefer port."

"Ruby or tawny?"

"Ruby."

"Good to know. I shouldn't have ordered for you. I'm sorry about that."

This time, I made a mighty effort to suppress the telltale signs of shock that would otherwise appear. What Lady Gaga song did my congressional boss chant when faced with a comparable political situation? Oh yes, "Poker face."

I decided to get to the point. "Mrs. Hollingsworth, did you want to talk to me about something in particular?"

"I believe I mentioned this before, but please call me by

my first name. I think of my mother-in-law when I hear Mrs. Hollingsworth."

"Thank you, Buffy."

"The reason I asked you to have a drink with me alone is that I'd like to talk to you about something quite important."

After Buffy's early suggestion that the Iron Gate would be the ideal location for the wedding, the remainder of the evening's discussion had focused on other topics. I should have known the respite couldn't last much longer. I braced myself for the inevitable wedding diatribe.

"Sure, go on."

"I'm worried about Winston getting railroaded for Grayson's murder."

Not what I expected, especially since she'd been so blasé earlier in the day.

In an upbeat voice, I said, "We established tonight there are other people who might have wanted Grayson dead."

"There's no guarantee the police will follow those leads. Even if they do, if Winston remains a suspect for long, his reputation will be shattered. A dark cloud will continue to hang over the Hollingsworth family."

"You have a point. But why talk with me? What would you like me to do?"

"Isn't it obvious? You need to figure out who really did kill Grayson Bancroft. Not simply talk about it, but actually investigate."

This wasn't the time to gloat, but my future in-laws were doing an about-face, and that change of heart needed to be spelled out. "When I've engaged in such investigations before, Doug made it clear that you and Winston didn't approve of my sleuthing."

Buffy clutched her glass of sherry and forced a smile. "Let bygones be bygones, Kit. The situation is dire."

I finished my sherry and waved off the waiter, who seemed eager to refill my glass. "I've already been discussing the murder with Doug. We'll plow ahead and try to figure it out. I want to be honest with you, Buffy. This case is complicated. We may not be successful."

Even though I'd tried my best to convey the gravity of the situation, Buffy ignored my warning. She jumped to her feet and gave me a squeeze that likely passed for a warm embrace among her set. "I'm so relieved!"

Feigning regret, I said, "I'm afraid the shopping spree tomorrow won't be possible. There's another lead I need to pursue, and that means attending the Mayflower Society trip to the National Archives."

A small pout disappeared as swiftly as it appeared. "I understand. Can I ask you what the lead is?"

"When I chatted with Cecilia Rose this morning, she mentioned that Kiki Bancroft and Professor Mansfield had a complicated relationship."

"It's the worst-kept Mayflower secret. No one is sure of the status, but it's worth scrutinizing. By the way, Kiki is arriving tomorrow."

"Why wasn't she at the conference?"

"She'd been away for several weeks on an exotic globe-trotting trip and decided to skip this year's activities. She was resting at their vacation home in Florida when she was notified earlier today about Grayson's death."

"I doubt she'll attend the scheduled activities, but it will be crucial to speak with her about who wanted her husband dead," I said.

Buffy tapped her temple. "I have an idea."

I eased back in my chair and glanced at my phone. Almost eleven. Would this day never end?

"Let's hear it," I said.

"I could ask Kiki if she'd like me to host a private dinner for her and our closest Mayflower Society friends tomorrow night. She'd appreciate the gesture."

Buffy might be on to something. Without my future mother-in-law's help, how would I approach the widow Bancroft to find out what she knew?

Excuse me, Kiki. Your husband was murdered a day ago and we've never met, but can you tell me who poisoned him?

"That's not a bad idea. Do you think Kiki will want to go out to dinner and face the public? Grayson was well known in Washington, and the local papers are going to cover this crime to death … uh, excuse me." I cleared my throat. Murder and death idioms seemed to be on the tip of my tongue these days.

"Normally I'd call the Blue Duck Tavern or Michel Richard at Central and we'd have a table like that." She snapped her fingers. "I doubt Kiki will want to risk an evening out on the town. Appearances are important, after all."

We sat without speaking for several moments. Buffy smacked her hands on the table. "I've got it! What if we hosted an informal get-together at your condo?"

I thought of my underwear drying on the laundry rack and the numerous outfits I'd thrown on the bed while trying to pack something appropriate for our Continental Club sojourn. "I'm not sure our condo is ready for dinner guests."

"Nonsense. We'll have a cleaning service take care of that tomorrow. Let me think. There will be ten of us. I'll deal with the catering in the morning, too."

Although hosting a dinner party for the Hollingsworths and their closest friends wasn't exactly on my bucket list, Buffy's idea had several advantages. If Kiki agreed, it might be a perfect opportunity to speak with her about Grayson. It also had the added benefit of allowing Doug and me to check out of the Continental Club tomorrow, as originally scheduled. At least Clarence would be pleased, although his exuberant canine presence at the evening soiree might present its own challenge.

"Let's do it. I'll tell Doug about our plan," I said.

Buffy clenched her fists in victory and then grabbed my hands. "Once this murder business is resolved, we can resume our discussions about the wedding. If we can find Grayson's killer, we can certainly find the perfect venue for your big day!"

I failed to see the connection between solving the murder of one of the wealthiest titans of business and planning the perfect wedding. There was no point in arguing with Buffy. After all, she had come up with a decent idea to keep the investigation moving forward.

"Sounds great, Buffy. I'd better head upstairs. Lots to accomplish tomorrow."

Buffy drained her glass and ended our conversation on a somber note. "Such as keeping my husband out of prison."

Chapter Twelve

―⚬―

THE NEXT MORNING, I awoke with the energy that presents itself after an exhausting day followed by a deep, restful sleep. It was six thirty, which gave me enough time for a jog around the neighborhood.

A few minutes later, I bounded down the stairs. The library and the area near the Franklin statue were still surrounded by yellow police tape. At least today no corpse lay on the ground.

Spring mornings in D.C. were beautiful and brisk. In a few weeks, I'd trade the long-sleeved hoodie for a tank top. The cool air was a relief after summer, which conquered the city with a humid vengeance.

I jogged along the landscaped side streets and headed north on Massachusetts Avenue. Eventually, I hung a right onto Belmont. This was an entire neighborhood of foreign embassies. The ornate buildings and tree-lined sidewalks provided gorgeous scenery. As I huffed and puffed along, my thoughts drifted to the murder and the day ahead. Doug had been asleep when I returned to the room last night. Before breakfast, I'd fill him in on the plans for a dinner party at our condo. This morning, there was a planned Mayflower Society excursion to the National Archives. Prior to Kiki Bancroft's arrival, I wanted to speak with Professor Mansfield. Did he have a motive to kill Grayson Bancroft? Something told me that the reserved Mansfield might prove harder to chat up than the others. I needed a plan or I could blow it.

I wove through the serpentine streets, passing by the consular headquarters of Turkey, Yemen, Thailand, Poland, Afghanistan, Syria, Macedonia, and Nepal. Each of these embassies hosted cultural events on a regular basis. When lucky enough to receive an invitation to an embassy fete, we made an effort to attend. Even Doug, who was more comfortable hiding inside Georgetown library stacks than frequenting a cocktail party, could be persuaded to take advantage of the splendid food, drink, and entertainment routinely found at embassy soirees.

As I cruised downhill via Connecticut, I thought more about Grayson's unfortunate death. Assuming poison had killed him, the concoction had been fast-acting. Grayson hadn't had time to scream or crawl for help. The stiff, unnatural position of his body made him appear to be frozen. *The poison had paralytic qualities.*

The instrument of delivery was also puzzling. They'd searched the Continental Club high and low and found only Winston Hollingsworth's syringes. Perhaps the murderer knew about Winston's diabetes and stole one of his syringes. Or the killer brought his or her own needle, knowing full well that Winston would be the prime suspect. If that was the case, how did the murderer get rid of the deadly instrument? The security cameras showed no one entering or leaving the building overnight.

As I rounded the corner and stepped inside the club, I was no closer to solving the mystery. But at least I felt better. If nothing else, the run had cleared my head … and hopefully burned off some of the calories from the previous night's indulgences.

Doug was still asleep when I reached our room. After

showering, I pulled off the covers and gave him a nudge. "Time to rise and shine."

Doug waved me off as he rubbed his eyes. A minute later, he sat up in bed, his glasses in position. "Why are you up so early?"

" 'Life moves pretty fast. If you don't stop and look around once in a while, you could miss it.' "

Doug loved my movie quotes. "Bueller? Bueller?"

"You got it. Get dressed. I have a lot to tell you."

Once he was settled, I told him about his mother's idea to host a dinner party at our condo tonight. He warmed to the ploy. "Gathering the suspects under our roof may give us a certain advantage."

"How so?"

"We can direct the conversation and probe them for information. After all, we're the hosts."

"Are we really talking about the same Mayflower Society people? This is not a crew that takes kindly to direction of any sort," I said.

Doug laughed. "Good point. I still think it's better to have them on our turf. After breakfast this morning, I'll go home with my mother and make sure the arrangements are settled for this evening."

"I'd better head to the National Archives outing. I don't want to miss an opportunity for careful observation." In imitation of DeNiro in *Meet the Parents*, I pointed at my eyes with two fingers. "I'll be watching Professor Mansfield. You'd better believe it!"

Doug laughed. "Good luck with that one. He's not exactly the friendly type."

"He's an academic. I think I understand academics." I gave Doug a playful punch in the arm.

"No, Kit. Even for an academic, James Mansfield has a reputation as a cold fish."

At Georgetown faculty events, I kept close to Doug's side.

Despite all the smarty-pants people who lived in D.C., there was a considerable divide between the Capitol Hill and university crowds. Not all PhDs were born equal in Washington. The policy wonks didn't speak the same language as the ivory tower intellectuals, resulting in a classic rivalry something like that of the Redskins and Cowboys.

"It's going to be hard for me to break through," I muttered, almost to myself.

"Is Trevor working at the Continental Club today?" Doug asked.

"Don't know. What are you thinking?"

"Trevor is the most pretentious person we know. Perhaps he and Mansfield would hit it off."

I considered his suggestion. "It might work. I could also see Trevor annoying Mansfield beyond belief."

"It's worth a shot, don't you think? I can't be at the Archives with you to run interference if I need to be at home preparing for tonight."

The dinner party aside, Doug couldn't help with Mansfield. Clearly the esteemed professor felt that Doug was treading on his turf. Whether his bristling in my fiancé's presence was intellectual, professional, or personal, it didn't matter. Doug's presence would hamper any shot I had with Mansfield.

"If Trevor is here, he'll be nearby in the Poets' Room," I said.

"Let's take a look." Doug opened the door, and I followed.

Sure enough, Trevor sat in exactly the same place as yesterday. "The dynamic duo who have yet to walk down the aisle. To what do I owe this honor?"

I ignored Trevor's impolite comment. He constantly nettled me about Doug. As far as I knew, Trevor had no significant other and didn't care one iota about our relationship status. Why did he continue to poke? Maybe, like many competitive Washingtonians, he couldn't resist the opportunity to expose and exploit the shortcomings of others.

"We have a job uniquely suited for you," said Doug.

Trevor closed his laptop. "I didn't know the President of the United States was resigning."

Only Trevor would self-appropriate himself as ruler of the free world. "Not quite as grandiose, I'm afraid. Can you join me at the National Archives later today for a tour?" I asked.

"This is starting to sound like the plot of a bad sequel to *National Treasure*," Trevor remarked.

"That ship has already sailed," I said. "The Mayflower Society will be visiting the Archives as part of their conference activities. It's a good opportunity to interrogate suspects. There's one in particular I want to focus on."

"Do you know Professor James Mansfield from Yale?" asked Doug.

"Not personally, but of course I'm a fan of his scholarly work."

I clapped my hands together. "Excellent. We need to talk to him at the Archives and figure out if he killed Grayson Bancroft."

Trevor raised a skeptical eyebrow. "You think Mansfield killed Bancroft?"

"We don't know. But he was close to Bancroft's wife, Kiki," I said.

Trevor fiddled with his tie. "He was having an affair with her?"

"We aren't sure, Trevor," said Doug. "That's where you come in. We need you to run interference with Kit and charm Mansfield so we can find out what he knows about the murder."

He cleared his throat. "I find myself in familiar territory. Kit's merry band of sleuths have mucked around again with a murder investigation and now require my assistance to make sense of it."

"That's not true!" I protested. "I caught the killer without your help both times."

"After I served you the suspects on a platter. No need to

become angry, Kit. I am willing to forego writing today and join you."

I held my tongue. No matter what clever retort I could devise, it would be in vain. Trevor would always one-up me. I remembered Buffy's plea from last night. Clearing Winston Hollingsworth was the priority, even if it meant putting up with Trevor's wisecracks.

Doug must have been on the same page. "Thank you for helping. It means a lot to my family." He extended his hand.

Trevor gave his hand a quick shake. "Why can't *you* interrogate Mansfield? You're both history professors. Doesn't that make you comrades in arms?"

"We're hosting guests at our condo this evening, and I need to assist with preparations," explained Doug.

Trevor wrinkled his nose. "A convenient conflict, no doubt. Kit, what time should we meet?"

I provided him with the necessary information, and we returned to our room. "If you pack now, I can take your suitcase with me," said Doug.

"Do you have to leave soon?"

"After breakfast. I need to make a stop on the way back to Arlington."

"Where?"

Doug hesitated. "I'd rather not say right now. But if memory serves, by tomorrow we might be able to learn more about Grayson's manner of death."

"Good luck. I'm at my wits' end concerning the poison. We need a break in this case."

"That's exactly what I'm hoping for."

Breakfast was a somber affair. The reality of Grayson's death had descended upon the Mayflower Society.

The Archives tour would depart in less than an hour. Doug conferred with his mother and made plans to meet her at our condo after the tour. I headed to an adjacent room to answer work emails before it was time to leave. On the way, I ran into Detective Glass.

"Ms. Marshall, just the person I wanted to chat with."

Hearing that line from a police officer never boded well. "Yes, Detective?"

"On Wednesday evening, did Grayson Bancroft spend a lot of time with a particular Mayflower attendee?"

"Not that I recall. He talked to everyone, exchanging pleasantries and making small talk," I said.

She wrote something in her notebook. "Do you know if the Hollingsworths hosted anyone in their room, perhaps for a drink?"

"I'm not sure, but I doubt it. We had drinks on the patio before dinner. The others were inside the bar."

"Are you sure you didn't hear anything Wednesday night after going to bed?" she pressed.

We'd been over this ground before, and I preferred not to remind Detective Glass how I'd been occupied. "No, I'm afraid not."

I ventured to ask a few questions of my own. "Have you determined what type of poison killed Grayson?"

"That's going to take a while. We'll get samples sent to the lab after the autopsy. We may not see results for a month."

Just as I thought. "Do you know how the poison was administered?"

Glass's pencil tapped her notepad. "Not sure I can say much more, Ms. Marshall."

"The last time we met, you searched Winston Hollingsworth's room and bagged his insulin syringes for evidence. Are you still pursuing that angle?" I asked.

"Let's put it this way. There's no alternative theory right now."

"The killer might have brought a needle and disposed of it. Wouldn't that make perfect sense? Winston's close friends knew he was diabetic. It would be the perfect frame-up."

"Plausible, but if that's the case, where's the used syringe?

We've torn this place up and searched everyone who was in the building at the time, and it's nowhere to be found."

"The murderer might have killed Grayson, exited the building, disposed of the needle, and returned to his or her room. It wouldn't have taken much time."

"It's a good theory, but it didn't happen that way. I think I mentioned this to you before: the Continental Club has a comprehensive security system monitoring its entrances. We looked at the footage, and no one entered or left the building from midnight until morning. As far as I'm concerned, the murder weapon is inside this building." She paused, and then added. "Or was."

She didn't need to finish her thought. That fact pointed further to Winston Hollingsworth as a suspect, especially since no other plausible explanations had surfaced.

Were the cameras so strategically positioned so that no one could possibly get around them without being detected? I wasn't convinced of that, but there was no point in continuing to argue. Better to end the conversation, or I might find myself digging out of a deeper hole. "Thanks for the chat, Detective. Doug and I will be returning to Arlington later today. You have our contact information."

"Will Winston and Buffy Hollingsworth join you?"

"No, they'll remain at the Continental Club for two more nights."

"Given the circumstances, a wise choice," she stated.

Should I have mentioned that my future in-laws would be coming over for dinner? I didn't see the point of volunteering too much. The detective naturally wanted her main suspect where she could keep a close eye on him. Under normal circumstances, I'd appreciate the toughness required to compete as a female detective. Unfortunately, the formidable Detective Maggie Glass had set her sights on my future father-in-law.

Chapter Thirteen

---·~·---

THE FAMILIAR COACH bus idled in the Continental Club
parking lot as Mayflower members boarded. Grayson's
death had left no one in charge of the society. Consequently,
I had no idea who to ask about Trevor tagging along. Many of
the attendees had already ditched the proceedings, and there
was no reason to believe the trend would reverse. More seats
were vacant on the bus today than when we traveled to Mount
Vernon. History buffs apparently drew the line at murder.

During breakfast, we'd told Winston and Buffy about Trevor
joining up for the Archives trip. The other Mayflower attendees
did a double-take when they saw a man other than Doug at my
side.

To prevent rumors, I decided to explain Trevor's presence.
"Everyone, I'd like to introduce my former Senate colleague,
Trevor. He belongs to the Continental Club and is interested
in joining the Mayflower Society. Hopefully you can answer
his questions."

Trevor shot me a piercing glance. I'd made up his supposed
interest in Mayflower membership on the fly, but it was a
credible ruse. Like many elite cultural organizations, Mayflower

benefited from the largesse of its older, wealthy supporters. To ensure future viability, it had to recruit younger members. Trevor fit the profile, and if others viewed him as a potential recruit, they might open up to him.

My clever ploy worked. Trevor engaged in several polite conversations as the bus wove its way through Dupont, Scott, and Thomas Circles to Ninth Street. A few minutes later, we arrived at the National Archives, wedged between Pennsylvania and Constitution Avenues.

The Archives is a revered spot in Washington. Those of us who lived locally didn't visit often, making opportunities like this one valuable. Unlike the Smithsonian museums or the National Zoo, it was nearly impossible to tour the Archives on a whim. To avoid waiting in line for hours, you needed reservations. Viewing the Declaration of Independence, the Constitution, and Bill of Rights required advanced planning.

As I suspected, Grayson had taken care of the details. We breezed past the long queue of visitors waiting to catch a glimpse of our nation's founding documents. As we entered the rotunda, I gazed at the two large murals flanking the huge glass cases housing the archive's most precious treasures. Painted by Barry Faulkner, the paintings had been restored over a decade ago. The mural depicted a fictional presentation of the Declaration and Constitution. George Washington didn't appear in the former—he was fighting the Revolutionary War in 1776—but he was the centerpiece of the second painting, regal in his magisterial cloak. At first glance, a casual viewer might believe that Faulkner chose to portray Washington in his mural as a king, perhaps a precursor to Napoleon. Such a facile interpretation couldn't have been further from the truth. Instead, Faulkner had sought to convey Washington's strong, unyielding belief in the newly created Constitution.

Our tour guide welcomed us to the National Archives and invited us to view the Declaration. Trevor sidled up next to me. "Having any luck with our suspects?" I asked.

"Not yet," he whispered. "They're too busy trying to find out if I'm made of money. Something tells me the Mayflower Society is in desperate need of funds."

"Grayson Bancroft propped them up. His death has thrown Mayflower for a loop. Bancroft's big donations greased the wheels. That's why we move to the front of the line at places like this."

"I figured. I can play along, for now. It's not difficult for me to pretend I'm an aristocrat."

"I always assumed you *were* an aristocrat."

He wrinkled his nose. "Don't mistake good taste for a privileged birth, Kit. It's annoyingly bourgeois."

Trevor was best tolerated in small doses. I returned my attention to our tour guide, who was talking about the writing of the Declaration of Independence.

"Jefferson was chosen by the Committee of Five to write the Declaration. After completing the first draft, he presented his work to Adams and Franklin, who made changes. The committee altered Jefferson's text in forty-seven places before submitting it to Congress. After voting for independence, Congress made thirty-nine more revisions. Finally the document was accepted and sent off for printing and dissemination."

"Blimey," I said, "I wonder how Jefferson felt about those edits."

Professor Mansfield overheard my comment. "Mutilations," he said.

"Excuse me?"

"You asked what Jefferson thought of the alterations, correct?" he asked.

"Yes, and your response sounded more like Dexter Morgan than Thomas Jefferson."

"I have no idea who Dexter Morgan is. But that's how Jefferson characterized the revisions made to his final draft of the Declaration. He called them 'mutilations.' "

Now it was making sense. "He thought they'd ruined his best effort," I said.

Mansfield nodded. "He held a grudge until the day he died."

Trevor spotted me interacting with Mansfield and joined us. He introduced himself to the professor, who politely shook his hand.

"I've read several of your journal articles on the revolutionary era," said Trevor.

His subtle attempt to ingratiate himself with Mansfield appeared to have the desired effect. The professor's face brightened considerably. "When you write for academia, you don't expect people to recognize your work outside scholarly circles."

"Your research transcends the constraints of academia, Professor Mansfield. I am truly honored to be in your presence." The words oozed off Trevor's tongue with enough sincerity to convince the object of his flattery.

After several more apparently successful attempts to beguile, Trevor got down to business. "Professor, forgive me for asking this question, but what do you know about the murder of Grayson Bancroft? As a member, I spend a great deal of time at the Continental Club these days. The crime is disturbing."

The professor looked suitably disturbed himself. "I don't know much about Grayson's death. As I understand it, the police have classified it as suspicious and are investigating the matter. I hope it's wrapped up quickly. I must return to New Haven on Sunday afternoon. I cannot miss my undergraduate lecture on Monday morning."

Just as I suspected, Mansfield was a bit reticent. But Trevor had done a good job of softening him up.

"How well did you know Grayson and his wife?" I asked.

If the professor was alarmed by my question, he didn't let on. "Quite well. I knew Kiki better than Grayson." He looked at me pointedly. "Anyone will tell you that."

"Was she at the Continental Club when Grayson died?" Trevor asked.

Mansfield waved both hands in denial. "She had returned from a long trip a short while earlier and decided not to attend the Mayflower meeting this year. She's been traveling the world lately," he added.

"By herself?" I asked.

"Yes. Grayson had little time for her. He had two passions—namely, money and history. At this point in his life, he made more money so he could fund his passion for American history. He was a benefactor of many museums, such as this one."

"Bancroft was a patron of the National Archives?" asked Trevor.

"More precisely, he planned to become one. Kiki told me he was in the process of negotiating a large donation to support a permanent exhibit on the Declaration and its political and historical legacy," said Mansfield.

"I wonder if the deal will fall apart," I said.

"Hard to say. Frederick Valdez might try to swoop in and make the Archives an offer instead. Of course, Lola is the history buff, but Frederick has his reasons for wanting it, too."

"To make up for losing out on the purchase of the *Capital Observer*, perhaps?" I said.

Mansfield raised his eyebrows. "You've been doing your homework."

I knew when to back off. If Mansfield was involved with the murder, I was dangerously close to putting a target on my back. I shot a look at Trevor to indicate he should take over.

He caught on quickly. "Professor, with your impressive intelligence, I'm sure you're able to hypothesize about who might have wanted Grayson Bancroft dead."

Mansfield hesitated, clearly torn between responding to Trevor's flattering challenge or letting it slide. He scanned the crowd. All of our Mayflower companions were viewing the historical treasures on display inside the rotunda. Then he leaned in.

"You're focused on the wrong relationship," he said cryptically.

I had no idea what he meant. "What relationship?"

He motioned for us to move closer still. I hoped he'd tell us his monumental revelation soon or I was going to become more intimately familiar with Professor Mansfield than I desired.

"You're fishing around to find out about me and Kiki. We weren't having an affair, if that's what you think," he said.

I dropped my eyes and stared at my hands. Trevor shook his head. "We never said you were, Professor," he stated.

Mansfield waved us off. "As you said, I'm a smart person. I know what you were trying to insinuate. Not only is it untrue, it's also leading you down the wrong track."

"How so, Professor?" I asked.

"You're focused on Kiki when you should focus on Grayson," he said.

He had my attention. "Grayson was cheating?"

"Not really. But he never got over his love affair with Cecilia Rose."

"So Cecilia and Grayson weren't an item, but he wanted her back?" asked Trevor.

"That's my understanding of the situation. Each book in her Savannah's Sultry Nights series rekindled the romance, at least in theory. You know that Savannah's main love interest is Grayson Bancroft, right?"

"That's not his character's name in the books, is it?" I asked.

Mansfield nearly rolled his eyes; at least I could tell that's what he wanted to do. "Cecilia based Savannah's love interest on Grayson. I don't know the details. I don't read erotic romance novels."

If Grayson still held a torch for Cecilia, then who might have wanted him dead? Thinking out loud, I muttered, "Drake."

"Correct, Ms. Marshall," said the professor.

"If Cecilia ever decided she wanted to get back together with Grayson, Drake would be out of luck," I observed.

"More like off the gravy train," said Mansfield. "Everyone knows he married Cecilia for her money."

"Wouldn't Drake get a nice settlement if Cecilia divorced him?" asked Trevor.

"The answer is no," Mansfield said. "Cecilia made Drake sign a pre-nuptial agreement. He lives the high life as long as they stay together, but he has no claim on her money otherwise."

"Murdering Grayson would eliminate the competition, especially if Drake thought Cecilia might have wanted to rekindle the flame," Trevor said.

I was skeptical. "You're right," I said, "but she didn't seem to be enamored of him at dinner the night he died. They traded barbs about her writing."

Mansfield waved away my doubts. "They were always like that, even when they were a couple. Grayson and Cecilia may have moved on to other relationships, but their attraction never went away," he assured me.

I wondered privately if it might be better described as a *fatal* attraction. Casually, I scanned the crowd. The Declaration and the Constitution had apparently failed to interest Drake. He fiddled with his phone, tilting it from side to side while touching the screen with his thumbs. He was likely playing a video game in the middle of the National Archives rotunda. Cecilia was standing near the Bill of Rights display. As I stared at her, she glanced in our direction. Was she monitoring our private conversation with Professor Mansfield?

"We've been chatting far too long," I whispered. "Let's move over to the exhibit."

"I've been here more times than I can remember. I don't need to look again," protested Trevor.

I grabbed his arm and guided him toward the Declaration.

Between clenched teeth, I said, "You're here because you love American history, remember?"

"Okay, okay, I'll play along," he said quietly.

We moved over to the titanium encasement, which might have been an extremely thick picture frame. Beneath the heavy, bulletproof glass resided the nation's first founding document. "I don't care how many times you've seen it, Trevor. It's amazing." We both bent over the case to get a better look at the parchment.

Our quiet moment of patriotic reverence was interrupted by a loud female voice. "I wish my husband could be here to see his closest friends enjoying our nation's treasures."

Trevor and I turned around immediately. A petite, attractive woman in her early fifties with perfectly coiffed blonde hair stood in the center of the rotunda. She was dressed in a black fitted sheath dress and a stylishly embroidered jacket. In her right hand, she held a delicate white handkerchief with the initials "KB" stitched in dark blue. The widow, Kiki Bancroft, had arrived.

"I didn't think we'd see her until later tonight," I whispered to Trevor.

"Something tells me no one puts Kiki in a corner."

"Trevor, are you a *Dirty Dancing* fan?"

He grinned. "In case you hadn't noticed, I'm full of surprises, Kit."

Touché. "I wonder why she wanted to come to the Archives instead of waiting to see everyone at the Continental Club," I said.

We edged closer to the throng of people who had formed a tight circle around Kiki. The typical condolences were offered, although I noticed Professor Mansfield kept his distance. Either he wanted to express his sympathy privately or he wasn't sorry Grayson was dead.

After several minutes of chatting with acquaintances, Kiki cleared her throat to speak. Everyone fell silent. The widow

Bancroft may not have enjoyed the closest relationship with her husband, but like him, Kiki certainly knew how to command a room.

"Thank you for honoring Grayson's memory by continuing with your Mayflower Society meeting this weekend. As you know, American history was his passion. Despite his untimely death, I am pleased to announce that his plan to establish a permanent exhibit at the Archives focused on the legacy of the Declaration of Independence will go forward as planned." Kiki gestured to the wing on her left. "We will break ground on construction of the Bancroft Gallery in less than six months. We hope many Mayflower Society members will join us for the opening of the exhibit."

Our tour guide burst into applause, and everyone else followed suit. A smile plastered across her face, Kiki nodded her head politely, almost like a robot. I shifted my position in the crowd so I could locate Frederick Valdez. Sure enough, he wasn't clapping. Instead, he looked furious. From the grave, Grayson had managed to best him again. Had Frederick's plans backfired? If he'd committed the murder to dethrone his rival once and for all, Grayson seemed to have had the last laugh.

Buffy and Winston had edged next to Kiki. My future mother-in-law motioned furiously for me to join them. Trevor muttered, "Duty calls."

I pushed past several people so I could join the Hollingsworths, who were politely expressing their condolences to Kiki. Buffy introduced me as Doug's fiancée before giving me the entrée I needed for tonight.

"Kit and Doug would like to invite you to dinner at their condo this evening. Isn't that right?" she said.

"Yes, my deepest sympathies, Mrs. Bancroft. We thought you might want to spend the evening quietly with friends in a private location. Doug and I are hosting a small dinner party in Arlington. Nothing too fancy." Recalling that I was speaking to one of the wealthiest women in the country, I added hastily, "But it will be elegant."

Kiki gave me a well-mannered hug, barely touching my left shoulder. "How kind of you, especially since we've only just met." Her smile exposed her bottom teeth, as though she'd forced her facial muscles to register pleasure. She turned toward Buffy and Winston. "I gather the usual suspects will be in attendance?"

Winston hesitated. "Yes, in a manner of speaking."

"Forgive me. It was a poor choice of words, given the circumstances. I'd be happy to join you this evening. It will be comforting to be near old friends during this time of tragedy." She raised her handkerchief to her eye to blot an undetectable tear.

"Is seven o'clock a good time for you?" I asked.

"Certainly. Please let James Mansfield know the address. I'll arrange transportation with him. Right now, I must briefly consult with the head of development at the Archives. They're eager for a firm commitment to fund the exhibit." With that, Kiki turned on her heel and walked swiftly toward several official-looking people in dark business suits waiting for her at the edge of the rotunda.

During the conversation, Trevor had been standing silently behind me. "Did Mrs. Bancroft share her husband's passion for American history?" he asked.

Winston rubbed his chin. "That's the odd development. Not really. She attended Mayflower Society meetings years ago. Most recently, she did not. She did not appear to share Grayson's interest in the Society or related philanthropic pursuits."

"I agree," said Buffy. "And yet, she was quick to fulfill his commitment to donate considerable funds for a new exhibit at the Archives."

"Perhaps she wants to honor her husband's last wishes," I said.

"Or maybe there's more to Kiki Bancroft than meets the eye," offered Trevor.

Trevor had a point, but Kiki had been almost a thousand miles away in Florida when her husband died. Unless she'd flown on a private jet, she could not possibly have killed Grayson and made it back to Florida in time to receive the news about his murder. Given the Bancroft's wealth, such an extravagant mode of transportation was certainly possible, but even private jets had to file flight path plans that were publicly accessible. Such a plan would be fraught with risk. Of course, Kiki might have joined forces with someone onsite. Professor Mansfield had been quick to implicate Drake. Had he genuinely wished to assist with our investigation, or just sought to redirect focus away from himself?

I stared at the mural featuring a supremely confident George Washington. At the time of the ratification of the Constitution, Washington must have had more questions than answers about the future of American democracy. Why had he appeared so sure of himself? Or had Faulkner merely depicted him that way to inspire patriotic devotion?

The rotunda's legendary mural had an underlying lesson to impart. Someone well acquainted with Grayson Bancroft, perhaps a friend, had killed him. Appearances were misleading, much like the impressive painting before me. The difference between masterful deception and reality could be hard to discern. The guilty party was putting on a good show, doing what was expected of him or her in the situation. George Washington's true feelings about the future of our republic might well remain a historical mystery, but I needed to figure out which member of the Mayflower Society was lying and why.

Chapter Fourteen

$\sim$

M Y PHONE BUZZED, and I tilted the screen inside my purse so I could see who had contacted me. Meg was checking in. I walked inside the Archives gift shop so I could focus on her text. Did women actually wear knee-high socks boasting the likeness of Abraham Lincoln? Perhaps I was missing out on the latest Washington D.C. fashion trend. I pulled out my phone and read her message.

Any progress?

I typed a response. *I'm @ Archives now.*

I waited for Meg's response. *Almost done?*

I answered. *Y.*

She wrote back immediately. *Oyamel in 30?*

Not a hard choice. *C U there.*

I chuckled to myself. Meg was better than a computerized app: no matter her specific location inside the Beltway, she could provide an instant suggestion for the closest happy hour within walking distance. Oyamel, a terrific Mexican restaurant and bar, was only two blocks away. Leave it to Meg to know exactly where we should go.

I looked briefly at a reproduction of the Magna Carta. In

1215, the rebels forced King John to agree that no ruler was above the law, and the resulting document was the Magna Carta. The 1297 version, which was impressive but not quite as valuable as the earlier copies, was on display at the National Archives. Perhaps a Magna Carta facsimile would make a suitable birthday present for Doug? Then again, given the heavy hand Doug used to run his history lectures at Georgetown, I wasn't quite sure he believed no ruler was above the law.

Trevor was waiting for me outside the gift shop. "What's wrong?" I said. "You don't want a Declaration of Independence t-shirt? Or a thousand-piece jigsaw puzzle of the Constitutional Convention?"

The edges of Trevor's mouth turned up slightly. Since he rarely smiled, my question must have amused him. "I'll take a pass."

"Where is everyone else?"

"They went for a brief tour of the Legislative Archives."

"I'm impressed." The treasures inside the Legislative Archives vault were only shown to VIP groups. A few years ago, I'd gone on a special Senate tour of the vault and we'd seen documents such as the House of Representatives roll call vote declaring war in 1941 and George Washington's first inaugural address.

"I would have joined them, but it's time for me to get back to my writing."

"Thanks for joining me today. Did you pick up any clues?"

"I'm not a smarter version of the Hardy Boys, Kit. I don't go around snooping with my magnifying glass to find a loose floorboard or a missing button."

"I think you mean a red wig."

"What do you mean?"

"In *The Tower Treasure*, the Hardy Boys search for a red wig. You know, to capture the suspect."

Trevor shook his head. "You read too many mysteries."

"You can never read too many mysteries. Did you gain any

insights from your conversation with Professor Mansfield? Anyone else?" I pressed.

"You've got a tough one on your hands. No one really liked Grayson Bancroft. He was tolerated due to his wealth and power. I'd keep an eye on Frederick and Lola Valdez. They both stand to benefit from his death, although for different reasons."

"Good point. They might have worked together to eliminate Grayson."

"Are they each other's alibis?"

"Yes. Quite convenient, isn't it?"

"Of course, the same could be said for your future in-laws."

I chuckled. "Are you insinuating that Buffy helped Winston kill Grayson?"

"The convenience of the alibis works for the Hollingsworths, too."

"Buffy would never stab someone with a poison injection. She might break a nail or stain her Hermes scarf."

"I don't like ruling out plausible suspects, but I take your point."

"What about Professor Mansfield? Any thoughts on him?" I asked.

"He's highly intelligent so it will be hard to catch him in an inconsistency or lie. You should follow up on the lead he gave you about Drake. If there was any chance that Cecilia and Grayson were romantically involved again, then Drake would have a definite motive for murder."

"I'll have to think about how to approach Drake. If he killed Grayson, he's smarter than he appears."

"And he deserves an Academy Award for best actor. He seems like a dim bulb to me."

"What about Mansfield and Kiki Bancroft? He denied they were having an affair."

Trevor considered my question. "Impossible to know right now. We don't have enough data."

As helpful as Trevor could be, he was often exasperating.

"You sound like my undergraduate statistics professor."

"I'm merely stating the facts, Kit. Mansfield denies having an affair with Kiki. The only way to evaluate that claim is to observe the two of them together."

"Good point. We're hosting a small dinner party tonight at our condo. They're both coming so I'll have to keep an eye on them."

"You're going to have a busy night ahead," Trevor observed.

I sighed. Doug and his mother undoubtedly had a handle on the catering and cleanup, but hosting duties were always onerous. The point of the dinner party was to gather more intelligence about the crime to exonerate Winston. If this was going to be a successful evening, I needed help.

"Would you like to join us, Trevor? You could be my eyes and ears."

"It's a tempting offer." He tapped his iWatch and brought up his calendar.

"You look like Dick Tracy." I giggled.

"Wearable devices are no joke, Kit. Soon we'll be wearing smart clothes and jewelry."

"Will they give me tips on fashion? I could use some."

He looked me up and down and wrinkled his nose. "No argument there. I'm free this evening. However, I must return to the club and write for several hours before joining you this evening in Arlington."

With that pronouncement, Trevor pivoted and sped toward the Archives exit. He wouldn't win any awards for congeniality, although I had to admit his social skills had improved since we'd worked together in the Senate.

I only had a few minutes before I had to follow Trevor out the door so I could meet Meg at Oyamel. Before leaving, I needed to check in with Buffy and Winston to make sure everything was set for this evening. I found them inside the East Rotunda Gallery, looking at an exhibit featuring flight documents and records from the Tuskegee Airmen.

"Damn impressive. Isn't that right, Kit?" Winston asked as I approached them.

"If you're referring to the airmen, then the answer is absolutely," I said.

"They fought on two fronts: the Nazis in the air and discrimination at home. Not easy wars to wage," Winston remarked.

Buffy beamed at Winston. "My husband is happiest when surrounded by objects older than dirt."

"That's right. Of course, that doesn't include you," said Winston.

For a moment, Buffy's face tensed at Winston's joke about her age. Then she burst into laughter. "I'm not that old. At least yet."

The Hollingsworths were certainly in a jolly mood. Perhaps they were a little too merry for their own good, given that Winston was still the prime suspect in a murder investigation. I'd bring them back down to earth.

"About tonight, are we set for dinner?"

"I just got off the phone with Doug. We're meeting shortly at a place called Liberty Tavern in Arlington. He gave me the address. They've agreed to supply the food and wine for this evening." She wrinkled her nose. "Doug swears by it, although I'm a little uncertain about having a tavern cater a dinner party."

"Don't worry," I said with a wave of my hand. "It's always ranked as one of the top restaurants in Arlington."

"I suppose we'll have to make do on such short notice," said Buffy.

Bored with our conversation about tonight's menu, Winston had apparently let his mind drift back to the Tuskegee Airmen. Buffy pulled me closer. "Have you made any progress on the case?" she whispered.

"Nothing significant, but keep your eyes and ears open tonight. Maybe we'll pick up some important information."

Buffy nodded. Then she said loudly, "Winston, I'm leaving. I'll see you tonight at seven."

Winston flicked his hand in acknowledgment, never taking his eyes off the exhibit.

"I'll walk out with you. I'm meeting Meg for a drink before returning to Arlington," I said.

We walked outside into the refreshing spring air. On the other side of Constitution, the National Gallery of Art Sculpture Garden was bursting with tourists. The ice skating rink had been dismantled for the season. Soon, the popular Friday concerts would begin, filling the area with jazz lovers sipping wine and enjoying the long summer twilight. Did the Sculpture Garden allow weddings? I glanced at Buffy, who had pulled out her compact and was fixing her coiffure. Better not bring it up. I'd finally gotten Buffy to focus on the murder and Winston's predicament. Mentioning the dreaded "W" word might take us back to square one.

"Do you need a taxi?" I asked politely.

"Of course not. The driver is picking me up." She scanned the traffic flying by on Constitution and spotted a black town car. "There he is." She squeezed my shoulder. "See you later, Kit!"

Oyamel was only three blocks north on Seventh Street. I passed the Federal Trade Commission and entered Indiana Square, the location of the Grand Army of the Republic Memorial. It probably wasn't on most touristy lists of "must see" monuments, yet its historical significance was considerable. Doug had told me the twenty-five-foot-high memorial commemorated GAR, which boasted a membership of over 400,000 Union veterans after the Civil War. The organization was responsible for securing pensions for Union soldiers—the first ever government-funded social welfare program in the history of the United States.

After crossing D Street, I spotted Rasika, one of the most popular restaurants in the District. Its modern Indian cuisine consistently received rave reviews. The president and first lady had dined there recently, increasing its popularity and the difficulty associated with securing a Friday or Saturday night reservation.

Oyamel was located next to Rasika. I opened the door and immediately spied Meg at the bar, drink in hand.

"Didn't care to wait for me?" I asked.

She wrinkled her nose. "Sorry. I was thirsty."

"*No hay problema, señorita,*" I teased.

"Aren't you sophisticated? Here's the happy hour menu. It's in English."

"Are you having a margarita?"

"Of course. When in Rome, Kit."

The bartender strolled over. "Make it another for me."

He nodded.

"Before we talk about the murder," Meg said, "I have to tell you about work today."

Meg launched into an animated story about one of our policy staffers who had gotten into a dispute with a representative from the North American Meat Institute about whether bacon consumption causes cancer. Congress was truly a battle over a million special interests, perhaps exactly how James Madison had envisioned American democracy. The public undoubtedly thought those of us who worked in Congress sat around thinking important thoughts and writing legislation. I doubted they knew the intrigue behind the supposed lethality of processed meats.

I listened to Meg's story without commenting. At the end, she asked, "Do you think I handled it right?"

I couldn't resist. "You did well today, Meg. You really brought home the bacon!" I burst into laughter and took a sip of my drink, which the bartender had delivered in the middle of her story.

Meg crossed her arms. "I'm glad you find it so amusing. It was quite stressful."

I put my hand on her arm. "I'm sorry. Thank you again for watching the shop while I'm on leave."

She sipped her margarita. "Apology accepted. Would you like to order tacos? They're on special for happy hour."

Breakfast seemed like a long time ago. There had been no opportunity for lunch after the Archives. On the other hand, I was sure Doug and Buffy were ordering a ton of food from Liberty Tavern for this evening.

"Before we order anything, would you like to come to dinner tonight at our condo? We're hosting a gaggle of Mayflower Society attendees, including the widow of Grayson Bancroft."

Meg fiddled with her phone. "I can come."

"You don't seem too excited about the invitation."

"I was supposed to have a date tonight, but he canceled on me." Meg stared at her drink.

"Someone from Capitol Hill?"

In a low voice, Meg said, "No."

"A happy hour?"

She shook her head.

"A stranger from your neighborhood?"

"I haven't actually met him in person," she paused before adding, "yet."

"You met him online?" I tried to hide the surprise in my voice. Meg had never pursued men online. Her attractiveness made her a magnet for male attention. As long as we'd been friends, she'd spent more time deflecting unwanted suitors than pursuing those she liked.

"I signed up for a dating site a month ago."

"There's no harm in that. Everyone dates online these days."

"I know, but it's new for me. Half the time, guys don't even keep the dates we plan."

"At least there's always another guy to choose from."

"Yeah, an endless supply of losers. It's been hard to rebound after Kyle."

Meg was referring to her most recent beau. They'd broken

up a couple of months earlier when political differences had forced a wedge between them.

"Come on, Meg. You can't seriously miss Kyle. He didn't want you to do your job because it clashed with his partisanship."

Meg signaled for another margarita. I'd barely touched mine. "You don't know how tough dating is these days, Kit. What do you care? You're engaged to Saint Doug and your biggest problem is convincing your in-laws not to spend a fortune on your wedding."

Meg's words stung, but she wasn't entirely off base. "Point taken. I don't always count my blessings."

My best friend looked at me for several seconds. "Well, at least you admit it."

"I'll confess something else."

"What? You secretly won Powerball last night?"

"Sometimes I envy you."

Meg twittered. "Me? Why would you envy me? You have the better job, a successful fiancé, and no financial problems."

"You're gorgeous and have guys fawning over you. You have a self-confidence I can only dream about."

"Confidence about what? My good looks? Give me a break, Kit." She circled her face with her index finger. "This won't be around forever."

I scoffed. "I think it will. You'll be stunning when we're eighty."

In a voice only slightly above a whisper, Meg said, "It's already happening."

I narrowed my eyes and leaned in closer. "What's happening, Meg?"

"Guys aren't that interested anymore." Her voice rose. "Look what happened tonight! Some moron I met online stood me up."

"You're making a mountain out of a molehill. It's one date. Happens all the time."

Meg sat back in her bar stool and took a long sip of her drink. "Not to me."

"Maybe in the past, but it's not about you. Trust me."

Meg pursed her lips. "And how would you know? When were you last on a date? Not including Doug."

"Actually, it was two months ago." I was referring to a staffer from the House of Representatives Sergeant at Arms office. I'd accompanied him to happy hour to interrogate him about a murder we were trying to solve.

With a dismissive gesture, she said, "He doesn't count. I don't even want to talk about how that turned out."

I frowned. "I don't have a lot of recent dating experience. But talk to the younger female staffers in our office. They'll tell you how online dating works. You might need to lower your expectations."

"All right," Meg said, her skepticism evident. "I'll ask around. In the meantime, I'm happy to help tonight with the investigation."

I squeezed her arm. "Terrific."

"One more question."

"Sure, go ahead."

"Do you mind if I order a taco?"

I smiled. Some things never changed.

Chapter Fifteen

~~~

M EG AND I parted ways outside Oyamel. She headed home
to her D.C. apartment to change clothes and squeeze
in a power nap. I headed northwest past the Shakespeare
Theatre, the Smithsonian Portrait Gallery, the International
Spy Museum, and the Martin Luther King Jr. Central Library
to the busy Metro Center subway station. Ten minutes later, I
descended inside the crossroads of the District's transit system.
Four separate lines were serviced at Metro Center, making it
the central hub for commuters and tourists. Rush hour had
begun, which was both a boon and a curse. It meant trains
arrived more frequently, but also that the ride home would
likely find me packed in like a sardine.

The annual Cherry Blossom Festival, which brought close
to one million visitors to Washington to gawp at the three
thousand blooming Tidal Basin trees gifted to the United States
by the Japanese government in 1912, had recently concluded.
I said a silent prayer of thanks the festival was over. During
the celebration, the swell in tourists made the daily commute
a nightmare. When the doors to my Orange Line train
opened, I was relieved to see a seat was available. Like a good

citizen, I plopped myself down only after making sure that an elderly, disabled, or pregnant passenger wasn't standing in the vicinity. It always irritated me when relatively young, able-bodied individuals took the seats when others who needed one were left standing. This time I was in the clear, which was lucky because during the ride I wanted to think clearly about Grayson Bancroft's murder. Rummaging through my purse, I found my trusty notebook and a pen.

First, I needed a list of suspects. That was easy: Frederick and Lola Valdez, Cecilia Rose and Drake, and Professor James Mansfield. Reluctantly, I added Winston Hollingsworth. After all, he was a suspect, despite being my future father-in-law. I also wrote down Buffy Hollingsworth. I doubt she'd murdered Grayson on her own, but in the unlikely scenario Winston had been involved, then Buffy might have been an accomplice. Was there anyone else? I included Kiki Bancroft. She hadn't been at the Continental Club the night Grayson was killed, but wasn't the spouse always a suspect?

More people got on the train at McPherson Square and Farragut West, two popular commuter stops, and the aisles quickly filled around me. Most passengers were federal workers, sporting lanyards with their identification badges around their necks. Though clearly exhausted, they all appeared able-bodied, so I continued writing.

There was no shortage of motives. Frederick Valdez viewed Grayson as a rival who had bested him for years. Purchasing the conservative newspaper from under his nose might have been the last straw. Lola detested the direction Grayson had taken with the Mayflower Society. With his considerable money and influence, he might have held the presidency for another decade. By then, Mayflower would have been transformed into something Lola abhorred. Perhaps the two of them had decided to work together to kill Grayson.

Drake acted like a pinhead, but appearances could be deceiving. If Cecilia took up with her former paramour, he'd be out on his can with nothing to show for it. Cecilia was even more of a mystery. She seemed to have a "love/hate" relationship with Grayson Bancroft. Did he want to rekindle the romance? Had Cecilia resisted his overtures? I put a question mark next to her name.

If Professor Mansfield and Kiki were having an affair, Mansfield would have had a strong motive for killing Grayson. He might have taken advantage of Kiki's deliberately orchestrated absence at the Mayflower Society. Perhaps he killed Grayson while she escaped scrutiny for the murder? After all, he'd tried to divert attention away from himself to Drake when Trevor and I had interrogated him at the National Archives. Had it been the clever ploy of a murderer trying to send us down the wrong path?

Of course, Winston Hollingsworth's motive was clear. He'd disliked Grayson and wanted to lead the Mayflower Society. Winston had publicly challenged Grayson only hours before his death and never hidden his disdain. The insulin syringes certainly pointed to him.

By the time we hit the Foggy Bottom station, the subway car had filled up. Despite the large volume of people, the Metro was almost always quiet. People listened to music, read books on their Kindles, or stared into space. However, Friday evenings were different. The crowd buzzed with chatter about weekend plans and the spring weather. Only ten minutes from my stop, I was able to tune out the surrounding din and focus on the case.

What did we need to learn at the dinner party? Since Trevor and Meg had agreed to join us, we should put them to good use. I studied the list of suspects and jotted down several notes. Before our guests arrived, I'd huddle with Doug, Trevor, and Meg.

The next stop was Clarendon. I got up to weave my way to the subway door. When I first started commuting, I made the mistake of remaining in my seat too long before my stop. Once the doors closed, there was no way to notify the train operator to reopen them. The only recourse was to double back at the next station.

Five minutes later, I was standing in front of the door of our condo, bracing myself. Clarence had a knack for knowing exactly when the door was going to open. He frequently waited on the other side, poised to escape. Never mind that his "escape" consisted of running down the long hallway of our building. He seemed to relish the thrill of it and take great delight in my feeble attempts to catch him.

But I'd gotten wise to Clarence. I opened the door slowly. Sure enough, I could see his floppy brown ears and black nose through the crack. In one swift move, I pushed through the door and slammed it behind me. Clarence's look of defeat was immediately replaced by excitement. He wiggled his butt with vigor and barked several times.

I shuttled Clarence to our oversized sofa and patted the seat next to me. He immediately jumped up and gave me a big kiss. After enjoying a speedy ear scratch and a hug, he rolled over onto his back for a belly rub. I could only imagine his thoughts. *Finally, someone who understands me is here. Thank goodness.*

Buffy appeared in the living room. She was dressed in a sleek black sheath dress with a fitted blazer and silver jewelry. I'd almost forgotten. This wasn't our normal Friday night out with Doug's Georgetown colleagues or my friends from Capitol Hill. I'd have to find something to wear in my closet pronto.

"Kit, what are you doing?" she asked.

"I just got home. Don't worry. I'm going to change my clothes before the party."

"I'm not talking about the clothes, although now that you mention it, you'd better change. Why is *he* on the couch?" She pointed directly at Clarence.

"Him? You mean Clarence?"

"Yes. Do you know we had this condo scrubbed spotless earlier today?"

I looked around. Now that Buffy mentioned it, the place did look cleaner than usual.

"Thank you for doing that. But Clarence is allowed on the furniture. We don't restrict him." He must have known we were talking about him. He cuddled up next to me and stretched across my lap.

Buffy drew herself up to her full height, as if poised for a fight. "What you do in your home is your own business. But not when I'm expecting friends here for a dinner party." She walked over to the couch and pointed to the ground. "Off the couch, Clarence. Now."

To my utter amazement, Clarence gave Buffy a sheepish look, hopped off the sofa, and put his face between his paws in defeat.

Buffy smacked her hands together. "Good boy. That's settled. Now Kit, let's go into the bedroom and find a suitable outfit for you."

Maybe Cesar Milan, popularly known as the Dog Whisperer, should hire Buffy as a guest host. Clarence regularly ignored Doug and me when we told him to behave. Although I couldn't know for sure, he seemed to respect Buffy's authority. Apparently her imposing personality transcended species.

Doug was in his office, pounding away at the keyboard. "What are you doing?" I asked.

"Trying to squeeze in a few hours of writing." He kept his eyes glued to the computer screen.

Yeah, right. More like avoiding your mother.

"Trevor and Meg are coming to dinner tonight. When they arrive, we should go over the plan."

Doug's gaze did not waver. "Sure, sounds good."

Buffy called from our bedroom next door. "Kit, I'm waiting for you."

I tapped Doug on the arm and mouthed silently, "Help."

He shrugged his shoulders. "Good luck," he whispered.

I grabbed a pen on his desk and wrote in large block letters on a yellow legal pad, THANKS FOR NOTHING.

He stifled a laugh while I stormed out of the office and into our bedroom. Buffy was standing next to our walk-in closet. At least she hadn't already picked out an outfit for me.

Foolish thinking. "Show me your suitable evening attire. Given the occasion, let's focus on black or darker colors," she said.

My clothes were arranged according to function. Fun, casual attire resided in the left-hand side of the closet. Work attire and suits were on the right. I wasn't sure how to classify this evening, so I gravitated toward the center where the two categories sometimes blended together. I chose a fitted black pantsuit, my classic LBD, and a flowing one-piece jumpsuit.

I placed the outfits on the bed. Buffy looked at the clothes and then sized me up. She did this several times before I lost patience.

"What are you doing?" I asked.

"Trying to imagine which one of these looks best on you, dear."

"They all look fine." Truth be told, I gained and lost the same ten pounds repeatedly. Right now, I was smack-dab in the middle. Nothing was loose, and nothing was tight. I'd vowed to reach the low end of my weight spectrum before walking down the aisle, but Buffy didn't need to know that.

"Of course. These are flattering cuts," Buffy said, in a polite yet patronizing tone.

I was tired of Buffy ordering me and my dog around. I snagged the jumpsuit off the bed. "I like this one. It's comfortable and appropriate for the season. I can dress it up with the silver necklace Doug gave me for Christmas."

Buffy looked surprised by my initiative. She started to speak, then stopped. Finally she smiled and said, "That will be lovely, Kit. With some bold makeup to complement your long brown hair, it will be enchanting." She touched me lightly on the shoulder. "I'll leave you to get ready."

Thank goodness. There were two ways to handle Buffy. One approach was doing exactly what she said, as Clarence had done. Of course, he was a dog, and I couldn't blame him. The other option was taking the bull by the horns. Even an alpha male (or female) respected a worthy challenger every once in a while. Hanging my pantsuit on the door handle, I congratulated myself on a small victory.

I glanced at my watch. With plenty of time before guests started arriving at seven, I decided to take a relaxing shower. As I was drying my hair, an appetizing aroma drifted inside the bathroom. Breakfast had been ages ago, and I hadn't ordered a taco with Meg. The blend of smells made it hard to discern what was on the menu. Dressed in my plush terry cloth bathrobe, I ambled down the hallway toward the kitchen. No surprise, Buffy had taken over and was supervising the arrangement of this evening's meal inside our dining room. A young man with a Liberty Tavern hat was trying his best to make her happy. Positioned at the edge of the dining room, Clarence waited patiently. The enticing aromas had undoubtedly drawn him to the food source, but Buffy's presence intimidated him. He licked his lips as drool oozed out of the corner of his muzzle. Clarence loved food and me, in that order.

"The chopped salad and the antipasti must go at this end. Guests will want to sample them first before the main dishes," Buffy declared. She pointed to the corner of our dining room table.

"Yes, ma'am."

"No, the cheese plate shouldn't be next to the appetizers. We'll put that over on the credenza inside the living room so guests can enjoy it while they have drinks. Are these labeled properly?" Buffy grabbed the assortment of cheeses from the delivery guy.

"Yes, ma'am."

"Put the gnocchi and the carbonara next to the salad. The shortribs and trout can go last."

No wonder I couldn't figure out what smelled so delectable. It was a veritable smorgasbord of victuals.

"You and Doug did a good job of picking all the favorites," I said.

Buffy looked surprised. She had been so consumed with her command and control performance, she hadn't realized I was even there. "Thank you, Kit. As I said before, we'll have to make do with pub food on such short notice."

The Liberty Tavern employee bristled but remained silent. Wise choice.

"Are you setting up a bar?" I tried to direct my question to our helper, but no dice.

"Absolutely," Buffy responded. "We'll use the granite countertop inside the kitchen for the wine selection." She frowned. "I do hope the wine order is correct." She put her hands on her hips again.

"Yes, ma'am."

Boy, this guy had nerves of steel—a bona fide professional. He arranged bottles of Meritage, Pinot Noir, and Sauvignon Blanc on the counter and placed several others inside the fridge.

"What's that?" I asked.

"La Grande Dame champagne," Buffy answered. "We'll toast Grayson tonight; he would expect nothing less."

I gulped. Hopefully Buffy and Winston had picked up the tab. One more box remained. Our trusty assistant removed two wrapped pans. The aluminum foil did not prevent the honeyed smell of dessert from filling the kitchen.

"Delicious," I muttered.

"Sweet corn panna cotta and toasted angel food cake," pronounced Buffy.

My stomach rumbled. If my future mother-in-law wasn't hovering like a hawk, I would have opened the corner of one of the pans and served myself a small piece. An appetizer of Italian dessert would hit the spot. But that was never going to happen.

I turned toward our helper. "Thank you very much for your work this evening," I said.

"Yes, ma'am."

A man of few words was an exceedingly rare asset in Washington D.C. My fellow chiefs of staff on Capitol Hill could learn a thing or two from him. I flashed him a warm smile and retreated back into the bedroom.

As I was applying my makeup, Doug appeared at the doorway. He scanned the room before entering.

"Don't worry," I said, "the coast is clear."

Relief washed over him. "Thank goodness." He flopped down on the bed.

"Tough day?" I asked.

"Within the scope of world crises, the Arab-Israeli conflict is more problematic. But not by much," he added wryly.

"Buffy gave the folks at Liberty Tavern a run for their money, I gather." I finished applying eyeliner. Mascara was next.

"Let's put it this way. I know you love their Vermont wood-fired pizza. But you might not want to show your face there with me anytime in the near future."

"No soup for you," I said.

"Very funny. That means no pizza for you."

"That's not amusing at all, Doug." I took my pizza consumption seriously. I hoped he was exaggerating about being blacklisted at Liberty Tavern.

Clarence ambled into the bedroom. Joining Doug on the bed, he immediately rolled over onto his back to expose his pink tummy. Clarence loved a good belly rub. Although I couldn't be sure, I was willing to bet a month's Metro allowance that Meg hadn't indulged him with a satisfying doggie massage while we were gone. As Doug petted him, Clarence uttered a growl of appreciation.

I scanned my row of lipsticks and selected a deep reddish brown. "Weren't you going to chase down a lead before the catering appointment with your mother? Any luck?"

"I was just going to tell you about it. I hope tonight's dinner doesn't last too long. We've got to be at the Natural History Museum tomorrow at eleven."

Blotting my lips, I asked, "The Smithsonian?"

"The one and only."

"I know you love museums, but do you really think we have time for a visit, given everything else that's going on?"

"We're going to the Smithsonian for research purposes."

"Squeezing in some legwork for your next book?"

"Wrong again. We're going to learn about poisons."

Doug had my full attention. "How are we going to do that?"

"*The Power of Poison* exhibit." He grabbed our iPad and showed me the screen. "It's wrapping up at the Smithsonian next week."

I took the device from him and scanned several pages. The exhibit focused on poisons in nature, legend, and crime. "Do you really think it could help us solve Grayson's murder?"

"I arranged for the exhibit's curator to meet with us. Maybe she can shed some light."

I checked my makeup and hair in the mirror one last time. "Can't hurt. I'm not sure Trevor and I made much progress today. Professor Mansfield denied having an affair with Kiki Bancroft. Instead, he implied Drake might have done it."

Doug frowned. "Drake? Why would he want to kill Grayson? He hardly knew him."

"Mansfield hinted that Grayson was still in love with Cecilia. If she ever decided to rekindle their romance, Drake would have been out the door with nothing but the clothes on his back."

"I suppose that's a plausible motive."

"It's as good as anything else I've heard. Also, Kiki Bancroft showed up today and announced she's going to honor her husband's commitment of a sizable donation to build a new gallery at the Archives. Frederick Valdez didn't seem pleased. With Grayson out of the picture, he probably intended to make a play for it."

"Are we going to discuss our sleuthing assignments for this evening? There's a lot of ground to cover."

"As soon as Trevor and Meg arrive."

As if on cue, my phone buzzed. After glancing at the text message, I said, "Meg will be here in ten minutes." I glanced at the time. "Trevor should arrive shortly, as well."

Doug nodded. "I suppose I should face the music and see if Mother needs any last minute help."

After Doug left, Clarence looked at me expectantly. "Don't worry, buddy. I'll save you a shortrib."

His eyes sparkled in reply.

The doorbell rang twice. Showtime.

Chapter Sixteen

I DIDN'T NEED to ask Doug who had arrived. The bickering voices of Trevor and Meg traveled from the entrance of our condo down the hallway to our bedroom. I couldn't find my fancy silver hoop earrings, but if I delayed much longer, we'd risk the launch of World War III. I grabbed another pair sitting on my nightstand and hustled to our living room.

"You are way over the line, Trevor." Meg struck a defiant pose, hands on hips.

"And you, *Megan*, suffer from delusions of grandeur." Trevor adjusted his horn-rimmed glasses. *Uh-oh.* Meg absolutely hated it when Trevor used her full name. Gadfly that he was, Trevor only did it to annoy her.

Where was Doug? I glanced around the corner, where he was hurriedly uncorking a bottle of wine. Smart move. Both of our early guests needed to take it down a notch.

"Hello, everyone. Thank you for coming to dinner this evening." I flashed a toothy smile in an attempt to diffuse the situation.

Trevor produced a bouquet of freshly cut flowers from behind his back. "For the host," he said.

"How beautiful, Trevor. I'll put these in water. Sit down." I pointed to the couch. "Doug is working on the drinks."

I joined Doug in the kitchen and asked him a low voice, "Why were they fighting?"

He shrugged. "Not sure. It had something to do with who was your true Dr. Watson."

I frowned. "What do you mean?"

"You know, who helped you more with solving the other murders," said Doug.

"You've got to be kidding me," I said, shaking my head.

Standing in the corner, Buffy had already poured herself a glass of red wine. "Lovely way to start the dinner party," she said sarcastically.

"Don't worry. They'll be fine once everyone arrives. They always fight like cats and dogs, but it works out in the end." I grabbed the two full glasses of wine from Doug. "This will help."

Doug followed me into the living room. At least Meg and Trevor were sitting peaceably on the couch next to each other. "Here you go."

After I handed off the glasses, Doug provided me with one. "Let's toast," he suggested.

The four of us raised our glasses. "What should we toast to?" asked Meg.

That was easy. "Solving Grayson Bancroft's murder."

Buffy snuck up behind us. "I can drink to that," she said.

"Let's discuss the strategy for tonight," said Doug.

I joined Trevor and Meg on the couch and Doug pulled chairs over for him and his mother.

"This is exciting," said Buffy. "What's the plan?" My future mother-in-law sparkled. Maybe Buffy needed to experience a thrill every once in a while. The routine of high-society dinners probably grew tedious. Although I knew she was worried about the veil of suspicion that had descended upon Winston, she also seemed to be genuinely enjoying herself.

"Meg, I think you should focus on Drake and Cecilia. See if you can figure out whether Cecilia still had feelings for Grayson and whether Drake has a brain in his head," I said.

"I can do that. Besides, I've read several novels in the Savannah's Sultry Nights series."

"Why am I surprised? Your literary choices speak for themselves," Trevor said mockingly.

I gave Trevor a little punch on the shoulder. "Romance sells, Trevor. Especially erotic romance. Don't knock it," I said.

Trevor sighed heavily. "No need to remind me. My editor wants me to write more about sex in my book."

The notion of nerdy Trevor writing about sex almost made me do a spit take. Instead, I forced myself to swallow my wine and maintain a poker face. "Trevor, can you chat with Kiki Bancroft and Professor Mansfield? Speaking of romance, see if you can detect whether Mansfield lied to us today about the supposed affair."

"I'll also try to figure out why she was so eager to go forward with the Archives donation," he said.

"Good idea." I turned to my future mother-in-law. "Buffy, you and Winston need to spend more time with Frederick and Lola. They both resented Grayson. Were they angry enough to kill him?"

"We've known those two for a long time. We should be able to figure something out," she answered.

"As hosts, Doug and I will make the rounds. Let us know if you need us," I said.

Our accomplices nodded. Buffy jumped up. "Where are my manners? Please, everyone, help yourself to the appetizers."

Meg didn't need to be asked twice. She made a beeline for the cheese tray and loaded up her plate. Clarence ran over to her and sat obediently at her feet. She patted him on the head and gave him a tiny piece of Vermont cheddar.

"He's your new pal," I commented.

"Once I agreed to share treats, we arrived at a truce," she said.

I was still laughing when Buffy interrupted our conversation. "It's time for Clarence to say goodnight," she said.

"What do you mean?" I asked.

"We cannot have a dog attend a dinner party," Buffy pronounced.

"Where is he going? You can't just turn him out on the street for the night." I tried to keep my voice even.

Counting our guests off on his fingers, Doug said, "We have twelve people coming this evening. It might be a good idea to keep Clarence inside our bedroom."

I looked at my mutt's face. He seemed to know we were deciding his fate. He cocked his head to the side and stared intently at me.

"We've never confined him to one room. He's not going to be happy about it," I said.

"Probably not, but maybe we can give him treats to sweeten the deal," offered Doug.

"That'll last about two minutes," I muttered.

Doug went inside the kitchen. I could hear him cutting up food and filling up Clarence's stainless steel bowl. I'd felt sympathy for Buffy after she'd implored me last night to solve Grayson's murder and clear Winston's name. But her dislike of Clarence—and perhaps all dogs—had gotten on my last nerve. I took a substantial sip of my wine in a feeble attempt to curb the anger rising within me.

Meg must have noticed. She reached down and petted Clarence. "He'll be fine, don't worry. We can visit him in between courses. It will give us a chance to compare notes."

I gave her a quick hug. "What would life be like without you, Meg?"

Without hesitation, she answered. "Booooring!"

"You're exactly right," I said.

Doug approached, a generous feast inside the doggie bowl. Clarence tilted his head upward and sniffed eagerly.

"Hey, buddy, do you want dinner?"

Clarence trotted down the hallway behind Doug.

There was a knock at the door. I moved to answer it, but Buffy was closer and beat me to the punch. *It's not even her home*, I thought.

Meg glanced at me with raised eyebrows. She whispered, "Kit, just remember. Serenity now."

"Thanks, Frank Costanza. I'll try."

Winston Hollingsworth entered, carrying a bouquet of flowers. "Good evening," he boomed out.

"Oh, it's you," said Buffy.

"You sound so enthused," said Winston.

"I thought you were one of our guests."

"Sorry to disappoint. Kit, please accept this as a paltry gift for hosting the best of the Mayflower Society tonight."

"Thank you. They're beautiful."

Doug appeared at my side and took the gift. "I'll put these in a vase."

Buffy grabbed her husband's arm. "Our assignment this evening is to figure out if Frederick and Lola Valdez killed poor Grayson."

Winston looked surprised. "I thought this was a dinner party for Kiki."

"Yes, darling. That's what we told her. But we're really trying to solve the murder. Please keep up."

"I'll try my best." Winston turned to Doug. "Can you pour me a Scotch? Balvenie?"

Doug nodded. "I believe we have a bottle of twelve year."

Winston blew out a resigned puff of air. "That will do."

Doug turned toward me and rolled his eyes. He kept a liquor stash for guests since we were wine drinkers, save my infrequent gin and tonic indulgences. Winston would have to put up with mediocre Scotch while we tried to prove his innocence.

Another knock on the door, and Buffy rushed to answer. I didn't even budge. It was Kiki Bancroft and Professor Mansfield. Buffy fawned over them and placed Kiki's purse in our bedroom for safekeeping.

After pleasantries were exchanged, Kiki approached me. She'd changed out of her black dress from earlier today into a fitted black pantsuit and an exquisite multi-colored scarf. Was it cashmere? I didn't have much time to ponder Kiki's fashionable accessories before she addressed me.

"When I met you earlier today, Kit, I hadn't realized you were the one who discovered Grayson's body on Thursday morning." Mansfield returned with a glass of wine. Kiki accepted the drink and waited for my answer. She had a steely blue stare second only to Superman's.

Caught off guard, I stammered, "Yes, I didn't want to t-tell you. Um, I mean, it didn't seem appropriate, given the circumstances."

Her expression remained unchanged. "Of course. We'd only just met."

What was I supposed to say? That Grayson looked like he'd been frozen stiff in the midst of a dying convulsion? Instead, I opted for a more benign version of events. "He seemed at peace."

Her eyes narrowed. "Grayson was never at peace. That's why he built a multibillion-dollar fortune." She sipped her wine. "But I suppose death is the great equalizer. Don't you agree, James?"

"All stories, if continued long enough, end in death," he said.

We both stared at him in uncomfortable silence.

"I didn't make that up," he protested. "It's Ernest Hemingway."

Kiki touched his arm lightly. "James, you're so intelligent. Always ready with a moving quote or observation."

Professor Mansfield blushed.

Trevor approached our group. After giving him a proper introduction to Kiki, I excused myself. Buffy was ushering in the next set of arrivals, Cecilia Rose and her husband Drake. I signaled to Meg that these were her targets for the evening. She was munching away on cheese and crackers while juggling a glass of wine, but she caught my drift and headed in our direction.

"Cecilia and Drake, may I introduce my best friend, Meg Peters," I said.

Meg was finishing her last bite of appetizer. She extended her hand as she chewed. After a big gulp, she smiled. "Pleased to meet you." She turned toward Cecilia. "I'm a big fan of the Savannah series."

In a bubbly voice, Cecilia said, "How delightful. Which one did you like best?"

Meg sipped her wine and thought for a moment. "I enjoyed *Savannah Sizzles*. But *Night of the Scoundrel* was pretty hot, too."

Meg's comment seemed a little off-color for a dinner party doubling as a wake. Cecilia didn't seem to mind. She piped up, "Fascinating! I love feedback from readers. What did you think of *Naked Cowboy*, by the way?"

Meg tilted her hand from side to side. "So-so, if you want my honest opinion. I'm not much for Western romance."

Cecilia nodded. "It was a diversion for the series. There are only so many hunks Savannah can sleep with in the South."

Meg laughed. "I see your point. Sometimes I think I've gone through all the guys in Washington D.C."

My bestie and Cecilia were two peas in a pod. I snuck a peek at Drake, who appeared absorbed in the conversation.

"What do you think of all this talk about romance novels?" I asked him.

"As long as it sells more books, I don't mind." Drake drained his glass. "Excuse me, I need a refill." He scurried off in the direction of the kitchen.

Cecilia sighed heavily. "Drake isn't a big reader. Then again, I didn't marry him for his intellect." She winked at both of us.

"When's your next book coming out?" Meg asked.

"I'm not exactly sure. Ask me after I've had a few more glasses of vino. I'd better find my husband. Ta-ta, ladies." She fluttered her fingers.

"What a trip," said Meg.

"Good job. Keep at it. After another drink, she might sing like a canary," I said.

With ten people carrying on lively conversations in the confined space of our condo, the rising din had prevented me from noticing that Frederick and Lola had arrived. "I'd better greet our last guests. Let's regroup soon," I whispered to Meg.

"I need more pecorino and another glass of Prosecco. Then back to the interrogations!" Meg declared.

At least she had her priorities straight. I weaved over to Frederick and Lola, who had been ambushed by Buffy. Winston stood next to his wife, fidgeting with his cufflinks. Despite his reputation as an ultra-successful attorney, perhaps Winston was uncomfortable with the prospect of interrogating suspects. I'd tried not to pay too much attention to the details of the elder Hollingsworths' lives, but I was almost certain Doug had told me his father made his fortune on corporate deals, not in the courtroom. Matlock, he was not.

Frederick spotted me first. "Thank you for hosting us this evening, Kit."

Doug appeared behind me. "We're happy to do it."

Lola had on a deep purple maxi dress and large hoop earrings. Not exactly the outfit I'd select for a wake, yet it fit her free-spirited personality.

After everyone had been provided a glass of wine, Winston said, "How'd you like the Archives visit today?" He gazed pointedly at Frederick. Maybe the elder Hollingsworth had decided to embrace the objective of the evening gathering.

Frederick adjusted the lapel of his sporty linen blazer. "Remarkable, simply remarkable."

His perfunctory response didn't satisfy Winston. With his eyes round and wide open, he asked, "Anything in particular, Frederick? What about the Declaration?"

I leaned back and whispered to Doug, "Your father's attempt to rile Frederick Valdez is a little obvious."

"Let him go. He's having fun. Just look."

Winston Hollingsworth did appear pleased with himself. He'd successfully suppressed a grin, but his entire visage glowed with anticipation.

"Yes, of course. It's not in good shape, though." He shook his head vehemently. "Too many years of exposure and getting jostled around. I'm not sure how much longer the Archives will be able to keep it on display."

That was exactly the entry Buffy needed. She'd watched the verbal volley on the sidelines in silence. A black panther cloaked in Prada, she saw her opening and pounced. Frederick Valdez was nothing but an unassuming antelope grazing on Italian cheese.

"I'd say long enough for Kiki to make sure the Bancroft wing of the Archives is built," Buffy said.

Frederick noted Buffy's smirk, and heaving a sigh, said, "It was a surprise to learn that Kiki is going forward with the donation."

"Yes, I thought so. Kiki never seemed that interested in Grayson's philanthropy," said Buffy.

"Why don't we find out why she decided to proceed?" asked Winston.

Buffy didn't need a second invitation. Kiki was standing only a few feet away, deep in conversation with Professor Mansfield, their heads only inches apart. If their relationship had been purely platonic thus far, it seemed to be taking a carnal turn. Perhaps I could persuade Doug to play Olivia Newton-John's "Physical" on our sound system to enhance the moment.

Nonetheless, the fairly obvious air of intimacy didn't deter Buffy.

She tapped the widow Bancroft on the shoulder. "Kiki, can you join us briefly over here? Winston would like to ask you a question."

The elder Hollingsworth grimaced. Kiki joined the conversation, the good professor trailing behind her. Winston cleared his throat. "Ah, Kiki. Once again, I'd like to express our sincere condolences." He paused, perhaps searching for the right words. "Grayson was a successful man. Many people admired him, and he certainly was devoted to the Mayflower Society."

Buffy rescued her husband. In a loud voice, she announced, "Hear, hear! That sounds like our first toast of the evening. Let's raise our glasses and drink to our dearly departed friend, Grayson Bancroft."

Kiki bowed her head in acknowledgment. After the toast, Winston picked up the conversation. "Some of us were quite," Winston faltered for a second, "*shocked* when we heard you wanted to continue with the commitment at the National Archives."

Kiki's face remained placid. "It's true that American history was Grayson's passion, not mine." She reached behind her and touched Professor Mansfield's shoulder. "But James convinced me the project was too important to abandon."

Mansfield's mouth fell open and his eyes shifted to those listening to the conversation. He started to speak but must have reconsidered. Buffy didn't let him off the hook so easily, though. "Professor Mansfield, you saved the Bancroft wing of the Archives. How delightful! Will you serve as a special history advisor to the project?"

"I'm not quite s-sure yet," he stammered. "There's a lot up in the air these days."

"Well put, Professor. I couldn't agree more," said Buffy.

Frederick Valdez said, "I hope you will have the time and

enthusiasm for the project, Kiki. It's no small endeavor."

Standing next to him, Lola nodded vigorously. I had a feeling she was responsible for Frederick's interest in the Archives donation. Had Lola also roped her husband into murder?

Kiki sipped her drink. "Now that Grayson is gone, I expect I'll spend more time at home. Trotting the globe doesn't seem appropriate." I noticed that she shifted her gaze ever so slightly in the direction of Professor Mansfield when she spoke. It was definitely an unconscious reaction, but perceptible nonetheless.

"In Washington? Or one of your other houses?" Frederick asked, a touch of annoyance in his voice.

"You know, here and there. Whatever strikes my fancy," she said nonchalantly.

"Our son is an esteemed professor of American history at Georgetown. He'd be happy to help with your Archives project. Isn't that right, Doug?" Winston raised his voice to get Doug's attention.

My fiancé raised his hand when he heard his name. His hands were full, quite literally, with drink refills for our guests. He definitely hadn't heard his father's offer. If he had, Doug would *not* have waved amiably in response. Doug had a one-track mind when it came to his scholarly work, and it didn't include acting as a consultant for tourist destinations.

"What a marvelous thought," said Kiki. The tightness in her face indicated the exact opposite. "Georgetown is a fine institution, but I hope to persuade Yale to take the lead. I hear the faculty is tremendously satisfying to work underneath." She moved closer to James Mansfield.

Everyone in our group stared at the professor, who glanced quickly at Kiki and then looked in the opposite direction. After a long moment, he said cautiously, "I'll have to discuss the proposal with the department chair."

Kiki's face fell. But she recovered almost instantly. "Of course. It's a big-time commitment, after all." She turned to me. "Darling, can I ask you for a refill?"

After asking what wine she was drinking, I made a beeline for the kitchen. Meg was pouring herself another glass of champagne while fiddling with her iPhone. If my best friend woke up one morning and found herself transformed into Supergirl, sparkling wine would be her Kryptonite. A close second might be prolonged separation from her smartphone.

"How's it going?" I asked.

"Do you have a minute to chat?"

"Sure. As soon as I deliver this refill to Kiki."

"Let's meet in your bedroom in two minutes."

"Is that a proposition?"

Meg hit me playfully on the arm. "Get your mind out of the gutter, Kit."

I giggled.

"And grab mine while you're there, too," Meg added.

Chapter Seventeen

———

I CAREFULLY CRACKED the bedroom door. Clarence was a master at escape, and I didn't trust him. I sneaked a peek and then swung the door open. Meg was petting Clarence on the bed.

"How's he doing?" I asked.

"I'm not sure. He seems antsy."

Sure enough, Clarence got up and paced back and forth. I sat down, caught him by the collar, and drew him close. "What's wrong, buddy?"

He nuzzled my neck, then drew back and jumped off the bed. Going over to the door, he sat next to it and growled.

Let me out.

I'd nabbed several doggie treats in the kitchen. "Clarence, come here." He froze, clearly torn between the promise of food or the possibility of escape. No big surprise, he opted for the food.

I fed him a treat and patted him on the head. "What did you find out, Meg?" I asked.

"I focused on Drake. He's definitely a piece of work."

"How so?"

She took a sip of her drink and then placed it on my nightstand. "For starters, he wasn't shy about telling me he's always preferred older women."

"Cecilia has to be twenty years his senior."

"Twenty-two, actually. She offered that detail." Meg wrinkled her nose. "I think she might view him as some sort of conquest. A boy-toy man trophy."

"You make it sound distasteful," I said. "Men boast about bedding younger women all the time."

"I know, I know. Gloria Steinem is going to revoke my subscription to *Ms.* But it's not any less obnoxious when a woman does it."

"Good point. He also mentioned another detail."

Clarence growled. I fed him a treat. "Go on. But make it quick. I'm running out of biscuits."

"Drake said something about Cecilia wanting to work on a new project instead of the Savannah series."

"Popular writers write standalone books all the time."

Meg sighed heavily. "Duh, Kit. I'm not stupid. What I'm trying to tell you is that Drake hinted about her ending Savannah's Sultry Nights."

That would be big news. "Was he upset about it?"

Meg reached back for her drink. "You betcha. He was not pleased. That series is a goldmine. By the way, he shared that tidbit when Cecilia left the conversation to use the restroom."

Clarence jumped up and leaned next to me. I squeezed him playfully. "Interesting, isn't it, Clarence?" He gave me a quick kiss on the cheek.

"Drake might have thought Cecilia and Grayson had a chance of getting back together," Meg said. "By eliminating the competition, he'd feel more secure. That makes him a good murder suspect."

"Precisely."

"But I'm not sure how the sunset of the Savannah series fits in," said Meg.

"Me, neither. Let's find out. By the time we have dinner, maybe Drake or Cecilia will be ready to talk."

"You know what they said during World War II?"

"What?"

Meg grinned. "Loose lips sink ships."

"We need someone with lips loose enough to sink an aircraft carrier if we're going to solve this murder. Let's drink to that." I raised my glass and clinked Meg's.

We got up from the bed. She turned back and looked at Clarence. "Are you sure he's okay?"

"He's fine. Doug had him out for a walk before the guests arrived. Clarence just doesn't want to miss out on the fun." I bent over the bed to ruffle his ears. "Trust me. Dealing with Buffy Hollingsworth is not a barrel of laughs."

Clarence responded with a low growl.

"See?" I said. "He understands."

Meg chuckled, and we left the room, making sure to close the door firmly behind us.

A line had formed around the dining room table as our guests helped themselves to the buffet. Doug and I hung back, making sure everyone had a full plate before we sampled the fare. Kiki and Cecilia passed by with their food. Kiki's plate was half empty, with a scoop of chopped salad and small piece of trout. Maybe she didn't like our dinner offerings or suffered from a food allergy.

"Kiki, did you find enough to eat? I'm afraid we didn't have time to check with you about the menu," I said.

Kiki waved me off with her fork. "Everything is delightful. It's time for me to lose the five pounds I gained during my recent trip."

I would have thought that her husband's unexpected death provided an excuse to abandon whatever diet she'd put herself on. If my boss's poll numbers dropped two points, I felt justified in eating a pint of ice cream. Of course, I doubted my willpower amounted to one-tenth of Kiki Bancroft's. She was twenty years my senior but maintained a killer physique.

Cecelia made a face. "Didn't you trudge through the Amazon for three weeks? Surely you burned serious calories."

"Yes, and I also feasted every night on grilled meat, chorizo, fried plantains, and exotic ice creams." Kiki patted her stomach. "It was worth it."

At least Cecilia hadn't shied away from the food. She'd loaded up with generous portions of antipasti, carbonara, and shortribs. "Save room for dessert," I reminded them.

Doug handed me a plate. Perhaps Kiki had a point. The past few days had been murder on my waistline. I opted for fish, salad, and a modest scoop of gnocchi. I plopped two ribs on my plate for Clarence. After spending his Friday night locked inside our bedroom, he deserved it.

Lola and Frederick were sitting with Kiki on our sofa. After maneuvering an armchair next to them, Lola said, "Please join us, Kit. We only started to eat this delicious food a moment ago."

"Besides planning the new Bancroft wing at the Archives, will you assume any of Grayson's other duties?" asked Frederick.

"If you mean business responsibilities, the answer is no. My husband knew I wasn't interested in such matters. His will outlines a clear line of succession for his corporation. Grayson has ensured his fortune will continue to grow. Of course, the profits will fund the estate," Kiki said.

"You're lucky Grayson was so prepared," said Lola.

Kiki picked at her food. "I had a long talk with my team of lawyers, financial advisers, and consultants before I flew up here. I'll be very comfortable. I have a few loose ends to tie up, and it should be smooth sailing."

"Best not to make too many changes at a time like this," offered Frederick. "The Archives construction will keep you busy enough."

Winston ambled over to our group. "Delightful dinner, Kit. Bravo! What are we discussing?"

"We've been discussing Kiki's handling of Grayson's estate and his various responsibilities," explained Lola.

"Not the least of which was his leadership of the Mayflower Society," said Winston.

"I'd not thought of that detail, Winston," said Lola. "I suppose we'll need to conduct an actual election before adjourning on Sunday afternoon."

Winston bent down and whispered in my ear, "No one ever opposed Grayson's election, so we've gotten used to selecting the president by acclamation. Not the most democratic practice in the world, for sure."

"More like a banana republic," I muttered, almost to myself.

Kiki cleared her throat. "Starting tomorrow, I will be consumed with final arrangements for Grayson. But I would like to be at the Mayflower Society business meeting on Sunday."

"You're welcome to attend," said Winston. "Fair warning, Kiki. It may bore you to tears."

"I'll manage. Correct me if I'm wrong, but I need to be present if I want to run for the presidency and succeed my husband. Correct?" She stared at Lola, Frederick, and Winston for an answer.

It was like watching a merry band of children who had just learned Santa Claus didn't exist. Winston's mouth fell open. Lola flinched, almost in a mini-convulsion. Frederick crossed his arms and frowned. The shock of Kiki's unexpected announcement reverberated around the room. No one uttered a sound.

Finally, I broke the uncomfortable silence. "I don't know anything about the bylaws of the Mayflower Society, but congratulations, Kiki. What makes you want to run for the presidency?" Then I added, "It seems like a lot of work."

"Since I'll be working on the new exhibit wing at the National Archives, it makes sense for the presidency to stay with the Bancroft name," said Kiki. "When I talked to the Archives development team this afternoon, they insisted I assume Grayson's position."

Winston, who had taken a sip of his Balvenie when Kiki was speaking, almost spit it out. "I mean no disrespect, but you cannot just assume Grayson's position. Lola, explain it to her."

Lola complied. "It's been a while since I consulted the bylaws. I did write them decades ago. If memory serves me correctly, Winston is right. There's no provision for assuming a position due to death or any other incapacity. We'll need to hold an election."

"Very well," said Kiki. "I certainly wish to abide by the rules. However, I'm sure the membership will want to continue the generous endowment to the Mayflower Society provided by my husband. It makes perfect sense to maintain the status quo during this troubled time."

Winston removed a handkerchief from his pocket and mopped his forehead. "Grayson Bancroft was generous with the club. I don't dispute that." He paused to catch his breath. "That's not the only criteria for selecting the next president of Mayflower." He looked at Frederick and Lola. "Don't you both agree?"

"Winston has a point," Lola said. She turned toward Kiki. "Your late husband's political beliefs were doctrinaire and oppressive. Do you plan to uphold his preferences? In my opinion, his ideology was ruining the society."

Kiki laughed. "Well said. I cannot dispute your description of Grayson. However, I didn't share his view of the world. No one has ever labeled me as overly rigid."

"Then what are you?" asked Frederick. "A Republican? A Democrat? An Independent?"

"A pragmatist. That's how I label myself. I'm someone who always looks for a way to solve a problem. When I'm elected, I'll make sure the Mayflower Society maintains its current esteemed stature in the historical and philanthropic community. Who can argue with that?"

Winston's features were twitching. He looked as though he would burst at the seams. Instead of torturing himself any longer, he left the group and headed toward the kitchen. I heard him rifling through our cabinets, no doubt searching for the Scotch.

It was time to extricate myself from the stressful conversation. "Excuse me for a moment. I need to check on the dessert."

Trevor stood right outside the kitchen with an empty plate in hand. I motioned for him to follow me inside. "How are you making out?" I asked.

He made an ambiguous gesture. "So-so. I haven't had the opportunity to spend much time with Kiki."

"That's okay. I've heard plenty from her. What about Professor Mansfield?"

"He's a hard nut to crack. I can't exactly ask him if he's been having an affair with the widow of a recently murdered billionaire." Trevor drained his drink and reached for a clean glass, which he filled with water from our fridge. He added, "By the way, every time I get involved in one of these murders, I end up drinking way too much."

"Water is a perfectly acceptable option. We don't force people to drink alcohol around here, Trevor."

"Just like Julia Child didn't force anyone to eat beef bourguignon," Trevor grumbled.

"Don't be a smart ass. Do you think Mansfield was having an affair with Kiki?" I pressed.

"Impatient, aren't we? I was getting to it." He took a long sip of his water. "They're definitely close. Mansfield let it slip that Kiki sometimes takes a detour on her famous trips, which involves a few days in his neck of the woods."

"I doubt New Haven is a convenient layover for any trip."

"Nope," said Trevor. "She definitely used the excuse of being away on a holiday to squirrel away private time with the esteemed historian."

"If that's true, it certainly gives Mansfield a motive."

Trevor nodded. "Yes, he has a motive, in my informed opinion."

"Thank you, Trevor. It's time for the dessert. Can you pass me an oven mitt?"

From our oven I removed the two wrapped pans, which had been set on a low heat to keep the treats warm and toasty. With Trevor's help, we cleared the dinner entrees from the table and replaced them with the dessert. Doug must have heard the commotion in the kitchen and appeared by my side.

"Can I help?" he asked.

"Let's make sure everyone has a drink of champagne so we can make a final toast and call it a night," I said in a low voice.

Doug let out a long breath. "Music to my ears."

I found Buffy and Winston chatting inside the living room and outlined my plan for wrapping up the evening. "Will one of you give the final toast?"

Buffy and Winston exchanged glances. Neither spoke immediately.

"If you don't want to do it, who do you suggest?" I asked.

Winston leaned in. "Not sure, darling. No one really liked Grayson very much. In the course of your sleuthing, you've figured that much out, right?"

The elder Hollingsworth seemed to be having considerable difficulty focusing on me. Just what I needed—an intoxicated future father-in-law on my hands. Where was Doug when I needed him? I scanned the room, but I didn't see him.

Cecilia was standing by herself, fiddling with her iPhone, while Meg appeared engaged in an animated conversation with Drake. Cecilia and Grayson had a history together. Maybe she'd help out.

"Cecilia, would you like to give a final toast in Grayson's memory before we serve dessert?" I paused, and then added emphatically, "It would be most appreciated."

Surely, Cecilia caught my drift. After all, the woman was

a bestselling romance novelist. She had to understand body language, tone, and innuendos.

She averted her eyes and stared into space for several seconds. Then she spoke slowly. "Absolutely. I'd be delighted."

"Thank you." I gave her a polite hug and raised my voice. "Can I have everyone's attention? Cecilia Rose, a longtime friend of Grayson Bancroft, would like to provide a final toast in his honor. After the speech, dessert will be served." I stepped aside and motioned for Cecilia to take the floor.

"I'll keep this short. Please raise your glasses in memory of Grayson. All of us who knew him were richer for the experience, literally and figuratively." A ripple of restrained laughter could be heard among the gathered guests. "Here's to closing old chapters and writing new ones."

She raised her glass, and the crowd responded, "To Grayson." Everyone took a generous sip of drink. Winston and Buffy looked unimpressed. Engaged in a private conversation, Frederick and Lola were touching heads, making them look like conjoined twins. Professor Mansfield stood behind Kiki, whose perfectly powdered face had turned the shade of a ruby red grapefruit. Her knuckles were white from the death grip she had on her champagne glass. Kiki hadn't liked something about Cecilia's parting speech. It was no *Ich bin ein Berliner,* but it hadn't been terrible, either. I was about to head in her direction to find out what she objected to when Doug tugged at my sleeve.

"What's wrong?" I asked. "I was about to say goodnight to Kiki Bancroft."

"It'll have to wait," he said. "Follow me." He marched across the length of our condo in the direction of our bedroom. I caught up to him as he opened the door.

The disturbing sight before me was nothing short of doggy Armageddon. Clarence sat on the bed, surrounded by a variety of objects that ostensibly came from the various purses, all lying open. Tissue paper was littered on top of it all, the coup de grâce of Clarence's canine protest.

I couldn't utter a word, let alone form a sentence. Doug had discovered the disaster before retrieving me from the dinner party, so he had no trouble speaking. "What are we going to do about this, Kit?"

Just as Doug spoke, Meg appeared inside the doorway. "About what?" she asked.

Then Meg noticed the mess. She covered her mouth with her free hand, the one not carrying champagne. "Holy moly guacamole!" she exclaimed.

At least Meg hadn't forgotten one of her favorite foods. I spoke slowly. "I'm not sure what to do."

Doug, Meg, and I walked over to the bed. Clarence's eyes were as big as half-dollars, and his ears shot to the back of his head. When I approached, he offered me a paw.

I'm sorry, Mom. But you locked me inside a room during a party. And you served ribs.

I reached out to grab his paw. Doug said, "Don't pet him. We shouldn't reward him for bad behavior."

I pulled my hand back, but seriously doubted whether my withholding of affection had any punitive effect. What's done is done. Clarence knew right from wrong. Oftentimes, he willfully listened to the devil puppy on his shoulder. In that sense, Clarence was no different from me or any other human. We were all repentant sinners, dogs and *homo sapiens* alike.

I picked up a Lancome compact and Aveda mascara. "There's no way of knowing where the items came from," I concluded.

"Even master sleuths couldn't figure this one out," Meg said. "I'm glad I brought my clutch this evening. It's sitting on your couch."

Clarence had apparently grown bored with our efforts to clean up the mess he'd created. He jumped off the bed and ambled toward the door.

"Should we stop him?" Meg asked.

I looked directly at Doug. "No point. He would have caused less damage if we'd let him join the party." Although I didn't add "I told you so," the smugness in my voice telegraphed it.

Doug shrugged. "Blame Buffy."

We examined several items, including a designer hairbrush, a pill case, a Montblanc fountain pen, a leather Coach wallet, and a pair of "Jackie O" Dior sunglasses.

"No tooth marks, thank goodness!" Meg said. "At least you know your guests have good taste."

"Of course they do." We all turned around as Buffy entered the room.

A second later, her jaw dropped open. "W-what happened?" she stammered.

Doug cleared his throat. "We had an incident with Clarence."

I couldn't resist. "We've never kept him confined to one room before. He didn't like it."

"That's an understatement." Buffy moved toward the bed and surveyed the damage, picking up several items for a closer inspection.

"Has the party moved to the bedroom?" Four heads swiveled as Drake entered the fray.

"We've had an accident with our dog," I explained. "We'll need everyone to identify their belongings, I'm afraid."

Drake burst out laughing. "This is the funniest thing I've seen all day."

The NSA must have heard Drake's loud guffaws, whether they were intentionally listening or not. Within sixty seconds, our remaining guests were crammed inside the room to find out what was so amusing. Clarence trailed behind, sitting politely in the far corner of the room.

"We're terribly sorry about this, but if you left a purse in this room during dinner, can you come forward to claim its contents?" Doug sounded apologetic yet completely in control of the situation, thank goodness. The last time Clarence had caused a mess in public, I'd had a giggle fit. That incident had involved a pepperoni pizza, a murder suspect, and a dog popularity contest. This screw-up may have surpassed the earlier debacle.

Lola, Kiki, and Cecilia joined Buffy next to the bed. Kiki clenched her jaw, but remained silent. She picked up a Tory Burch black shoulder bag and placed several stray items inside.

Cecilia's eyes darted back and forth. She gathered up several possessions and zipped up her bag. "I certainly hope nothing was broken," she huffed.

"I don't think so," said Doug evenly. "Everything is childproof these days. Luckily, that means it's dog proof, too." The corners of his mouth edged upward in a strained smile.

Cecilia grunted in reply and examined the designer pen carefully. "I keep this pen in my purse for when fans approach me for autographs. No apparent damage, except your dog's slobber." She extracted a wet wipe from her purse's zippered compartment and carefully cleaned the pen.

Lola clasped her hands together in relief when she saw her sunglasses. "Thank goodness! I just love this pair." She took the opportunity to remove them from the case and put them on. "Do I remind you of a certain first lady?"

Certainly, except for the flowing gray hair, the flower child outfit, and the extra fifty pounds. Otherwise, Lola was the spitting image of Jacqueline Kennedy.

I pushed those snarky thoughts aside. "Absolutely. You just need some white riding pants and a headscarf."

Lola laughed. "Kit, you're so quick-witted. No wonder you've been successful as a congressional staffer. I bet nothing gets by you!" She shook her finger at me.

Doug put his arm around me. "Not much." Then he turned to the rest of the crowd. "Once again, we apologize for Clarence's bad behavior. Has everyone claimed their possessions?"

Hearing no objections, Doug announced that dessert would be served with after-dinner drinks. The sweet smell of corn panna cotta and angel food cake, plus the promise of port or some other equally yummy digestif, was enough to lure our guests back to the dining room. The last person to leave the bedroom, I found myself alone with my naughty dog.

"Clarence, what am I going to do with you?"

He presented me with his paw, and this time, I took it. I scratched him on the head, and he gave me an apologetic lick. It reminded me of a saying my dog-loving boss in the Senate liked to quote when someone in the office screwed up.

"To err is human. To forgive, canine."

Chapter Eighteen

Thirty minutes later, our guests had departed. Doug opened the sliding glass door to our outdoor balcony, and we joined Meg, Trevor, and Clarence outside for some fresh air. I pulled on a light cardigan over my jumpsuit. Soon enough, the cool evenings would be replaced with muggy summer nights. Springtime didn't last very long in Washington.

"I'm glad that's over," I exclaimed after flinging myself onto our comfy chaise.

Meg swung back and forth slowly in our single-seat hammock fastened to the deck above us. "I thought it was quite successful," she said. "Except for Clarence's faux pas, of course." Our dog's ears perked up at the mention of his name.

"That's an understatement," said Doug. He'd poured himself a half-glass of port, a clear indicator the stress of the evening had worn on him, too.

"Dogs will be dogs, I suppose." Trevor wrinkled his nose. Although we'd managed to convert Meg to a Clarence fan, Trevor had a long way to go. "Nonetheless, I have reached a conclusion about the alleged relationship between Professor Mansfield and Kiki Bancroft."

Meg leaned in, always eager to hear gossip about sex. "Go ahead, Trevor. Spit it out."

"After observing the two people in question, I have inferred that Kiki's romantic attachment to the professor is asymmetrical," he said.

Meg rubbed her forehead. "I need a translator when I'm speaking with you, even though you seem to be speaking English."

I giggled. Trevor had a knack for making things sound more complicated than they actually were. "I think what Trevor is trying to say is that Kiki likes James much more than he likes her."

"Thank you, Kit, for that fifth-grade version of events. I'll reiterate the point I was trying to make," Trevor said. "She's pursued him more than the converse."

"I'm not surprised. Kiki is a woman who gets what she wants," said Doug.

"Her comments tonight certainly angered your father," I said. "She wants to succeed Grayson as the president of the Mayflower Society. That really upset Winston."

"She also upset Frederick Valdez," said Doug. "Kiki has indicated she wants to continue Grayson's legacy of philanthropy for historical causes. Even with less money, Frederick could have replaced Grayson as the new donor about town. But that won't happen if Kiki continues to make big bequests using the Bancroft name."

"Which brings us back to my original point," said Trevor. "Kiki knows she can sustain Mansfield's interest if she keeps shelling out big bucks for the causes he cares about."

"Like the National Archives exhibit," I said.

Trevor snapped his fingers. "Exactly."

Meg raised her hand. "If I had to guess, I'd finger Kiki Bancroft for her husband's murder," she said. She finished her glass of champagne and tipped her glass. "Is there any more of this? It's fabulous."

I pointed toward the kitchen. "Yes, please finish it." Meg ambled inside. Once Clarence noticed she was headed to the kitchen, he followed.

"There are two things in nature that cannot co-exist," said Doug

"I'll bite. What's that?" I asked.

"Meg and an open bottle of sparkling wine," he answered.

Trevor actually smiled. "I couldn't agree more."

Meg returned with a full flute and Clarence on her heels. She'd grabbed a leftover sparerib. "Has Clarence had a treat lately?"

"No, but I'm not sure he deserves one," I said.

"Come on, Kit. Have a heart." Meg pouted.

"Go ahead. Just don't give him the bone."

Clarence licked his lips as he saw Meg carefully remove the meat.

"You know, I found out something important tonight, too," she said.

"That's right. When I talked to you in the bedroom earlier this evening, you said Cecilia was considering wrapping up the Savannah series. Did you learn anything more?" I asked.

"Sure did." Meg petted a satisfied Clarence, who licked her fingers for any last trace. "Just as I thought, Cecilia was ready to dish after a drink or two."

"More like three," I said.

"Probably," Meg agreed, "but who's counting? She told me she's ending the series with the next book."

The news surprised me. "Why? Most authors would give their right arms to have such success."

"She's tired of the characters. She mentioned some nonsense about maximizing her creativity and writing a science fiction series," said Meg.

Trevor perked up. "Cecilia Rose said she wants to write science fiction?"

Meg downed her last sip of champagne. "I didn't pay much

attention, but she went on and on about it. When she didn't mention any steamy scenes, I lost interest."

"I imagine you won't be her only reader to tune out," said Doug.

"How can you say that? Maybe she will be great at science fiction," I said defensively.

"She might be a terrific writer," Doug said. "But whatever she writes in that genre is unlikely to sell as well as her romance novels."

"So that's why Drake doesn't want her to end the Savannah series," I said.

Meg nodded. "You got it. Drake has romanced older women before. But he got Cecilia to marry him. He doesn't want his lifestyle to change one bit, and those romance novels provide him with a generous allowance."

"But how does Grayson's murder fit in?" asked Trevor.

"Good question," said Meg. "Here's the last detail. Grayson owned Cecilia's publisher, and he wanted her to keep writing the Savannah books. He wasn't going to support her lofty literary aspirations unless she kept writing the books that made him a lot of money."

"That makes sense," I said. "He wanted to talk to her about it before he was murdered, but Cecilia put him off."

"Don't forget they were romantically involved years ago. It sounds like a complicated relationship," said Doug.

"Or maybe a love triangle with Drake," said Meg.

"Now you sound like a romance novelist," I said, laughing.

Meg stood up. "You never know! I'm full of surprises."

She and Trevor made their way to the front of our condo. After exchanging goodnight pleasantries, Doug and I turned to assess the condition of our condo.

"Not too much of a mess," I remarked.

"It was a tame crowd." Doug glanced at Clarence. "For the most part."

"Don't blame me. I told you not to lock him inside the bedroom."

"I didn't say a word. Let's clean up before bed. We need to get up early tomorrow for our appointment at the Smithsonian."

"I almost forgot. Do you really think it's worth it?" I asked.

"Have you got any other leads? We've established motives, but right now, we don't know how Grayson died. Short of Detective Glass and the CSI wizards providing us with evidence, my father still looks good for this." Doug loaded up the dishwasher and turned it on.

"Based on tonight's revelations, don't you think Kiki Bancroft might have done it?"

"I see what you mean, Kit, but she wasn't anywhere near the Continental Club on Wednesday night." He tied up the trash and moved it near the door.

"She was *supposedly* in Florida," I said. "But do we know that for sure?"

"Surely the police have checked her alibi."

I sighed. "You're right. I'm grasping at straws because I want to clear your father of suspicion."

He stopped cleaning and came over to give me a hug. "I appreciate it."

"I go back to work in two days. My boss returns from China on Sunday night, and that means I'll need to focus on her."

Doug's forehead creased. "That's not the deadline I'm worried about. We need to find the murderer before Detective Glass decides she has enough to charge my father."

We finished tidying up and then went directly to bed. Exhausted from the long day, I fell into a deep sleep. In my dream, I was inside the lavish ballroom of the Continental Club, dressed in an old-fashioned flowing gown reminiscent of the one worn by Gertrude Harper in the striking portrait. Doug was decked out in a classic tuxedo. When we turned to admire ourselves in the full-length mirrors that adorn the ornate walls of the ballroom, instead of our reflections, we saw a huge hourglass. The sand was plummeting precipitously, and there was no way to stop it. Winston Hollingsworth was running out of time.

Chapter Nineteen

⌐≈⌐

THE COMBINATION OF exhausting days and a fitful night's sleep took its toll. Doug and I slept in later than usual. Clarence was dog-tired, too. When I finally opened my eyes, he was snoring on his side, nestled between us.

I slipped out of bed without disturbing the two sleeping beauties. It was actually a perfect photo. I grabbed my phone and snapped a picture for social media posterity, although I didn't think Doug would let me post it unless I'd edited him out.

It was almost nine, so the comatose duo would need to be woken soon. In the meantime, I busied myself with coffee and the online *Washington Post* morning headlines.

Ten minutes later, Doug ambled into the living room to join me. We did a round of rock-paper-scissors to see who would take Clarence out for his morning walk and bathroom break. I lost, which was only fair because Doug usually attended to him during the week as I scurried to get ready for work on Capitol Hill.

When I returned, Doug was already showered and dressed. "How quickly can you be ready to leave for the Smithsonian?"

"Why? Our appointment isn't until eleven, right?"

"Yes, but we could squeeze in a fun springtime activity beforehand, if you're game."

"What do you have in mind?"

Doug smiled. "You're wasting time. Just get ready so we can take off."

Years of hitting the snooze button had prepared me for this challenge. In less than fifteen minutes, I returned to the living room, raring to go. "Fast enough?"

He glanced at his phone. "Not bad. We'll have plenty of time before our appointment at the museum."

We said goodbye to Clarence and headed to retrieve our Prius from the garage. Five minutes later, we were barreling eastward on Route 50 toward downtown. We were on the road early enough to beat the tourist crush, which swelled in the afternoon hours.

Doug found a parking spot on Madison Drive in front of the Smithsonian American Art Museum. As Doug carefully maneuvered the car, I commented, "An auspicious start to the day." It was near impossible to find parking in this part of the city.

"Let's hope it's a sign of great things to come," he said.

"I've been a good sport. Where are we going? It can't be far away." It was a quarter past ten and our appointment was scheduled for eleven.

Doug chuckled. "We're already there." He pointed ahead past the intersection of Seventh Street and Madison.

I followed his finger with my eyes. "The Sculpture Garden!"

"Not just the Sculpture Garden," he said. "Breakfast at the pavilion inside the Sculpture Garden."

I smiled from ear to ear. "Thank you. I love the evening jazz concerts here in the summer."

He put his arm around my waist. "How could I forget? I know the past couple of days haven't been a walk in the park. The least I could do was give you the real thing."

We strolled past the open-air installations situated inside a small fenced-in area that served as an outdoor extension of the National Gallery of Art. My favorite was the huge bronze spider sculpture, but Doug preferred the pop art Lichtenstein house. The artists had painted the freestanding structure as an optical illusion. The side of the house appeared to project both toward you and away from you at the same time, changing perspective as you walked around it.

We arrived at the Sculpture Garden Pavilion Café and ordered a delightful brunch. A few minutes after finding a spot inside the glass restaurant, we had been served our order of steel cut oats, scrambled eggs, croissants, mimosas, and two coffees.

"This should fortify us for the day," I said while digging into my oatmeal filled with cranberries, nuts, and brown sugar.

"No doubt." Doug sipped his mimosa and clinked his plastic glass to mine.

I finished a bite of buttery croissant and wiped my mouth. "So what do we hope to accomplish at the Smithsonian this morning?"

Doug chugged his coffee and cleared his throat. "We haven't focused on how Grayson died. I don't think the police are going to have too many answers for us. We can't wait around for forensics to tell us what happened."

"Even if they had the answers," I said, "it's not like I can email Detective Glass and ask her for a copy of the toxicology report."

"Precisely. But that doesn't mean we can't use our deductive powers to make an educated guess."

I stifled a gasp. Was this really the man I was engaged to marry? The same historian who refused to write a sentence without checking multiple sources? Even Doug's endnotes had footnotes.

In my most neutral voice, I said, "Doug, no offense, but educated guesses usually aren't your style."

He downed the rest of his mimosa. Morning drinking, even champagne drowned in orange juice, also wasn't Doug's style. This murder had him upside-down.

"What choice do we have? A colleague of mine at Georgetown put me in contact with the chief of the Science Reading Room at the Library of Congress. She was helpful and mentioned the Smithsonian was winding up an exhibit on poisons. She referred me to the curator at Natural History responsible for the displays."

"Our cultural institutions at their finest moment," I remarked.

"Don't knock it. Their collaboration benefits us."

"I'm not. We're lucky the exhibit is at the Smithsonian."

Doug nodded. "We caught a break there. Who knows? It might lead to nothing." He studied his plate and pushed his eggs around.

I reached over and took his hand. "Hey, don't worry. We'll figure this out."

He glanced at my Fitbit. "What time is it? We don't want to be late for our appointment."

I hit the button. "Twenty to eleven. Time to go."

It was only a short walk across Ninth Street to our destination. The cherry blossoms had already peaked so the crowds were smaller than they had been only a week ago. Even so, a line had formed outside the main entrance. Several recent updates to permanent exhibits had caused attendance to soar. With over seven million visitors last year, Natural History was easily the most popular Smithsonian museum and a "top five" D.C. attraction.

After clearing security, we found ourselves face to face with an enormous pachyderm inside the first floor rotunda. "That's the biggest elephant I've ever seen," I remarked.

Doug pointed to the information placard. "You're absolutely correct! It's the biggest mounted specimen of the largest land animal in the world. Behold the African bush elephant."

"It's comforting to know he's keeping an eye on everything," I said.

"If there's any truth to *Night at the Museum*, I don't want to be around when he wakes up."

We laughed and walked around the perimeter of the rotunda. When we reached the Hall of Mammals, I glanced at the time. "We have ten minutes before our meeting. Can we do a quick tour?"

"It will have to be fast."

We pushed our way through the crowd to catch a glimpse at a tiger leaping out of the ceiling, a giraffe stretching to eat a leaf, a fully upright brown bear, and a hippo with its enormous mouth wide open. The heavy traffic of tourists and sightseers prevented us from taking a closer look, which didn't matter since we had only minutes to spare.

As we emerged from the exhibit, Doug shook his head in wonder. "Even if you live in D.C. area, you need to take a day off work to visit the Smithsonian. These weekend crowds are a killer."

"Speaking of killers, let's find our contact. What's the name?" I asked.

Doug consulted his phone. "Celeste Martin. Research biologist and assistant curator. Doctorate from UC Berkeley."

"Sounds impressive. I'll follow you."

We headed up the stairs, and after consulting a visitors' guide on the wall, we discovered the *Power of Poison* exhibit tucked away in a quieter corner of the second floor. The displays were divided into several categories: "Poison in Nature," "Poison in Myth," "Poison Plants," and "Poisonous Villains and Victims." We had started to examine a display featuring Cleopatra when a slight middle-aged woman wearing jeans, a Smithsonian polo shirt, and large wire-framed glasses approached us. "Are you Doug Hollingsworth?" she asked softly.

Doug turned around. "That's me. Celeste?"

"Yes. My friend at the Library of Congress said you'd drop

by this morning and that you had some questions about our poison exhibit," she said politely. She avoided direct eye contact, although she didn't appear rude. If I had to wager, I'd guess that Celeste suffered from an acute case of shyness, particularly around strangers.

I extended my hand. "I'm Kit, Doug's fiancée. We haven't had a chance to view the exhibit yet, but perhaps you can help us."

She straightened up. "You'd like a private tour, then?"

"Not exactly," said Doug. He hesitated for a moment before continuing. "We're investigating a murder."

Celeste crossed her arms and raised her eyebrows. "A murder? I thought you were a historian from Georgetown?"

"I am," said Doug. "We attended a conference over the past several days at the Continental Club, and unfortunately, someone died under suspicious circumstances."

Celeste leaned forward, all shyness gone. "How so?"

"We believe the victim had been poisoned," I said. "There was a small puncture wound on his neck, perhaps from an injection. When I came across him—"

Celeste interrupted me. "You discovered the body?"

"Yes. That's one of the reasons why we want to figure out what happened." No need to tell Celeste that Doug's father was the prime suspect. She seemed intrigued by our story, but we couldn't afford to spook her.

"That must have been terrifying." Celeste's face softened. "Can I ask you a few questions?"

"Sure. Ask away," I said.

"How long did it take for the victim to die?"

Doug and I looked at each other. "We can't be sure, but it must have been pretty fast. He was killed inside the library of the Continental Club. If it was slow-acting, he could have screamed for help or stumbled downstairs."

Celeste scratched her neck. "Interesting. Was his face contorted?"

With too much enthusiasm, I said loudly, "Yes! His legs and arms were spread out, almost like he was frozen in place."

"Was it likely he had convulsions before he died?" she asked. "I know these are difficult questions, but the answers might be important."

Doug frowned. "I don't think so. Kit?"

"I doubt it."

"Were you close enough to the body to detect a smell?" asked Celeste.

"I was," I said. "I bent down for a closer look. I thought he might have had a heart attack. He wasn't overweight, but he could have been a smoker. I didn't smell cigarettes, though."

"No almond smell? It would be a bitter almond, not sweet."

I shook my head. "I would have remembered something so distinctive."

Celeste turned around and motioned for us to follow. "I'd like to show you a couple possibilities."

We trotted behind her until we reached a large, brightly colored photograph of a small, yellow frog. This guy only vaguely resembled his more famous cousin Kermit, who resided at the neighboring American History Museum. His bulging black eyes stared ominously at us.

Celeste pointed to the pesky amphibian. "Meet *Phyllobates terribilis*. He's more commonly known as the golden poison arrow frog."

"You think he could be our culprit?" I asked.

She nodded. "Perhaps. Of course, he didn't do it on his own. He had some help."

Clearly intrigued, Doug approached the photograph for a closer look. "Tell us more."

"They're the most poisonous animals alive, much more so than snakes or spiders, even though they get all the attention. This frog contains enough poison to kill ten human beings."

"It's not easy being green. Or yellow," I said.

Celeste chuckled. "I've heard that one before. The poison

inside these frogs causes paralysis and cardiac arrest. It's much more powerful than strychnine." She added, "Death would be swift."

"So you don't think our victim might have been poisoned by strychnine?" Doug asked.

"I don't mean to be impolite, but you've been reading too many Agatha Christie novels. It's not readily available these days, and even if your killer got his or her hands on it, the victim would have experienced violent convulsions and seizures. It doesn't fit your description of the crime scene." Celeste indicated that we should follow her down the hallway to another part of the exhibit.

"She's in the wrong profession," I whispered to Doug. "The D.C. police should be calling her for a job interview."

"No kidding," he replied. "I wouldn't want to get on her bad side." He made a slicing motion across his neck.

"One wrong move and you'd find a lethal frog in your bed," I said in a low voice.

Celeste waited for us next to an exhibit case with a clay pot inside it. "That doesn't look too dangerous," remarked Doug.

She wagged her finger. "You wouldn't want to touch the contents. May I present the Amazonian poison known as curare?" We both looked at her with blank stares. She continued, "It's an alkaline, like the poison from the dart frog. Not quite as powerful, but certainly lethal. It immobilizes its victims." She said the last sentence with more enthusiasm than I was comfortable with.

"So victims die from asphyxiation?" I asked.

"Technically, paralysis. When the muscles used for breathing are immobilized, the victim suffocates," said Celeste, matter-of-factly.

"Is it from an animal?" Doug inquired.

"No, it's from two different woody plants. The vines are crushed and condensed into a resin. Curare loses its potency if it's exposed to air, thus the need for pots to contain the poison."

"It doesn't sound like something that could be injected," I said.

Celeste nodded. "Good point. It's too thick for a syringe. Instead, South American hunters and warriors coated arrows with it to kill their prey." She added ominously, "Whether human or some other unfortunate animal."

"Why do you think curare might have been used in the murder we're trying to solve?" I said.

"Two reasons. If administered directly into the bloodstream, curare works quickly. Death can occur in a matter of minutes," explained Celeste. "Also, the description of the body sounded like paralysis to me. The first muscles immobilized are facial. Didn't you say he almost appeared frozen?"

"Yes, like he was surprised," I said.

"That's because he was," Celeste replied. "By the time he realized he'd been fatally poisoned, it was too late. His skeletal muscles were unresponsive."

Doug studied a picture adjacent to the curare pot inside the display. It was an old photograph of an Ecuadorian native preparing curare-tipped darts next to a rustic fire. He turned to Celeste. "This is fascinating, but it seems like making curare might be a lost art. Are people still producing it today?"

"Absolutely," answered Celeste, again with a degree of enthusiasm that made me queasy. "It was first discovered by the conquistadors in the 1500s. Curare was eventually adapted into an early form of anesthetic for medicinal purposes. But South American indigenous populations still use it for hunting wild game."

"How can they eat the animals after the poison kills them?" I asked.

Celeste's face became even more animated, if possible. "You're really paying attention! That's the cool thing about curare. It's only dangerous in the bloodstream. There's no problem if it's swallowed."

"If someone was injected with curare, it would be impossible for them to call for help," I said, thinking aloud.

Celeste grew somber. "Death from curare is not pleasant. The victim would be awake, but unable to move or speak. He or she would be cognizant of the increasing paralysis. Eventually, they would suffocate."

"These are pretty exotic poisons," said Doug. "I understand the crime scene doesn't support the use of strychnine. What about arsenic? Cyanide?"

"The victim's time of death and his reaction to the poison don't match. The lack of a bitter almond smell makes cyanide unlikely. Furthermore, cyanide is typically swallowed or inhaled, not injected," she said.

"Doug, I think Celeste is the expert. She would have considered the more likely explanations first," I said.

"Was I mansplaining again?" Doug asked sheepishly.

"Not exactly. But you came close," I said.

"It won't happen again." Doug turned toward Celeste. "Thanks so much for your time."

Celeste's shoulders slumped. "Don't you want to see the rest of the exhibit?"

Doug and I exchanged a brief glance. "Of course!" I said, drumming up my enthusiasm. "Would you mind showing it to us?"

"Absolutely! Follow me down the corridor." She took off for the next display case. "Here are some of the most famous poison victims in history." She regaled us with stories about Cleopatra, Napoleon, Socrates, Hitler, Alan Turing, and Viktor Yushchenko. Then we turned to poisons found in snails, spiders, scorpions, insects, and snakes. We finally found ourselves at the starting point of the exhibit.

I offered my hand. "Celeste, thank you again for your time. I'm not sure how we can repay you. Maybe you'd like a tour of Congress?"

To my surprise, a wide grin spread across her face. "I'd love it. It's not that far away from this place, but I've never been inside the Capitol."

"You got it." We exchanged cards, and I promised to provide her with a first-rate tour during the next congressional recess.

We had begun to walk away when Doug turned around suddenly. "Celeste, I have one more question."

"Sure," she said, "fire away." Although I noticed she sneaked a peek at her watch. We'd already monopolized the better part of an hour. Surely a Smithsonian curator had better things to do than play twenty questions with a modern-day Tommy and Tuppence.

"Where would one obtain these poisons?" he asked.

Celeste gave the matter some thought. "It's hard to say," she said, finally. "It's not like you can go buy them at your local drugstore … or make them yourself. The various recipes for curare are passed down from generation to generation. And with the poison dart frog, let's just say you don't want to be an amateur handling one of those pesky little guys."

"What region of the world are we talking about? You mentioned the Amazon," I said.

"The golden poison dart frog lives on the coast in Colombia. Its habitat is shrinking, so they're becoming increasingly rare. Less lethal species occupy a larger region." She paused. "Curare can be made from a number of plants that grow in Central and South America. The indigenous people who know how to make the poison from the native vines are found throughout the continent, particularly the Amazon basin." She counted several countries off on her fingers. "I imagine you could find tribes making curare in Brazil, Peru, Ecuador, Bolivia, Venezuela, or Colombia."

Doug nodded. "It would be hard to find, right?"

"Yes and no. I've never gone looking, actually." Celeste laughed—a curious, whinnying sound. "It's my experience that if you have a good guide and a lot of money, it's not terribly difficult to get your hands on anything, even exotic substances."

"Could it be transported easily?" I asked.

"It would require care and attention. Like I said before, the poison can't be exposed to the air or it loses potency. By the way, some tribesmen mix the poison from the plants with venom from the dart frogs."

"They don't need doctorates in chemistry?" I asked, a little flippantly.

"They're pretty advanced. Many of them have experimented with various ingredients over time. It depends on what they are planning to hunt."

"Like a human," Doug muttered.

She held up her hand. "That's why I mentioned the mixture. For your victim to die so quickly, the poison would have to pack a powerful punch, no matter what it was. Your murderer wasn't messing around."

Doug and I stared at each other. The evidence was stacking up against the killer. But there was a big wrinkle. Our number one suspect had an airtight alibi for Grayson Bancroft's murder.

Chapter Twenty

———

After thanking Celeste profusely for her assistance, Doug and I made our way through the crowd. The popular Hope Diamond, almost four hundred years old, was responsible for the tourist swarm on the second floor. The *Washington Post* reported that over seven million people viewed the blue gem each year at the Harry Winston Gallery, making it the most popular Smithsonian attraction in Washington.

We edged our way downstairs to the rotunda and found a seat on a bench at the periphery of the African elephant.

"Quite a morning," I said.

Doug turned to face me. "Are you thinking what I'm thinking?"

"I'm no mind-reader, but I'd guess we're on the same page."

"Let's find out. On the count of three, we'll both say the name of the person we think killed Grayson," said Doug.

This whimsical suggestion was out of character for Doug, but I wasn't going to complain. His voice sounded less worried, and his eyes were bright with hope. We'd finally had a break in the case. It wouldn't be enough for a conviction, but it might cause Detective Glass to reconsider slapping the cuffs on Winston Hollingsworth.

"Okay," I said. "I'll count. One, two, THREE!"

With the precise unison of a master a cappella duo, we both bellowed "Kiki Bancroft!" in loud voices. Several Smithsonian visitors glanced quizzically in our direction.

"Shhhh," I cautioned, putting a finger to my mouth. "We don't want to draw attention to ourselves."

"Most of these people have never heard of Kiki or Grayson Bancroft," said Doug.

"I know, but this is still Washington D.C. You don't know who could be standing right around the corner."

"With these many tourists, I'm not sure you could overhear anything, even if you tried," said Doug.

I took his hand and gave it a little shake. "We shouldn't celebrate just yet. If Celeste is right and the killer used an exotic paralytic poison from South America, then Kiki looks good for it. She was on a long trip there, and with her considerable resources, she could easily have found someone to make a lethal concoction. But there's a big problem with that theory. Kiki was at their house in Florida when Grayson died. Your mother told me."

"Maybe she flew to Washington, killed Grayson, and then flew back. I'm sure she has access to a private jet. It's not like she has to wait for the next American Airlines flight out of National Airport."

"I agree, but there's still an issue. Remember what Detective Glass told me yesterday about the murder weapon."

Doug's forehead wrinkled. "I'm not following your line of reasoning."

"We were talking about the syringe, and she said the police had examined the security footage monitoring the doors and exits. No one entered or left the building at the time of Grayson's murder."

The corners of Doug's mouth turned downward. "So Kiki

couldn't have arrived after everyone had gone to bed."

"Unless the Continental Club has a secret entrance. It's a little far-fetched, but everything about this murder has been off the wall, in my opinion."

Doug rubbed his chin. "It's possible. For all the famous and high-profile members, a secret entrance would be a valuable perk."

"Let's face it. If Kiki could get her hands on a poison made by South American natives, she could also figure out a way to get inside the Continental Club without being noticed."

Doug laughed. "Good point. What should we do next?"

"I don't have anything else to suggest. Do you?"

"Nope. The Smithsonian was all I had."

I rubbed my hands together. "Well, it was a big deal. It might just be the break we needed to solve this case. I think we should head over to the Continental Club. Is the Mayflower Society going on any more field trips?"

"I don't think so. But let me check." Doug pulled up the schedule on his iPhone and scrolled with his finger until he found today's events. "A series of historical lectures. Everyone should be there."

"Let's poke around for a way Kiki might have gotten inside the building unnoticed. If we find something, we can tell Detective Glass. Even if Kiki used a private plane, there should be a record of the flight. After all, she had to land somewhere near Washington."

We left the building and walked into the bright sunshine. From the top of the museum's outdoor steps, we could see clearly across Independence to the Sculpture Garden. That reminded me of something. When we were enjoying brunch at the pavilion, I'd wanted to raise the topic of our wedding. With the craziness of the past two days, the controversy over when, where, and how we'd get married had fallen by the wayside. Before we found ourselves consumed with sleuthing once again, I wanted to share an idea with Doug.

Doug stepped down toward the street, and I put my arm out to stop him. "Wait a second."

"Shouldn't we head to the club to find out if Kiki could have possibly killed her husband?" he asked.

"Before we go, what do you think of the Sculpture Garden? Do you like it?" Squinting in the sunlight, I shifted left and pointed across Ninth Street.

"Sure. I took you there for brunch this morning. Remember?"

I ignored his smart-alecky question. "I wonder if they allow weddings."

Doug jerked his head back. In a playful voice, he asked, "Did you voluntarily mention our wedding?"

I punched him lightly on the arm. "It was never about avoidance. But I want our wedding to be on our terms, not someone else's."

Doug grabbed my hand and lightly touched my engagement ring. "Seems fair. And to answer your question, I *do* like the Sculpture Garden." He kissed my cheek. "Very much, especially if you want to get married there."

"Okay," I said breathlessly. "I'll check it out when I have some extra time."

Doug laughed. "That's like a chocoholic promising to forgo sampling Kisses during a tour of Hershey."

I clenched my jaw. "That's not fair. I can't help it if I'm a busy person."

Doug released my hand and put his arm around me. "I'm teasing you, Kit. We'll figure it out. I'm not in a big rush. But we should find a place for our wedding that makes both of us happy." He paused. "Our opinion is what matters."

A huge wave of relief washed over me. We were finally on the same page. "Thank you for making that clear," I said.

"I should have done it earlier. But sometimes it can be difficult with my parents. They're ..." he searched for the right words, "forceful people."

"That's one way of putting it. I think your mother and I have reached a détente."

"Equivalent to easing of Cold War tensions?" he teased.

I smirked. "Not in magnitude but maybe in complexity."

"Buffy Hollingsworth isn't easy to deal with. Believe me, I know from years of experience," said Doug.

"She may not approve of the Sculpture Garden as our venue of choice."

Doug's arm tightened around me. He whispered, "She doesn't have a presidential veto."

I couldn't help myself. "As a congressional staffer, I simply could not hear more magical words."

We walked arm in arm to the car, then headed to the Continental Club.

During the fifteen-minute drive across town, we didn't speak much. Alone with my thoughts, I considered the conversation with Doug. Perhaps the cloud of suspicion surrounding his father had given Doug new perspective. Or maybe Buffy's aggressive overtures had pushed him over the edge. Quite frankly, the explanation didn't matter that much. Doug and I would figure out wedding arrangements on our own terms. That realization was enough to make me giddy.

Unfortunately, there was no time to celebrate. We pulled into the Continental Club valet parking, tossed our key to the attendant, and strolled inside. Just as we cleared the covered entrance, we were bombarded by the annoying blare of sirens. The din grew louder, destroying the typical air of quiet splendor. The Continental Club neighborhood didn't witness much police action. Something was amiss.

Heading toward the lobby, we rounded the corner and almost ran into Maggie Glass.

"Sorry, Detective," I sputtered. "How's the case coming along? Any leads?"

Her eyes appeared glazed over as she said, "Which one?"

"Grayson Bancroft, of course," answered Doug.

She shook her head slowly. "He's got company. We just found another victim."

Doug and I both sucked in our breath. Had we heard from Winston and Buffy this morning? If Doug had communicated with them, he hadn't mentioned it.

"Who is it, Detective?" I asked, more than a hint of desperation in my voice.

She crossed her arms. "I shouldn't divulge that information. I'm waiting for reinforcements to arrive." She started to walk past us.

Doug put his hand out to stop her. "I'm sorry, Detective. But my parents are staying here. You need to let me know who has been killed."

Detective Glass stared at us for a long moment. She put her hands on her hips and faced us. "It's not either of your parents. That's all I can say."

We both exhaled a sigh of relief. "Thank goodness," I said.

Detective Glass hurried toward the rear entrance of the club, where I guessed the ambulance and authorities were arriving. If what she said was true, the emergency medics had barreled down Massachusetts Avenue for a very brief visit.

"We should find your parents. Do you want to text them?" I asked.

"Let's check one place before I do that."

I followed Doug down the hallway. After he turned left down a corridor, I knew where he was going. It was a safe bet.

Sure enough, a healthy quorum of the Mayflower Society had decided that when the going got tough, the tough opted for daytime cocktails. They weren't settling for wine or beer, either. Charles had two stainless steel cocktail shakers in front of him, and he was busy pouring booze into both. Tom Cruise had nothing on this guy.

Doug spotted his parents in the corner of the bar. Buffy saw us as we approached. "Doug, Kit! Thank goodness you're here."

She tapped her almost empty martini glass. "Will you be dears and get us another round?"

Doug stopped in his tracks. Under his breath he muttered, "I suppose it's five o'clock somewhere."

"Not on the East Coast," I whispered.

"No point in fighting it," he answered. "I'll get you a drink, too. You'll need it, believe me."

He turned on his heels and waved to Charles, who could hopefully replicate their earlier order. I had a feeling Charles might be serving quite a few second and third rounds this afternoon.

I maneuvered through the crowd and arrived at my future in-laws' table. Winston stood and gave me a kiss on the cheek, and Buffy bestowed a polite shoulder hug. After taking a seat, I asked, "Rough morning?"

"It's been a nightmare!" Buffy buried her face in her hands.

Winston leaned over and gave her a hug. "This ordeal has been too much for her," he explained.

Uh-oh. Buffy was coming apart at the seams, and we had another dead body on our hands. My hand crept into my purse, searching for my iPhone. My fingers itched to text Meg and provide her with details. Before I could try to sneak a message off to her, Doug arrived at the table with our drinks.

"I need to go back to the bar to retrieve one more," he said. "Did my parents tell you who was murdered?"

"Not yet. We got sidetracked," I said.

Buffy recovered sufficiently from her temporary nervous breakdown to sip her drink. "A terrible tragedy! A dynasty wiped out over the course of a few days." She paused for dramatic effect and fingered her pearl necklace. "It's almost Shakespearean."

Now I was utterly confused. Perhaps we had been too sanguine in our assessment. Was this Buffy's second drink or had there been more than one earlier round?

Doug saw the perplexed look on my face. "Mother, you're

talking in riddles." He pointed at her martini glass. "May I suggest you consume your current drink more slowly than the previous ones?" Buffy glared at Doug but remained silent. Winston's hand covered his mouth to stifle a laugh.

Doug turned to me. "You're not going to like what I have to say, especially since we thought we had Grayson's murder solved."

I took a gulp of my drink. Buffy wasn't the only one who could benefit from a little liquid courage. "You can tell me," I said. "I'm not getting any younger."

"Let's put it this way. Kiki Bancroft won't be getting any older."

Yikes. Nothing screws up a murder investigation more than finding out your supposed killer has become a victim.

Chapter Twenty-One

———※———

Doug scurried off to pick up the remaining libation. Buffy might have reached her limit, but I had only just begun. The euphoria I'd felt following the identification of the poison at the Smithsonian drained out of my body, replaced by the dread of defeat. We were back at square one. I'd been supremely confident we'd solved the case and cleared Doug's father. Perhaps we'd met our match. This murderer had killed twice, right under the noses of his or her closest friends.

Doug's parents did look out of sorts. Buffy was biting her lip, thus spoiling the effect of the carefully matched lipstick that accented her pleated taupe crepe dress. Winston tapped his foot on the ground nervously as he fiddled with his tumbler, swirling the amber liquid I could smell from across the table. He wasn't settling for twelve-year-old Scotch today.

"I take it you knew about Kiki, right?" I asked.

Buffy snorted. "*Knew*? We were there."

I took another belt of my G&T. "You were *what*?"

Winston leaned in. "We found her, Kit."

I was almost afraid to ask the question, but curiosity overrode my desire to stay sane. "And where was she, if I may ask?"

Holding his drink, Doug rejoined the table. I recounted the minor detail concerning the discovery of Kiki's body. "They were just about to tell me the location," I said.

Buffy looked pointedly at Winston, who cleared his throat before speaking. "The Poets' Room. It's across the hallway from our chamber."

"I know what you're talking about." It was the small, cozy alcove where I'd discovered Trevor working on his book.

"Wait a second. Where was Kiki staying?" Doug asked.

"At first," Buffy said, "she didn't want to stay at the Continental Club, but then she decided to run for Grayson's position during tomorrow's business meeting. She told several of us at your dinner party that she'd arranged for a room."

"And do you know where her room was?" I asked, dreading the answer.

Winston shifted in his chair. "She took the only available room at the club—the one you and Doug had stayed in."

Doug blinked several times. "So she was right next door?"

Buffy answered quickly. "We already told that pesky policewoman we have no information on her whereabouts last night. We came back from your party and went to bed right away."

"I hope you didn't say it as defensively as that," said Doug. "You might as well help the police put the cuffs on Father."

My palm-out gesture was meant to put a stop to Doug's destructive train of thought. "Hold it. Before we get carried away, let's establish a few facts," I said. "When did you find Kiki?"

Buffy was eager to respond. "Around noon. She wasn't at breakfast or the first lecture. No one thought anything of it. Kiki wasn't exactly the early-to-bed, early-to-rise type."

Winston picked up the thread. "Before lunch, we went upstairs to our room to freshen up. I needed to check my blood sugar to make sure it was under control."

Buffy shook her finger. "The stress of the past several days hasn't helped your father's diabetes. His numbers have been way too high."

"As much as I hate to admit it, she's right." Winston sighed. "Plus, I've had way too many of these." He shook the contents of his glass.

"He doesn't like me to hover when he's doing his test. So I told him I'd wait for him outside. That's when I wandered into the Poets' Room ..." said Buffy.

"And you discovered Kiki," I finished.

Buffy nodded. "I screamed, of course. Winston came running out of the room. Unfortunately, he had a syringe in his hand."

"My blood sugar reading was too high. I needed to give myself a shot of insulin before lunch. I was just about to do it when I heard Buffy's yell," he explained.

Doug's eyes widened. "So when Mother screamed, you came running." He pointed at Winston. "And then everyone and their brother came out into the hallway."

Winston muttered, "That's about right."

Doug continued, "And besides finding Mother hovering over the body, everyone saw you with a syringe in your hand."

Winston shrugged his shoulders. He looked defeated, like a Washington Nationals fan at a New York Mets rally. His eyes normally sparkled with excitement; now his eyelids drooped from exhaustion. He couldn't take much more of this. If we didn't solve the murders pronto, the situation was going to deteriorate rapidly.

I asked the obvious question. "Did Detective Glass see you with the syringe?"

Winston wiped his forehead, now glistening with light beads of sweat. "No, she wasn't there when it happened."

Buffy broke in. "She arrived about ten minutes later. Apparently she was already headed to the club to continue investigating Grayson's murder."

"But she knows the unfortunate circumstances?" Doug asked.

Winston nodded grimly. "When she arrived at the scene, several people provided her with the details."

"You saw Kiki's body?" I asked Buffy.

"Of course. You wondered why I didn't stop at one of these." She raised her glass.

"Speaking from experience, discovering dead bodies is traumatic," I said.

We all chuckled. Our laughter thankfully lightened the mood, which had gotten more depressing than a Senate committee hearing to solve the national debt crisis.

We could wait to talk to Detective Glass and press her for important details, but we had a star eyewitness sitting right in front of us. I decided to forge onward. "This might be difficult, since you've known Kiki for a long time, but can you describe what she looked like when you found her?"

Buffy pressed her lips together and rested her chin in her right hand, deep in thought. After a few seconds of what appeared to be reflection, she said slowly, "Her face was twisted in pain, as if she was caught by a painful surprise. She wasn't crumpled in a heap. Instead, she lay flat on her back, limbs straight and extended." Buffy demonstrated by raising her arms overhead.

Doug brightened. "That's helpful, Mother. Was anything disheveled or messy, like she might have had a convulsion before she died?"

"Not that I could see. She looked …" Buffy searched for the right word, "paralyzed. Except she wasn't paralyzed. She was dead."

Doug and I locked eyes. We had to be thinking along the same lines. The South America poisoner had struck again. But there was a major problem with that theory. Kiki Bancroft had been the likely supplier of the deadly concoction. Had her death been an accident?

I lowered my voice so only Doug could hear. "Do you think

Kiki ingested the poison mistakenly? Or spilled it on herself somehow?"

He whispered back, "That would be a convenient solution to this whole mess, but I don't think so. Remember your question about curare to Celeste. It's only dangerous if it hits the bloodstream."

I hit my forehead with my hand. "How could I forget? This mystery has too many crazy details."

Doug smiled. "That's where I come in."

I had to admit that Doug's help had been invaluable. He really had a knack for sleuthing, although I'm sure he couldn't wait to return to the comfort of his carrel in the Georgetown Library and his writing desk in our condo. Both had been neglected for several days, and his next book wouldn't write itself. The quicker we figured out the killer, the sooner he could get back to his precious footnotes and folios.

"We're dealing with another injection, I would imagine," I said.

"I know. My father gallivanting up and down the hallway brandishing a syringe doesn't help matters," muttered Doug.

"That's an understatement," I said.

Doug turned from our private conversation back to his mother. "Did you happen to notice a mark on Kiki's neck? Remember, Kit saw a small puncture wound on Grayson's body when she found him."

Buffy smoothed her hair and narrowed her eyes. "Darling, I'm not sure how Kit noticed something like that on Grayson, but I didn't hang around to examine poor Kiki. I screamed for your father, who appeared seconds later."

Doug faced Winston. "And I suppose you didn't notice anything on Kiki's neck?"

"Sorry, son. I took one look and pulled your mother out of the room. Then others arrived at the scene."

"Who showed up?" I said.

Buffy and Winston considered my question for a moment

before answering. "Frederick and Lola were there," Buffy said.

"Cecilia and Drake," added Winston.

"Anyone else?" asked Doug.

"Unfortunately, Professor Mansfield also appeared," said Buffy.

"Was he upset? How did he act?" I probed.

"It's hard to tell with James," said Winston. "He's so restrained. But he did seem unnerved. He pushed past us and stared at Kiki's body for a minute or two. Then he returned to his room. I don't think he said a word."

I looked around the bar. Professor Mansfield hadn't joined the rest of the crowd. If he was hiding from his Mayflower brethren, was it due to guilt or grief? Perhaps he'd killed Grayson to be with Kiki, but after the deed was done, she'd had second thoughts about their relationship.

"What happened next?" I asked.

Winston replied, "Frederick said something about notifying the police. He dialed 911 with his cellphone. Lola ran off to inform the Continental Club staff."

"Cecilia noticed you had a syringe in your hand," said Buffy. "She made a snide remark."

"Yes, she said something about it being deadly coincidence. She was being dramatic, as usual," said Winston. "Cecilia can't help it. It's the novelist in her."

Buffy broke in, "Lola returned with a manager from the club. He said he'd stand outside the Poets' Room until the police showed up. That's when Cecilia suggested we head to the bar for a drink."

Winston broke in, "No one wanted to be there a moment longer. So it seemed like a good idea."

"We don't know when she was killed," I said. "We'd have to find out if Detective Glass has an approximate time of death. If she's willing to share," I added.

Doug laid a hand on my arm. "That's true, although all the possible suspects were staying at the Continental Club last night and were here this morning for the meetings. I'm not sure the precise time of death will matter that much."

"Good point," I said. "We should focus on finding out if Kiki was killed in the same manner as Grayson."

I was just about to tell Doug it might make sense for me to walk upstairs and find out if Detective Glass might be willing to share a few details of the latest murder with me. Before I could speak, Frederick Valdez approached the table and grabbed an empty chair next to mine. "Good to see you again, Kit. Sorry that your introduction to the Mayflower Society has been so deadly." He winked at me playfully.

Buffy bristled. "Really, Frederick. Is it appropriate to make light of two murders?"

His voice boomed. "I was doing nothing of the sort. Simply reciting the facts." He surveyed the table. "Everyone looks so glum. Let's cut to the chase. With Kiki out of the way, Winston is a lock for tomorrow's election."

My future father-in-law sat up straight in his high-backed wooden chair. Winston's voice sounded cold and unfriendly. "What are you implying, Valdez?"

Frederick snickered. "It doesn't take Sherlock Holmes to put two and two together. I'm merely stating the obvious."

Doug shifted closer so he could speak directly to Frederick. "Are you accusing my father of involvement in Kiki's murder?"

Frederick assumed a convincing air of skepticism. "Don't get carried away. A few days ago, Grayson Bancroft was killed. That freed up the presidency of the Mayflower Society. Until," he paused dramatically, "his widow showed up and declared she wanted to assume her husband's position. It would have been impossible for Mayflower to pass her over. But now that's not a concern, is it?"

I couldn't keep my mouth shut. "That sure sounds like an accusation to me."

Buffy had watched the verbal volley without comment. Like me, she'd heard enough. "How about another version of events,

Frederick? With Grayson out of the way, you and Lola have the opportunity to take over as the grand philanthropic couple of Washington D.C. That is, until Kiki decided she was going to keep the Bancroft tradition going. Maybe you only planned on killing Grayson, but then Kiki complicated matters. She left you no choice." Following her accusations, Buffy glared pointedly at the cellphone magnate.

Frederick slapped his knee, threw his head back, and laughed. "Touché, my dear Buffy. You're cleverer than most people think. But if your story is true, how did I kill Grayson? A police search of our room yielded no plausible instrument to deliver whatever God-awful poison the murderer used. The same cannot be said for the search of your room."

Frederick's last words quieted the Hollingsworths. Doug shifted uncomfortably in his chair while Buffy and Winston stared at their drinks. Frederick had a point, and we all knew it.

I broke the awkward silence, whispering to Doug, "I'm going to find Detective Glass and see if she'll share any information about Kiki's death. I'll be back in a few minutes. You should stay here in case anyone else decides to accuse your father of a double homicide." Doug nodded. Leaving his parents would have been tantamount to throwing them to the wolves.

I hustled up the two flights of stairs to the guest rooms. The narrow hallway was filled with police, EMTs, crime scene techs, and other official-looking personnel. The Poets' Room had been barricaded with yellow police tape. With so much confusion in the confined vestibule, no one paid any attention to me. I peeked around the corner to catch a glimpse of the murder scene. I couldn't see much, but Buffy's description of poor Kiki seemed dead on. This was certainly a repeat of Grayson's murder.

Kiki's body was too far away from the entrance, so I couldn't zero in on a puncture wound. I did notice she was dressed in workout gear. Had she been on her way to the gym when the killer attacked her? As I craned my neck in hope of spotting more precious details, I felt a firm tap on my shoulder.

I had a pretty good guess who'd busted me. *Uh-oh.* I turned around slowly and sure enough, my fears were confirmed. Detective Maggie Glass stared up at me. She did not seem pleased.

"Ms. Marshall, may I ask why you are here? If I didn't know better, I might think you take some pleasure in hanging around dead bodies."

Her expression was stern, but I detected a hint of humor in her voice. "Not at all. My future mother-in-law found Kiki's body. The way she described it, I wondered if the manner of death was the same as the first murder."

"And your conclusion?" asked the detective.

"Looks like the same MO to me."

"That sounds reasonable." She pointed toward the staircase at the end of the hallway. "Now I have to ask you to leave."

"Can I ask you one more question?"

"If you must." When I didn't move, she put her hand on my arm and guided me in the right direction.

"Did you find a puncture wound on Kiki's neck?"

"No."

"Then how was the poison administered?" I asked.

We'd reached the staircase. "That's another question, Ms. Marshall. You should have asked if we found a puncture wound anywhere on her body."

I needed a lesson in semantics like a hole in the head. "Sorry, Detective. You're right. So you found it somewhere else?"

Detective Glass pointed to her upper arm.

"Ouch. So I suppose you're looking for another syringe? Before you jump to any conclusions, Winston had just checked his blood sugar before Buffy found the body. He was about to give himself a shot of insulin when she screamed."

I could swear Detective Glass rolled her eyes. "Mr. Hollingsworth's running around the scene of yet another murder with a syringe in his hand is grounds for suspicion," she said. I started to interrupt her, but she held up her hand to cut me off. "Let me finish. I was going to say that we got a preliminary report from our medical examiner on our first victim. The working theory is some type of paralytic poison. But the method of delivery is giving us trouble."

Now she had my attention. "Really? What kind of trouble?"

She put her hands on her hips. "I hope Detective O'Halloran from the Capitol Hill Police hasn't been feeding me a line of bull. He told me I could trust you."

Good old Detective O'Halloran. I'd have to buy him a jelly doughnut the next time we crossed paths inside the House of Representatives cafeteria.

I crossed my heart. "Girl Scout's honor."

"As long as you don't try to sell me another box of cookies. I've already eaten my annual allotment of Do-si-dos."

"Tagalongs for me. They're killing me."

The corners of Detective Glass's mouth tilted upward. "Our medical examiner doesn't think Grayson was injected with a syringe."

"Not a syringe? Then what?" I asked.

"Exactly. The ME still thinks the red spot on his neck was the entry point for the poison. When she examined it closely, the puncture wound was too big for a needle."

I gave this new detail some serious thought. "Some other sharp object delivered the poison. But it wasn't a knife wound."

"That wouldn't fit. Now you can appreciate our dilemma."

"I'll have to ponder this new piece of information, Detective Glass. Does this mean Winston Hollingsworth is off your list of suspects?" If I could deliver that news to Doug, it would take a load off his mind.

"Not so fast. He may not have used his insulin needles to kill Grayson and Kiki. That doesn't rule him out as our perp."

The detective's logic made sense, but Winston was still off the hook as much as anyone of the other immediate friends of the deceased. "At least he's not your prime suspect any longer."

Detective Glass kept a sphinx-like demeanor. "I can't confirm or deny that statement, Ms. Marshall. I need to return to the crime scene." She turned to leave and then spun around quickly. "One more thing. If you uncover something important, I want you to tell me immediately. Do you understand?"

"Certainly, Detective."

"As I recall the stories Detective O'Halloran shared with me, you have a way of figuring these things out, but the resolution includes collateral damage," she said.

"Don't worry, Detective Glass. Those days are over for me. After all, I want to make sure I survive my wedding." I raised my left hand to show her my engagement ring.

Clearly still skeptical, she said nothing, and hurried down the hallway. Thank goodness she hadn't seen my right hand, hidden behind my back with fingers crossed.

Chapter Twenty-Two

———∞———

I TOOK THE stairs two at a time so I could tell Doug the news about the murder weapon. Winston and Buffy would be relieved, too. Then I stopped abruptly as an alternative scenario hit me. My next move required skillful strategizing.

Should I tell my future-in-laws about my conversation with Detective Glass? If I did, they'd jump to the misguided conclusion that they were completely off the hook. Buffy would certainly resume the discussions about our wedding, and I'd find myself in another uncomfortable meeting with wedding planner extraordinaire Tammy and her accomplice-in-arms Bonnie. No way did I want to relive that convo.

The smarter option would be to tell Doug about the development and leave his parents out of it. That way, we'd guarantee the elder Hollingsworths' fullest cooperation until we found the murderer. My instincts were almost always correct. Of course, the couple of times they hadn't been spot on, I'd almost became the next victim of the murderer I'd been chasing.

I grabbed my phone and texted Doug. All the social rules about restricting cellphone use to certain areas were out the window. With two dead guests, could the club afford to be concerned about etiquette? I didn't want to seriously ask that question. After all, Miss Manners was a longtime member.

Luckily, Doug had thrown caution to the wind as well. He responded within seconds and said he'd meet me at the portrait by the ballroom.

I stared at the impressive replication. Gertrude knew who killed Grayson Bancroft. She'd witnessed everything. I wished she could whisper the answer to me.

"Any luck with the police?"

I jumped a foot in the air. I'd been so entranced by the portrait, I hadn't noticed Doug sneaking up on me.

"Are you crazy? There's a murderer running loose and you're slinking around?" I asked.

He chuckled. "It was hardly unannounced. We agreed to meet here a few minutes ago."

"Fine. There's no point in arguing. I need to tell you what I found out from Detective Glass."

I recounted the details of the confusion over the murder weapon. As Doug listened, he nervously bit his lip.

"So my father isn't the prime suspect any longer. The syringe tied him to the murder. Now he's in the clear."

"Not exactly. He may not have used a diabetic needle, but Detective Glass still thinks he could have killed Grayson and Kiki. He had motive."

"I understand. But it's a step in the right direction." He let out a big breath.

"I'd say so. But I don't think we should tell your parents yet about this development."

"Why not? It would lower their blood pressures, for sure."

"I don't disagree, but we might need them to still think they're suspects, especially if we want to try to solve these crimes. We need them to remain," I searched for the right word, "focused."

Doug cocked his head as he considered my reasoning. I could practically see the smoke emanating from his ears as the gears of his brain whirred. Finally, he said in a slow, deliberate voice, "You may have a point."

I took Doug's hand and led him into the library, where the yellow police tape had been removed. We sat down at one of the beautiful oak tables. "It may seem harsh, but it's impossible to know how this is going to be resolved."

"Kit, I get it. You don't want my mother to return to her bridezilla persona. Well, I know she isn't the bride, but she acts like she is. The nomenclature I'm looking for doesn't exist, as far as I know, not for controlling future mothers-in-law or pushy mothers of the groom."

"Thanks, Doug," I said. "I appreciate your understanding. Besides keeping her mind off the wedding, we need both of them to keep their ears to the ground."

Doug rubbed his chin. "They'll lose interest if my father isn't the prime suspect."

"Exactly. We always knew he didn't do it. But two people are dead, and we're starting to put the pieces together. I don't want to stop sleuthing until we figure out whodunit." I stated the last sentence forcefully. Doug was always hesitant about Meg and me participating unofficially in homicide investigations. I hoped he wouldn't lose his nerve now.

"Don't worry, Kit. I'll see this through with you. To be completely honest, it's been pretty exciting."

I grabbed Doug's arm. "Did I hear you correctly? Have you been bitten by the detective bug?"

Doug chuckled. "I wouldn't go that far. But I see why you've wanted to get to the bottom of these mysteries."

"I'll take it. So we'll keep quiet for the time being?"

Doug mimed a zipping motion across his mouth. "My lips are sealed."

We returned to the Continental Club lounge, which was buzzing with conversation. Poor Charles was racing from one end of the bar to the other in a frantic attempt to keep up with the drink orders.

Thankfully, Buffy and Winston were still sipping the drinks Doug had brought. Cecilia and Drake had joined them, so Doug and I found empty chairs and squeezed into a free spot at the table.

"I'm telling you, I'm not spending one more night in the place," Drake insisted. He took a slug of his tall beer. At least he wasn't hitting the hard stuff.

Cecilia put her hand on Drake's upper thigh and squeezed it. "Darling, there's nothing to be worried about. Clearly the murderer had something against the Bancrofts. Now that they're both dead, why would anyone else be in danger?"

I broke in, "Do you think it was a vendetta against Grayson and Kiki?"

"It can't be a coincidence. A husband and wife murdered within days of each other? Someone wanted to wipe them out in one fell swoop." Cecilia made a dramatic gesture with her arm that encompassed the whole room.

"Unless the killer only intended to kill Grayson, but then decided Kiki knew too much," I said. "It might not have been in the original plan to murder two people."

"Who knows? I can't be concerned with such details. Either way, we'll sleep soundly tonight like always, won't we?" Cecilia purred.

Drake clenched his jaw. "Speak for yourself. I'm going to keep one eye open."

"Don't be silly. Finish your drink, dear. I need to call my publisher and have a chat with the club's membership office."

"I forgot you're a member here," said Doug.

"Yes, and I need to make sure they issue me a receipt for my recent donation. It seems to have gotten lost in the mail." Cecilia tugged at her husband's sleeve. "Let's go before the police corner us."

Drake guzzled the rest of his beer and stood up. "Duty calls." He gave us a salute and followed Cecilia.

Buffy raised her eyebrows. "That woman is a born storyteller."

"That's an understatement, given the success of her books," I said.

"She doesn't stop at romance novels," Buffy said. "Cecilia likes to portray her life as rosier than it really is."

"What do you mean?" asked Doug.

"Cecilia acts like she has the perfect marriage." Buffy changed her voice to mimic Cecilia's: " 'We'll sleep soundly like we always do.' " In her normal tone, she added, "That's hogwash. She sleeps soundly because she takes sleeping pills."

"How do you know that?" asked Winston.

With a wide grin, Buffy said, "Clarence told me."

"I didn't know our dog could speak English," said Doug.

"Very funny. After Clarence's meltdown last night in the bedroom, I popped open a designer pill case lying on the bed. There was Ambien inside. Believe me, I know those magic pills when I see them." Buffy clicked her tongue in disapproval. "Cecilia claimed them as hers. So typical. Sometimes I think she's blurring reality with her fiction writing."

I turned to Doug. "Speaking of Clarence, we'd better head back to our condo to check on him."

"Let's go before we get caught up in the police interrogations that are sure to come this afternoon," he said.

Buffy looked panicked. "You're not staying? What are we going to tell that detective when she tries to pin Kiki's murder on your father? Or both of us?"

Doug patted his mother's hand. "First, tell the truth. Second, I'd stop drinking those," he pointed to her empty cocktail glass, "and order some lunch and a tall glass of water."

As we left, Doug's parents sat stiffly in their chairs, staring at each other wordlessly, expressions pained. Their despair was palpable, but for the first time in days, I felt a glimmer of hope.

Chapter Twenty-Three

———

AFTER A LEISURELY walk around our Arlington neighborhood with Clarence, I decided to take advantage of the downtime and watch a mystery movie. Whenever a good one was scheduled to air, I recorded it on my DVR and watched it at those times I needed to unwind. This one was about a female sleuth who owned a pie shop. In between creating sweet, mouth-watering concoctions, she managed to solve murders in her small New England town. She was a younger Jessica Fletcher who could bake, which made for quite a talented combo.

Usually, I enjoyed my made-for-television mystery flicks with the enthusiasm of a shopaholic let loose in Harrods of London. This afternoon, I couldn't give myself over entirely to my brain candy. Thoughts of the Continental Club double murder cluttered my mind. I switched off the movie and texted Meg. Sometimes talking through the scenario helped. Bizarrely, my texts went unanswered. So I grabbed a notebook and a pen.

How was it done? The poison was likely an exotic paralytic of some sort, potentially from South America. Still, we didn't know the method of delivery in either killing. If not a syringe, then what? It had to be something sharp that could inject the deadly substance directly into the bloodstream.

Who had motive? I went through the suspects. James Mansfield, certainly, but why kill Kiki? Frederick and Lola Valdez wanted to get Grayson out of the way, but did their motive extend to Kiki when she decided to keep up the Bancroft philanthropy? Cecilia had a tumultuous romantic and professional history with Grayson. She and Drake each had reason to kill Grayson. There was definitely no shortage of motives to murder Grayson, but none to explain Kiki's death.

Who had opportunity? This was a tough one. All the suspects had stayed at the Continental Club and had access to the library and Poets' Room. Two of the couples provided alibis for each other. That left James Mansfield, who had no one to vouch for his whereabouts. It was worth noting that he could easily have committed the crimes without having to cover his tracks.

What was Kiki's role? After our meeting this morning at the Smithsonian, we'd thought Kiki might have killed her husband. If that were true, then why would Kiki have turned up dead, murdered with the very poison she used on her husband? That made no sense. It seemed more plausible that Kiki had an accomplice who killed Grayson. Then, for some reason, her partner in crime turned on her. But if so, who was the murderous conspirator?

I looked at my questions and answers. There was more to the story, but I didn't know how it all fit together. I turned to a fresh page in my notebook and wrote down every detail I could remember from the past three days. I forced myself to record any conversational tidbit, observation, or fact, even if it seemed insignificant. Something told me I had almost all the pieces of the puzzle. After I was done, I reread my handwritten notes, which filled two pages. Nothing immediately grabbed me, except that my penmanship was seriously in need of improvement.

Maybe this had been an exercise in futility. I sighed, grabbed the remote, and returned to my pie-baking sleuth.

Doug emerged from his office as the movie wrapped up. "Enjoy your mystery?"

"Not as much as usual," I admitted. "I kept thinking about the Continental Club murders. We're missing something important."

Doug sat next to me on the couch. "I agree. I had the same feeling while I was working on my book."

My thoughts shifted to more important matters, like dinner. All the delicious-looking desserts in my afternoon movie had caused my stomach to grumble. "Are you hungry?"

Doug studied his phone. "My parents just texted me. They'd like us to join them for dinner in the city. Apparently the police interrogations about Kiki's murder are finished and they want to leave the Continental Club. They've been sequestered there all day."

With a healthy dose of skepticism in my voice, I asked, "Where do they want to go?"

Doug smiled. "I think you'll be pleased. Le Diplomate."

I did a double-take. "How did they get reservations?" Le Diplomate was a popular French bistro on Fourteenth Street. Usually, reservations were required weeks ahead of time, particularly for a Saturday night.

"My father knows the owner. Apparently he did legal work for him when he considered opening a restaurant in Boston."

"You don't have to ask twice," I said. "Give me a half hour, and I'll be ready."

"Plenty of time. We'll meet them there at seven."

Soon we were searching for a parking space in the trendy Logan Circle area. Luckily, we found a spot on nearby R Street, which was primarily residential. After walking a few blocks south, we approached the standalone corner restaurant and edged our way inside the busy entrance underneath its classy, bright sign. The bread table was right near the door. I inhaled the enticing smell of freshly baked baguettes.

"If I close my eyes, I could pretend I'm in Paris," I muttered.

"Don't close your eyes. The décor is the best part!"

I turned around to see Winston Hollingsworth's beaming face.

After we exchanged greetings, Winston pointed upward. "My client made sure the ceilings had been sandblasted to give the appearance of a tobacco-stained ceiling. His attention to detail is impressive."

"I'll say so." My gaze drifted to the Tour de France bicycle decorating the bar and the antique opacity of the dining room's silver mirrors. To my surprise, I spied Professor Mansfield with my little eye.

"I didn't know you were joining us," I remarked.

"I invited James," Winston said. "It's been a difficult day for him, and he hadn't eaten anything. He could use some entertaining company."

The other times I had seen Professor Mansfield, he had been the picture of neatness and order. Today, he was disheveled and his eyes drooped with weariness. He looked like a man who had suffered a major loss. Alternatively, he might want to appear as such.

The five of us were seated outside in a prime patio spot. Heat lamps provided the warmth we needed for springtime early evening dining. Fourteenth Street had nothing on *Saint-Germain*-des-Prés. If we could conjure up a modern-day Sartre and de Beauvoir, Washington D.C. had gotten pretty darn close to perfecting the French café experience.

"Does it remind you of Paris?" I politely asked Buffy.

"I know the shops better than the cafés." Buffy tugged at her brightly colored scarf. "My latest Hermès purchase does look appropriate."

Forget the apparel. My mouth watered as I saw the waiter deliver roasted leg of lamb, beef bourguignon, and steak frites to the table next to us. The waiter took our order for appetizers. The crudités would have been the wise choice. Instead I opted for the onion soup gratinée, which I'd heard was simply divine. Buffy raised an eyebrow when I ordered, but remained silent. You only live once, and this week had been unexpectedly stressful. Rather than watching every bite, Kiki would have indulged more and worried less about her waistline, had she known the end was nigh.

"You survived the police questioning, I gather?" asked Doug.

"It's clear they have no clue about who killed poor Grayson or Kiki," said Buffy.

"I hate to admit it, but your mother is right," said Winston. "Now they're telling us we may not be able to go home on Sunday."

That made me sit up and take notice. "You won't return to Boston tomorrow?"

Buffy sipped her Sancerre. "Not if the police feel as though we need to stay for additional questioning. They'll let us know tomorrow, but it doesn't look good."

I gulped my ice water. "Where will you stay?" Visions of the Hollingsworths taking up residence in our condo for an indefinite period flashed before my eyes.

Buffy waved her hand dismissively. "We could remain at the club if they're not booked. Or move to the Hay-Adams. The Four Seasons or Willard, in a pinch."

I couldn't restrain the whoosh of air I exhaled in relief. Doug's face tightened in minor irritation. To cover my obvious faux pas, I said quickly, "Thank goodness you'll be comfortable if you're stuck here."

Professor Mansfield broke his silence. "It's a damn inconvenience. I'll end up missing my lectures next week." His face softened. "I'd really like to return to work to get my mind off what has happened."

Patience was wearing thin. No one said anything in response to the professor's pronouncement. A few minutes later, our first course arrived, and I dug into my soup. It was worth every blasted calorie.

Satisfaction with our food seemed to improve the sour mood. After the waiter removed our empty dishes, I turned to Professor Mansfield, who was seated next to me. "I don't think I properly expressed condolences about Kiki," I said quietly.

Moisture glistened in the corners of his eyes. Was it real waterworks or crocodile tears? I continued to size up Mansfield. If Larry David could stare down Richard Lewis, couldn't I break a Yale history professor?

Mansfield was silent for a long moment. Then he said softly, "Thank you. Most people knew I enjoyed her company." He paused again, perhaps to choose his words carefully. "Our relationship was complicated at times, but it wasn't the sordid affair perpetuated by the rumor mill."

I leaned closer. "What was it, then?"

"We were kindred spirits. Most people didn't know that Kiki also loved the study of history and culture. Her husband chose to give money, often in very public ways, to promulgate his causes. Kiki preferred staying out of the limelight. Most people viewed her as uninterested, but that wasn't the case."

"She enjoyed talking about history with you," I said.

Mansfield nodded. "Very much. Recently, we liked to travel together. I provided the knowledge, and she provided the resources. It was mutually beneficial."

The professor had given me the perfect opening. "But you didn't go with her to South America for her most recent trip?"

"I wish I had," he said. "It was during spring break. She only told me about her plans a day before her departure. There was no way I could join her." He frowned. "Quite frankly, I'm not sure she even asked me."

"She didn't tell you why she wanted to go?"

"I'm not sure what the purpose of the trip was, except she hadn't been there before. Usually she shared the details of her trips with me. This one, not so much."

That helped to confirm Kiki was on an expedition to bring back a fast-acting, difficult-to-trace poison to murder her husband. The accomplice and the weapon were still elusive. For all I knew, Mansfield had concocted the whole elaborate back story about Kiki to cover his tracks.

Our entrees arrived, and I inhaled deeply, savoring the delicious aroma emanating from my moules-frites. A Belgian specialty also enjoyed by the French, the pot of mussels and accompanying french fries were steaming hot. Doug had gone for the burger Americain, which had been called the best cheeseburger in Washington D.C. Nothing like letting the French beat us at our own game.

Buffy had gone for the healthy trout amandine. She was picking at the food, but her focus was on me. "Kit, this trip has been a disaster for our wedding planning."

After slurping a mussel, I mustered a half-hearted smile and tried to keep the sarcasm in my voice to a bare minimum. "We didn't get very far with it. Solving two murders tends to take the focus off wedding planning."

Buffy sipped her wine. "Circumstances were clearly beyond our control. But don't fret." Buffy opened her purse and withdrew her iPhone. "I've consulted my calendar, and I can return to Washington soon. This weekend will seem like a distant nightmare by then."

Buffy put on her reading glasses, pecked at her phone, and smiled broadly. "I have an entire week in May that's free. We can get a lot done with five straight days of planning."

What could I do? Sure, I'd dodged a bullet this weekend, but Buffy wasn't giving up. I could see myself in an elaborate sequined wedding gown, walking down the staircase at the Continental Club with two hundred pairs of eyes on me. Our wedding was a snowball careening down Mount Everest. There was no way to stop it once Buffy put it in motion.

I looked helplessly at Doug, who I expected to respond with a resigned shrug of the shoulders. Instead, his nostrils flared and his facial muscles tightened. He wiped burger juice from the corners of his mouth with his napkin and said, "Mother, I'm not sure that's a good idea."

Le Diplomate is a noisy restaurant. As I recall, the *Washington Post*, which assiduously monitors the decibels at local eateries, listed it as a "must speak with raised voice" establishment. Despite the endless chatter of other patio diners enjoying their meals, I could have heard a pin drop at our table. Winston chewed his hanger steak with trepidation in his eyes. Professor Mansfield's expression blended surprise with a hint of admiration. No one told Buffy Hollingsworth "no." It didn't happen. Except it had just happened.

Buffy looked as though someone had told her Chanel had gone bankrupt. Her hand trembled as she placed her fork next to her plate. "Douglas, tell me why this would not be a good idea."

Doug's cheeks flushed. He glanced toward Mansfield. "Perhaps it's not the time or place to have this conversation."

Buffy wasn't going to let him off so easily. "Don't be ridiculous. James is an old friend. You don't mind if we talk about the wedding, do you?"

The professor blinked several times. With a bit of an amused smirk, he replied, "Not at all, Buffy." He added, "I love weddings."

Yeah, right. Professor Mansfield loved weddings like I loved fresh fruit for dessert. The repartee between Doug and his mother had provided him with an entertaining distraction from his grief.

"Mother, Kit and I need to decide what type of wedding we're going to plan. After we figure those details out, we'll let you know." Doug wasn't asking for permission. He was telling.

Winston watched the verbal back-and-forth as if it were the final round of Wimbledon. After Doug's pronouncement, he put his hand on Buffy's. "Dear, let's let Kit and Doug have time to themselves. I seem to recall a bride forty years ago who didn't want her mother-in-law planning her wedding, either."

Buffy pulled her reading glasses off her nose and adjusted her scarf. "Fine. I'll await your decisions." She took a long plug of her wine and returned her attention to the trout remaining on her plate.

Point, set, and match. Doug sighed in relief. I reached under the table and squeezed his hand, and he grinned in response.

The conversation drifted to topics of politics, history, and the future of the Mayflower Society. With the latter in such disarray, no one knew what would transpire at the business meeting tomorrow. It was scheduled to take place after the morning brunch at the Continental Club. With the topic of our wedding disposed of, at least for now, Doug chatted amiably with his parents. As I nibbled on my mussels and fries, my mind drifted back to the murders. If Kiki traveled to South America to obtain the poison, who did she recruit to administer it? And how?

When I turned my attention back to the table conversation, Doug was recounting our trip to the Smithsonian earlier today, carefully avoiding any details that could make Professor Mansfield uncomfortable, such as our conclusion that Kiki likely obtained the deadly poison during her recent trip.

As I half-listened to Doug describe the exhibit, my brain strained to recall the details I'd written down earlier while I watched the mystery movie on television. Suddenly, I put two and two together. Was I remembering everything correctly? With my fellow diners ensconced in conversation, no one noticed as I fished through my purse to find my trusty notebook. I flipped to the appropriate page and checked my facts. Sure enough, I'd remembered the details correctly.

My conclusion was based on circumstantial evidence, but I was almost completely certain who killed Grayson and Kiki Bancroft. Now we just needed to prove my hunch was right.

Chapter Twenty-Four

⟨⟨⟩⟩

AFTER EXCUSING MYSELF, ostensibly to use the restroom, I bolted for the chaotic bar area of the restaurant, nestled myself in a corner, and pulled out my phone. Meg hadn't replied to my earlier texts but hopefully she'd respond now.

Break in case. Need to chat.

I waited. After a long minute, three dots appeared. She was replying. *Where?*

I'd imagined Meg was out for the night. *Are you near Continental Club?*

She wrote back immediately. *At home. I can meet u there.*

Sheesh. I couldn't remember a Saturday night when Meg didn't have plans. Maybe she wasn't exaggerating the dry spell in her dating life. This was definitely not the time to poke the bear.

30 minutes or so. Meet in the bar.

The prospect of a free drink must have buoyed my best friend's spirits. She sent back a smiley face.

If we were going to execute the plan I was formulating, we'd need all hands on deck. I whipped out my phone again and texted Trevor.

Where are you?

Writing. Not in my usual spot.

That's right. Trevor's favorite location was now the scene of a homicide.

Want to help solve these murders? Meet at the bar.

Trevor answered a few seconds later. *Anything to get back into my room.*

Forget bringing criminals to justice or getting my future father-in-law off the suspect list. Trevor was interested in one thing only, namely himself. At least he was predictable. In this case, his narcissism worked in my favor.

Now I needed to rally the troops. Before returning to the table, I took a moment to strategize but was easily distracted by the surrounding din. Two men were drinking a bottle of Cabernet Franc as they loudly debated the merits of vaping in bars. It wasn't Paris, but at least people were drinking good wine and contemplating the finer points of public policy.

I didn't want to tell Buffy and Winston about my hunch. If a plan came together to expose the killer, it would be better if they didn't know. What about Doug? A few months ago, I might have left him out of the picture, as well. As the son of the prime suspect, he'd certainly been strongly motivated to unmask the true killer. Earlier today, when I told him a syringe couldn't have been used to deliver the poison to kill Grayson and Kiki, he hadn't backed away from pushing forward to solve the murders. Furthermore, he'd stood up to his mother at dinner when she tried to take control of our wedding. I'd seen a new side of Doug these past few days, and I hoped his prudent adventurousness and cautious defiance—not intentional oxymorons—wouldn't disappear after we solved the Continental Club crimes.

When I returned to the table, my dinner companions had finished their entrees. Winston motioned the waiter for a dessert and digestif menu. No way could we get roped into another course. Trevor and Meg would be waiting for us, and they detested each other. They'd only last five minutes unchaperoned before their irritation with each other erupted into a massive fight. I didn't want either to become murder victim number three.

Putting my hand on Doug's arm, I told his parents, "You should enjoy an after-dinner drink with the milk chocolate pot de crème. I hear the desserts are fabulous. Doug and I need to get back to the Continental Club." I tugged his sleeve.

Doug jerked his head back. "We can't stay for dessert? I wanted the crème brûlée."

"I'll make it for you at home," I said sweetly.

Now Doug looked really befuddled. He knew I couldn't make crème brûlée if Jacques Pepin whispered the instructions in my ear. "Why do we need to go back to the club?" he asked.

"Trevor needs to speak with me," I said.

"Trevor? What does he want? Why can't you talk to him on the phone?" Doug was making this more difficult than necessary.

I'd have to get creative. I said the first thing that popped into my head, "Women troubles. He needs my advice about a love interest."

Doug wrinkled his nose. "I never knew Trevor had any romantic interests."

Doug was right, but that didn't stop me. "That's why it's so important I speak with him about it. He's a novice."

My fiancé gave me a skeptical sideways glance but stood up. "We'd better go. Sorry to eat and run," he said emphatically.

"Yes, it's very rude of us. Of me, rather." Buffy stared at me blankly. Maybe she wouldn't be too upset about Doug's rebuff on the wedding planning. Given my boorish behavior, she probably didn't want me anywhere near a white dress if her son was involved.

I pulled Doug toward the door as we exchanged perfunctory goodbyes with his parents. The springtime night air was brisk, giving me a welcome shot of energy.

As soon as we hit the sidewalk, Doug halted. "Okay, Kit. 'Fess up. What was that all about?"

"Sorry about the white lie. I had to get you moving. We need to meet Trevor and Meg at Continental Club. Pronto." I pulled his hand toward the direction of the car.

"And why do we need to dash off to meet them?" Hands on hips, Doug planted himself firmly on the corner of Fourteenth and Q.

Admittedly, I'd simply assumed Doug would follow. If I expected him to join my sleuthing efforts, I needed to play fair and deal him in.

I inhaled deeply. "I think I know who killed Grayson and Kiki."

Doug covered his mouth in surprise. "How'd you do that?"

I told Doug how I gathered all the details together this afternoon. At dinner, the final piece of the puzzle fell into place. After I told him the identity of the killer, a grin spread slowly across his face.

"Kit, I think your instincts are right. But the evidence is mostly circumstantial. How are we going to prove it?"

"I'm glad you asked that question. That's why we need to meet with Meg and Trevor. To plot the next course of action."

Doug rubbed the back of his neck. "Okay. I'm game, although I'm not sure how we're going to trick the killer into confessing."

"Oh, ye of little faith," I joked.

"You don't need to get biblical on me," said Doug. "I know you can come up with a good plan. I'm less certain about the ability of a certain dynamic duo in orchestrating this masquerade."

"Us?" I asked innocently.

"Hardly. I mean Trevor and Meg."

"Don't worry. Meg has a flair for the dramatic."

Doug rolled his eyes. From observing our close friendship over the years, he knew too well about Meg's quirky, yet lovable, histrionics.

I continued, "And Trevor, well, he never fails at anything. He's Type A all the way."

Doug laughed at my description of Trevor. "That's an understatement."

"Let's get going so we're not late," I said. I reached for Doug's hand and once again tugged it in the direction of the Prius.

Ten minutes later, we drove into the Continental Club parking area. Upon entering the bar, I cast my eyes about, searching for our friends. They were in a corner booth, sitting on opposite sides and glaring at each other with the vitriol usually reserved for health care reform debates in the House of Representatives.

I whispered to Doug, "Hurry up and get us some drinks. It looks like they're already at each other's throats."

I hustled over to the table and willfully ignored their steely gazes. "Good evening. Thanks for joining us tonight," I said a little too loudly.

Meg and Trevor didn't speak for close to a minute. I gave up. "Okay, is someone going to tell me what's wrong?"

"This one," Meg pointed a manicured nail at Trevor for emphasis, "claims we're wasting our lives working for Congress."

I shook my finger. "Trevor, did you say that? It's very insulting."

Trevor addressed his response to me. "Your best pal has not changed since our days in the Senate. She hears one thing and concludes another. I said no such thing."

Maybe Doug was right. How were we going to fool the killer when our crackerjack sleuthing team couldn't speak a civil word to each other?

Doug appeared with our drinks. After everyone had a glass of wine, I excused myself and found my trusty bartender Charles. Before we began our meeting, I needed to check on an important detail.

I whispered a question in his ear. We scanned the bar,

focusing on a particular location. Then he murmured an answer in a low voice. I asked another question and cupped my hand around my ear to make sure I heard his response correctly. I grinned and thanked Charles for his help.

"What was that all about?" asked Meg.

"Just needed to check a few facts before we hatch our scheme," I said.

"What will this plan accomplish precisely?" asked Trevor.

I straightened up in my chair. "It's going to set a trap to catch our killer."

We exchanged thoughtful, silent stares. Finally, Meg said, "Well, that's something we can agree on."

Our gaze shifted to Trevor. He rubbed his chin. "Count me in."

We raised our glasses in a toast. "To catching the notorious Continental Club culprit," said Doug.

"Hear, hear," chimed in Trevor.

After we pulled our chairs closer together, I explained my idea for trapping our killer.

"With a little luck, we should this solved by noon tomorrow," I concluded.

"Perfect," said Meg. "Plenty of time for us to hit the mall afterward."

"You have a burning desire to go shopping?" I asked.

"Not really," said Meg, "but you owe me a pair of sandals. Remember what Clarence did to mine?"

"I almost forgot. You got it, Meg. Murder and then the mall. It's a deal," I said, giggling.

"We'll need a miracle to pull this off," muttered Trevor.

"I wouldn't worry," said Meg absently. "Nordstrom is having a sale."

Trevor rolled his eyes but remained silent.

Chapter Twenty-Five

———❧———

I SHOWED DOUG my clothing options for Sunday brunch. "What should I wear? It's either the yellow Calvin Klein belted dress or the light blue pantsuit with the pastel ruffled blouse."

Doug studied the two outfits. "It depends. Which one is better attire for catching a double murderer?"

I considered. "I think I'd better go with the suit. Just in case we need to make a fast getaway."

Doug laughed. "I hope that's not the case. If it is, something has gone seriously wrong."

"Let's keep our fingers crossed that our suspected killer takes the bait."

We'd already been awake for several hours. We went over the plan again during our morning walk with Clarence. Then I called Detective Glass to clue her in. If our harebrained scheme actually worked, we needed someone from law enforcement to witness it. She'd sounded dubious over the phone. After a little cajoling, she agreed to participate.

"No one else has a better idea," she'd admitted. Not exactly a ringing endorsement.

We jumped in the car and headed yet again in the direction of the Continental Club. At this point, I had the route memorized.

Brunch didn't start until eleven. We'd agreed to meet Trevor and Meg beforehand to review everything one more time. I glanced at my watch. Right on schedule. The garden bar wasn't usually open during the day, but Detective Glass said she'd take care of it. Sure enough, we walked right in. Trevor and Meg were waiting for us.

"Ready for the ultimate test of your acting chops?" Meg was dressed in perfect spring brunch attire, a tropical green and white shirtdress with sling-back wedges.

"I'll invoke my inner Cate Blanchett," I said.

"For what you have planned, it sounds more like Tina Fey and Amy Poehler," said Doug.

Trevor blew out a skeptical puff of air. "Let's not give them too much credit," he said dryly. "At least not yet."

"Thanks for the vote of confidence, Trevor. Your part in all of this isn't nearly as difficult as mine," Meg groused.

"Enough! Stop arguing. Let's keep it together," I said.

"Kit is right." Doug's voice was surprisingly calm. "We only have one shot at this. We've got a good theory about who killed Grayson and Kiki, but it's not going anywhere unless we get the police some proof."

Trevor and Meg glared at each other but said nothing.

"Very good," I said. "Let's go out to the main dining room now. The Mayflower Society will be gathering for brunch, and we need to make sure we get good seats. Doug, perhaps you can arrange it so that the right characters in the cast are seated together."

"Sure thing." Doug smiled devilishly. "I wonder what my parents are going to think of this."

"You could have called them this morning to explain," I said.

"Nah. My mother can't keep a poker face. She might give it away."

"One thing's for sure," I said.

"What's that?"

"After this morning, I doubt your mother will bug us again about planning our wedding. She won't even want to think about us walking down the aisle."

We entered the large Continental Club dining room. The back portion had been reserved for Mayflower Society members. Not many remained. Grayson's death had scared off a good number, and Kiki's murder only made matters worse.

Doug guided Meg and me toward a large round table. He surveyed the room and swiftly guided Professor Mansfield, Frederick and Lola Valdez, Cecilia Rose, and Drake to our table. Trevor found Doug's parents and sat with them at an adjacent table. There was no need for them to have a front row seat for our shenanigans.

We exchanged pleasantries with our tablemates, and I reintroduced Meg, who didn't really need it. Most people who met Meg remembered her.

Our waiter approached the table. I nudged Meg, and she grimaced in acknowledgment. As embarrassing as this was going to be, we needed to swing into action.

"Good morning. My name is Jeffrey, and I'll be your server today. Welcome to the Continental Club brunch. Please help yourselves to the buffet inside the MacArthur Room. In the meantime, can I offer you a glass of champagne?" He smiled and waited for our response.

Meg took the opening. "My friend and I would love some champagne." She smiled sweetly at Jeffrey. "We plan to enjoy our brunch this morning."

After our tablemates had placed their beverage orders, we walked to the buffet. Continental Club host Bonnie hadn't exaggerated when she'd recommended the brunch days ago upon our arrival. The MacArthur Room was filled with a wide assortment of breakfast and lunch entrees, freshly carved meats, a seafood bar, and a made-to-order omelet station.

Meg saw me stacking my plate with waffles, eggs, and a slice of bacon and hurried toward me. "What are you doing, Kit?"

"Getting breakfast. What does it look like?"

"Don't eat too much. Aren't we supposed to seem like we're getting wasted?"

"That's the plan. So what?"

"You get drunk faster when your stomach is empty, not when it's full."

"Meg, we're not really supposed to drink too much. We're going to appear like we've had too much. Remember?"

She threw her hands up. "I guess I'm the only one taking my acting role seriously!" She marched off in a huff, grabbed a plate, and selected a few pieces of lettuce and three carrots. Meg exhibited all the qualities of a great *artiste*, including a tendency to exaggerate.

We returned to our seats, where our champagne was waiting. Meg raised her glass. "It's been such a stressful week. Thank goodness for bubbly!" In one magnificent chug, Meg emptied the flute.

Professor Mansfield's eyes narrowed, but he said nothing. Drake appeared to enjoy Meg's antics and joined in.

"I'll drink to that!" he announced.

I needed to at least try to keep up with Meg. All I could manage was a simple "cheers" before I drained my glass.

Lola Valdez glanced at Meg and then angled toward me. With a fake tone of politeness, she asked, "It's so nice your friends could join us again, Kit. Is there a particular reason?"

I'd already thought this one through. "Absolutely. Both Meg and Trevor are considering membership in the Mayflower Society. As I understand it, Mayflower is recruiting younger people."

Frederick Valdez burst out with, "Absolutely! What fantastic news. Will you join us for our business meeting after brunch?"

It was a perfect setup. "I was certainly planning on it, Mr. Valdez. Thank you for asking me to join," said Meg.

Jeffrey appeared at the table. "It looks as though we may

need refills on the champagne. Shall I pour another round?"

With a hearty dose of enthusiasm, Meg, Drake, and I said, "Yes!" simultaneously.

"Darling, perhaps you should slow down," said Doug with a patronizing tone. If he wasn't playing his part to perpetuate our little ruse, his comment would have been extremely annoying.

Meg didn't give me time to respond. "Don't be such a wet blanket, Doug. Kit is still trying to recover from the traumatic experience of discovering the poor murdered man's body in the library." She patted my hand affectionately.

"Thank you, Meg. I'm glad someone understands." I shot pseudo daggers at Doug.

Jeffrey reappeared with the champagne. As soon as hers was poured, Meg reached for her glass and downed it. She nudged me under the table. I steeled myself and followed suit in a big gulp.

Professor Mansfield grimaced. "I take it you're no longer investigating the death of Grayson Bancroft? Or Kiki, for that matter?"

"I tried my best. But I'm no closer to figuring out the murderer than I was earlier in the week." I allowed my shoulders to slump. "Sorry I couldn't be more help."

Doug put his arm around me. "Don't feel too badly, Kit. The police have no idea who did it, either. At least that's what I heard from my parents."

Mansfield grumbled, "I certainly hope we're allowed to leave later today, despite the lack of progress."

"We're definitely leaving this afternoon," said Cecilia. "I have an important business matter to settle, and I can't wait around for the police to bungle through their investigation."

"Anything we'd like to hear about, Cecilia?" asked Frederick.

Cecilia's eyes sparkled. "I suppose there's no harm in announcing it. My agent is negotiating a publishing deal for a new book. Hopefully it will be the start of a brand new series."

"Will it be different than the Savannah books?" asked Meg.

Cecilia played with her dangly silver earrings. "Oh, yes. It's a science fiction erotic romance. A coming of age story set in another galaxy." She grinned broadly. "Like *Star Wars* meets *A Catcher in the Rye* meets *Fifty Shades*."

Seven pairs of eyes stared at Cecilia in uncomfortable silence. No one wanted to tell her the description sounded like the wackiest mixture of genres for a novel. When the silence continued, Cecilia said, "Of course, it will be better written than *Fifty Shades*." Everyone nodded politely.

"Sounds like a winner to me," said Drake. "As long as the books keep flying off the shelves." He pinched Cecilia's cheek affectionately.

"If you'll excuse me, I'm going to visit the buffet for dessert," said Professor Mansfield. Others quickly agreed.

"You go ahead," said Meg. "I'll make sure our waiter gives us a refill." She winked conspicuously at me.

I grabbed my purse and ducked inside the restroom located right outside the MacArthur Room. I whipped out my phone and texted Meg.

Getting tipsy for real. No more drinks!

I paused to wait for her response.

Don't worry. I'll take care of it.

I didn't know what her reply meant. She was definitely scheming. After exiting the ladies, I piled a couple cookies on top of a slice of cheesecake and hightailed it back to the table.

Meg must have flagged down Jeffrey and persuaded him to pour us another round of champagne. When we'd all returned to the table, Meg raised her glass.

"I'd like to propose a toast to the Mayflower Society. For a bunch of older people, you definitely know how to party," she announced.

Our fellow diners looked stunned but raised their glasses nonetheless. Then Meg pointed in the opposite direction. "Isn't that Supreme Court Chief Justice Roberts?"

Everyone followed Meg's direction. While they were

scanning the crowd, she grabbed both of our drinks and flung the contents into the potted plant next to the table.

"We still need to play the part, remember?" she whispered in my ear.

I nodded and tried my best to suppress a chuckle.

"I don't think that was him," said Professor Mansfield.

"Sorry, my bad. No big deal. If you've seen one Supreme Court justice, you've seen them all."

Drake spied our empty glasses. "No fair! You finished before me." He chugged his champagne. His face flush, he inconspicuously tried to conceal a burp.

Meg giggled. "Good luck in keeping up. We're professional champagne drinkers, aren't we, Kit?" She elbowed me.

Doug crossed his arms. "What's gotten into you two this morning?"

Meg waved him off like a pesky mosquito. "Doug, can't you let Kit have some fun? Besides, who said American history has to be boring and stuffy?"

"This has certainly been an entertaining brunch," Lola remarked in a low voice.

Bonnie from the Continental Club appeared at our table. I glanced at my watch. Her timing was perfect, just as we'd planned earlier this morning.

Smiling warmly, she said, "We hope you've enjoyed our brunch. Before you adjourn to your business meeting upstairs, please join us in the bar. There's been a request for a final toast to commemorate Grayson and Kiki Bancroft."

Frederick frowned. "I hope this won't cause too much of a delay. We have important decisions to make at our meeting today."

"Is my future father-in-law going to be elected the next president?" I asked.

Doug shushed me. "Really, Kit? You know that's a sensitive subject."

Lola sniffed dismissively. "It's impossible to say how the vote will go. He's certainly qualified. But there is an air of suspicion around Winston Hollingsworth."

"What do you mean, Lola?" asked Meg, feigning ignorance.

She averted her eyes. "With the murders, of course. No disrespect to your father," she said to Doug, "but the police view him as a suspect."

Doug removed his napkin from his lap, folded it, and stood up. "I'm confident he will be cleared of any wrongdoing."

Taking Doug's cue, Meg and I followed him out of the dining room and back inside the bar. The rest of the Mayflower Society members were trickling in and finding seats. I glanced in the direction of the courtyard. Sure enough, Detective Glass was lurking outside, in the perfect position for the final act. It was show time.

Chapter Twenty-Six

W HEN CHARLES THE bartender spotted us, he gave me a surreptitious thumbs-up. I'd clued him in last night before we left and convinced him to volunteer for the supposedly impromptu gathering on Sunday. Doug sidled up to the bar.

"Need drinks for the ladies?" asked Charles.

"How could you have possibly guessed?" said Doug, with a heavy dose of feigned innocence.

"A little birdie told me," said Charles.

Doug leaned in and whispered to him. Charles winked, and then announced loudly, "Two stiff gin and tonics, coming right up, sir!"

Doug passed us our drinks, and I sipped mine immediately. Thankfully, it was carbonated water. But with a lime, stirrer, and Charles's proclamation, everyone would think we were continuing to booze it up.

Doug drifted a few feet away to speak with his parents. Out of the corner of my eye, I could see Buffy bending his ear. No doubt the rumor mill about our inappropriate brunch behavior had already reached the Hollingsworths. Hopefully our performance would work. Otherwise, we'd have an awful lot of explaining to do this afternoon.

The din inside the bar increased as Mayflower Society attendees chatted amongst themselves and ordered drinks. It gave me a moment to check my prop, situated next to the bar. Sure enough, its arrangement appeared exactly as it should. Seven red darts were stuck on the board. The wing of one of the darts, which aficionados call a "flight," was pear-shaped. The others closely resembled a pointy diamond. To the untrained eye, this minor distinction didn't matter one bit. For a sleuth looking to identify a sharp murder weapon, it made all the difference in the world. Trevor had also done his job and persuaded our "guests of honor" to sit in the desired position, conveniently next to the dartboard.

Bonnie glanced at me, waiting for her cue to begin. I gave the slightest hint of a nod, which she accepted as the high sign.

Clapping her hands together, she said, "May I please have your attention? Before we move this meeting upstairs, the Continental Club suggested the Mayflower Society might want to offer an official toast to two of its longtime supporters, Grayson and Kiki Bancroft, who so recently met their untimely deaths. On behalf of the esteemed membership of the Continental Club, I want to extend our sincere condolences." She paused briefly in an apparent attempt to find the right words. "We are deeply saddened that these deaths occurred at our beautiful mansion."

Apparently, no one in the Mayflower Society held the Continental Club responsible for the murders. The bar erupted in applause, with several people commenting, "Long live the Continental Club!" and the like.

"At this point in time, I'd like to turn the floor over to Professor James Mansfield, a close friend of the Bancrofts," she said.

"He was certainly a *friend* to Kiki Bancroft," Meg said, loud enough for the crowd to hear.

I punched her lightly on the shoulder. In a slurred voice, I said, "Shut up, silly. Other people can hear you!"

She raised her glass in response. We clinked our tumblers and giggled.

Professor Mansfield, who was not clued into our ruse, shot us a dirty look.

Meg wobbled on her high heels. "Now we're in trouble," she said.

"SHHHHH!" I put a finger to my mouth as if attempting to quell the misbehavior of my best friend.

Out of the corner of my eye, I monitored the crowd. Horrified stares returned my gaze. The most appalled belonged to Buffy and Winston Hollingsworth. *God, I hope this works*, I thought. Otherwise, I would be in the doghouse more than Clarence had ever been.

Ignoring us, Mansfield proceeded with his speech. "As many of you know, I had a special connection with the Bancrofts, particularly Kiki."

"That's one way of putting it." Meg slugged down a gulp of her supposedly alcoholic drink.

Mansfield gave us another angry sideways look but continued without comment, "We were kindred spirits, united in a common love of American history."

"United in other ways, too," I said.

Meg smiled and gave me a sloppy high five. "Good one, Kit."

That was enough for the professor. He turned toward us. "Excuse me, ladies. May I finish my comments uninterrupted?"

Doug had covered his eyes with his hands. Maybe we were overdoing it.

"Of course, Professor Mansfield," I said, staggering a bit as I rose to my feet. "Please continue. We'll stay quiet." I plopped back into my chair and jabbed Meg in the side with my elbow.

Mansfield droned on, telling stories about his trips with Kiki and lauding Grayson for his generous donations to preserve American culture and history. Most college professors in my experience loved a captive audience, and James Mansfield was no exception to the rule.

Finally, he finished and Bonnie asked if there were any more remarks. Everyone looked around, hoping that the silence would hold. When no one spoke up, Bonnie announced the business meeting would start in fifteen minutes upstairs.

Meg grabbed me by the arm. "It's now or never. Are you ready?"

"Let's do this," I said. "Otherwise, our crazy behavior will have been for nothing."

Carrying our fake drinks, we sauntered over to Cecilia and Drake's table. Trevor and Doug were seated directly behind them. Doug gulped. He knew we were about to spring into action.

Meg aimed a sexy smile at Drake. Standing next to his chair, she draped her arm around his shoulder. With a heavy purr, she asked, "Do you like to play darts, Drake?"

Drake, who had apparently continued to drink the real stuff, slurped on his half-full martini. In her fitted floral dress, Meg was hard to resist, even with his wife sitting right next to him.

"Sure," he slurred. "I love darts."

"Maybe we should try to squeeze in a game before that boring business meeting," said Meg.

Drake appeared dazzled. She could have offered to drive him to the moon. He didn't care, as long as she continued to pay attention to him.

I went over to the board and removed all the darts. "I'll play, too," I said.

"Of course," said Meg. "It'll be a threesome. You'd like that, wouldn't you Drake?"

Drake looked as though he'd just won the lottery. He nodded his head vigorously while Cecilia sat stone-faced next to him.

I handed Meg three of the darts, including the one with the distinct-shaped wing. She waved them in her right hand, which was coming dangerously close to Drake's exposed neck. "Anyone else want to play?"

That was enough for Cecilia. "Watch what you're doing!" she said.

I positioned myself on the other side of Cecilia. "What's wrong with you?"

She straightened up in her chair. "Nothing, except your friend is acting like a drunken idiot with those darts in her hand."

I grabbed the pear-shaped dart. "Are you afraid of darts or something?"

Cecilia recoiled as I pointed the dart at her. "Don't be ridiculous."

A small circle of onlookers had gathered around us, tracking our conversation with amusement, curiosity, or both.

Meg stomped around the table and approached me from behind, holding her tumbler in one hand and the remaining darts in the other. "This is stupid. Are we going to play darts or what?" Meg appeared so authentically sloshed, I felt like we were in a Tennessee Williams play. She stumbled in her stiletto heels and pushed me toward Cecilia and Drake. The dart was pointed directly at Cecilia's exposed upper arm. I made sure the pointed end contacted her skin.

Cecilia looked down at the red mark on her arm and screamed, "Help me!"

After I straightened myself up, I asked, "Why are you so worried, Cecilia? I only grazed you with the dart."

She shrieked, "You have no idea what you just did." She gasped for air. "I can't breathe."

"Do you need some sort of medical attention?" I asked. I was no longer pretending to be drunk, but Cecilia was too distraught to notice.

Pointing to her mouth and hyperventilating, she said, "I need CPR."

"Well, you're in luck, because the police just happen to be around the corner," I said. "Detective?"

Maggie Glass opened the glass door connecting the bar with the outdoor patio. She approached Cecilia. "Ma'am, what's wrong?" she asked.

"I ... can't ... breathe," she sputtered.

Detective Glass picked up the dart and examined it. "I can't imagine why that would be the case. This is an ordinary dart, and it only scratched you."

"That's ... enough," she croaked.

"Enough for what?" asked the detective.

"To kill me, you dolt," stammered Cecilia.

Detective Glass leaned closer. "And why would a minor scrape from a dart kill you?"

Cecilia clawed at her throat. "There's poison on it."

Detective Glass raised her eyebrows in feigned surprise. "Poison? And how would you know about that? Unless you put it there?"

"Who cares how I know? Just get a paramedic here before it kills me!" Cecilia's face was drained of color and beads of sweat appeared on her forehead.

"No need to worry about that," I said, with a heavy dose of smugness.

Cecilia scowled. "What do you mean?"

"I'm glad you believed our performance," said Meg. "It was perfectly staged, if I do say so myself."

Cecilia glared, and her face went from deathly pale to red.

"We would have never allowed Kit and Meg to wave around a dart with the remnants of a lethal poison on the tip," said Detective Glass. "So I switched out the deadly dart earlier this morning with this replica." She picked it up from the table and ran the tip back and forth over her hand. "It's perfectly safe."

Doug spoke up. "The other dart, however, is on its way for forensic analysis. I'm sure the crime scene investigators will find a fatal South American concoction on the tip. Perhaps curare? Or the poison dart frog?"

Drake was three sheets to the wind, but even he knew this wasn't looking good for Cecilia. "Are you a murderer?" he asked. Then he hiccuped and covered his mouth.

"Shut up, you fool," she said. "I'm not saying another word until I talk with my lawyer."

"A wise choice," said Detective Glass. "Please come with me." She took Cecilia by the arm and guided her toward the exit.

The other Mayflower Society members had watched the scene unfold. After the police left with Cecilia, the crowd erupted in applause. Meg and I curtsied and took a bow.

Winston Hollingsworth came over with Buffy in tow. He put his arm around me and gave me a squeeze. "Good show, Kit. We didn't doubt you for a minute." He shook his finger at me. "I knew you were up to something!"

From the look of utter shock on Buffy's face, she'd definitely doubted me, especially when Meg and I kicked our stunt into high gear at the end. Despite her astonishment and without saying a word, my future mother-in-law embraced me. And it wasn't the polite hug I was accustomed to receiving from Buffy. Instead, she gathered me up in a big bear hug. She squeezed me so tightly, I almost couldn't move my arms.

"Th-thanks," I stammered. Buffy tousled my hair and pushed a strand out of my eyes.

"No, thank *you*, Kit. Without your help, an innocent man, my husband, might have been subjected to countless days of suspicion and heartache. Now we can return to Boston without a cloud hanging over our heads." She smiled and took Doug's hand in her own. "You've picked the right person to marry."

Doug put his arm around my waist. "I know, Mother. Believe me, I know."

Chapter Twenty-Seven

***

A N HOUR LATER, we sat inside a wood-paneled room as the Mayflower Society convened its annual business meeting. Doug, Meg, Trevor and I had been invited to join the gathering to provide a coherent explanation for the events that had unfolded inside the garden bar.

I looked around the wood-paneled room. "Hard to believe we ate dinner here four days ago. It seems like an eternity."

"With two more people alive," said Doug.

In the absence of a president, Professor Mansfield served as the chair for the meeting. After waiting while the acceptance of the minutes from the last gathering and a brief treasurer's report were read, Professor Mansfield turned to the four of us.

"This annual gathering of the Mayflower Society will be considered the most unusual and tragic of our meetings. No more eulogies for Grayson and Kiki Bancroft will be given today. There will be another time and place for that. However, as a learned society, we are entitled to understand what happened to our members, or so I believe. Luckily, we had several enterprising sleuths who worked with the police to solve these horrific crimes. I turn the floor over to the them so they can provide us with an explanation." He motioned for us to stand and take the floor.

The whir of the air conditioner was the only sound in the room. Thirty pairs of eyes shifted on us as we approached the podium. Because of the murders, only a small fraction of the members had stayed for the entire conference. Those who remained were the diehards, the true supporters of the Mayflower Society. Professor Mansfield was right. They deserved to know what had transpired over the past several days.

Doug kicked us off. "Many of you know my parents, Winston and Buffy Hollingsworth. My fiancée Kit and I live nearby and joined them for the annual Mayflower Society gathering. Things started to go south when Kit found Grayson Bancroft's body early on Thursday morning."

I provided several details about my unfortunate discovery and our initial interactions with Detective Glass. Then came the more interesting part, namely, how we solved the crimes.

"Unfortunately, several of you had reason to want Grayson Bancroft dead, including Doug's father." Winston Hollingsworth broke into a hearty belly laugh when I mentioned his name.

"There was no shortage of motives. Once we knew the murderer couldn't have entered from the outside, we had to focus on whoever was already present and determine how Grayson was killed and who might have had access to the weapon, whatever it was—"

Meg interrupted me. "And how that person pulled it off in the middle of the night without anyone knowing."

I smiled. "Good point, Meg. While visiting Mount Vernon, we realized that the timing of Grayson's death was significant. As we all know, George Washington died quickly after catching a cold during an early morning ride around his property. Grayson couldn't have lingered long, either. That posed a problem. Most poisons are slow acting. This one wasn't."

Trevor chimed in, "Then we went to the National Archives, where the plot thickened."

"We met Kiki Bancroft and learned she wanted to honor the generous donation her husband had pledged. But that wasn't the most important clue we gathered that day." I cleared my throat. "Instead, Professor Mansfield said something that started to make me suspicious."

Professor Mansfield raised his eyebrows. "I did?"

"Yes, but you didn't know it at the time. Nor did I. You mentioned that Thomas Jefferson detested the edits made to the Declaration of Independence. When I thought about our conversation later, it was the first time I became convinced that Cecilia Rose might have a legitimate reason to want Grayson Bancroft dead. Writers really hate other people messing around with their books." I added, "Or historic documents, for that matter."

"Cecilia wanted to stop writing the popular Savannah books, but Grayson wouldn't allow it," said Doug. "She had other ideas for novels, but she was chained to the series by its popularity."

"Jefferson didn't kill anyone, but he was pretty darn angry, too," Trevor added.

"However, none of that matters if you didn't figure out how Cecilia killed Grayson," said Meg.

"Absolutely," I said. "That leads us to our third stop, the Smithsonian. Doug and I spoke with a curator of their current exhibit on poisons. She provided us with a lot of valuable information."

I briefly recounted the description of curare and the poison dart frog and the significance of the South America connection. Then Doug took up the thread. "That led us to think Kiki Bancroft had somehow killed her husband, even though she wasn't in Washington at the time of his death. Imagine our surprise when we rushed to the Continental Club, only to find out that Kiki herself had become the next victim."

"That was truly baffling," I admitted. "But then Buffy

Hollingsworth gave me the final clue I was looking for."

Buffy squealed. "Me? *I* solved the mystery?"

"In a way, you did," I said. "Or maybe the credit should go to Clarence, our dog."

Laughter erupted in the audience. Little did they know that Clarence had helped us solve a murder on Capitol Hill only a few months earlier.

"After Kiki's murder, you mentioned that Clarence had uncovered a pill case full of Ambien from Cecilia's purse during the dinner party we hosted at our condo," I said. "But Cecilia had made a point of telling me earlier what sound sleepers she and Drake were. Something didn't add up."

"When Kiki was killed, we knew she had to have an accomplice on the inside," explained Meg.

Meg was getting ahead of herself, bringing up Kiki's involvement. A murmur rose in the crowd when a few people realized what we were implying. All in good time.

I went on, "And we had evidence that one person had made sure her partner didn't wake up during the night. In fact, Drake told me he didn't remember anything from the night Grayson died until the alarm went off." I paused. "It didn't matter much at the time, but the sleeping pills made a lot of sense once I knew about them."

Professor Mansfield was listening intently from the front row. "It all adds up, but it doesn't seem like enough to go on."

"I almost forgot," I said. "There was another important clue. I picked up on this one. Charles, the Continental Club bartender, told me the dartboard inside the bar had been recently donated to the club. After Kiki's death, Cecilia excused herself from our table, claiming she needed to talk to someone from the club about getting a receipt for a recent donation."

"That's when Kit started to put the pieces of the puzzle together," Doug said proudly.

"Almost. That detail didn't make sense to me until later that day when we went home and I was able to review my notes from all our conversations. We still had no idea how the murderer killed Grayson and Kiki. If it wasn't a syringe, then what was it?"

Professor Mansfield slapped his knee. "The dartboard! She donated it so she could plant the murder weapon."

"Now you're catching on," I said. "Kiki wanted her husband dead. Likewise, so did Cecilia—Kiki's husband, that is. They conspired to kill him, and Kiki came up with the idea to use this particular poison."

"Cecilia agreed to do the dirty work at the Mayflower Society gathering," said Doug. "Once Kiki had supplied the deadly concoction, Cecilia came up with the ingenious idea of donating the dartboard. After she used the tip of the dart to kill Grayson, she simply placed it on the board inside the bar. She had the perfect place to hide the murder weapon in plain sight."

"The sleeping pills *and* the unusual donation to the Continental Club was too much coincidence," I said. "It had to amount to something. But there was no way to prove it."

"That's when Kit called on us to help," said Meg.

I nodded. "We had to set a trap," I continued. "The only way we could get Cecilia to admit she'd poisoned the dart was to threaten her own life."

"So that's why we pretended to have too much to drink this morning," said Meg. "We don't usually act that way." She paused. "Well, certainly not on a Sunday morning."

"We needed an excuse to act crazy when we moved to the bar after brunch," I said. "How else could we justify almost stabbing her in the arm?"

Doug explained further, "Kit made sure Detective Glass knew what we were doing. She watched the whole scene unfold from behind the glass doors to the courtyard."

Meg broke into a wry smile. "I guess we must have been pretty convincing."

Trevor commented dryly, "It wasn't a big stretch of your

acting skills. You two put the 'happy' in happy hour."

Meg shot Trevor a dirty look, but kept her mouth shut.

"Bravo," exclaimed Professor Mansfield. "Your sleuthing skills and historical expertise are commendable! I shall use this story in my class at Yale."

The crowd gave us a round of fervent applause. The four of us bowed politely and returned to our seats.

"Any last words, Ms. Marshall, before we proceed to the business portion of our meeting?" asked Mansfield.

I stood up quickly. "Yes, Professor. Although I'm not officially a member, I would like to propose Winston Hollingsworth as the next president of the Mayflower Society. I truly believe he's earned it, and you couldn't find another person with more enthusiasm for the organization."

I sat down and looked over my shoulder at my future father-in-law, whose smile stretched from ear to ear.

Chapter Twenty-Eight

⸻

"KIT, WE NEED to leave in ten minutes."

Meg's voice traveled down the hallway of our condo and into the master bedroom. There was time for one final hair and makeup check in my full-length mirror.

The reflection staring back gave me a moment's pause. I was wearing a long, white-silk dress with a sleeveless bodice and a scooped neckline. My long brown hair had been swept into a loose up-do with wispy tendrils framing my cheeks and chin. I had on more makeup than usual, but thankfully it looked natural. The taupe and peachy tones gave my skin a healthy glow, perfect for a beautiful Saturday morning in early June.

My dress wasn't long, so I could walk comfortably in my one-inch sandal heels. Meg was waiting for me in the living room, clutching a beaded purse in one hand, and of course, a glass of champagne in the other.

"How can you possibly drink this early in the morning?" I asked, perhaps naively.

"How could you not have a drink, given what you're about to do?" Meg retorted.

"Good point. I'll take a sip."

Meg giggled as I grabbed her glass.

"Are you sure you want to go through with this? It's a little crazy, even for you," she said.

"What? Getting married? Not everyone is an expert dater like you, Meg."

After a dry spell, Meg had rebounded. In fact, she'd had so many online dates in the last month, I'd teased her she was aiming for a world record.

Meg finished off the champagne, headed to the fridge, and poured herself a refill. "Getting married is nutty enough. But I'm talking about your wedding plan. I hope this works."

I followed her into the kitchen. "We've gone over it several times. And it's exactly the type of wedding Doug and I want."

"I've heard of pop-up stores before," said Meg. "Just not pop-up weddings."

"You make it sound like we're selling Christmas tree ornaments or something. I told you before. It's a *creative* wedding, Meg. Not traditional."

"Hopefully we won't end up in handcuffs," muttered Meg.

"Don't be silly. No one is going to arrest me while I'm wearing this thing." I grabbed the flowing skirt of my dress and shook it.

Meg made a clicking sound with her tongue. "Famous last words. Who's going to bail us out? Trevor?"

I laughed at the thought. "We're not going to get caught. Besides, Doug's father is a lawyer."

"Yeah, that did him a lot of good when he was accused of double homicide. As I recall, we were the ones to get him out of that mess."

"True, but Buffy and Winston are being pretty cool about our wedding, so I suppose it all worked out, didn't it?" I squeezed Meg's shoulder.

She glanced at her phone and punched a few buttons. "Our ride is arriving in five minutes. I even ordered an Uber black car for you." Meg grinned. "After all, it's my best friend's wedding day."

Twenty minutes later, we were approaching our drop-off location, the corner of Seventh and Madison Avenue Northwest, right next to one of the many entrances to the Smithsonian Sculpture Garden.

Meg looked at the clock inside our car. "Five minutes after eleven," she said.

"Perfect," I whispered.

Our Uber driver, his interest already piqued due to our fancy garb, gave us a sideways glance. "What are you ladies up to this morning, if I may ask?"

Meg pointed at me. "She's getting married inside the Sculpture Garden."

Our driver shook his head. "I don't think that's allowed. Do you have a permit?"

"My fiancé and I hired a company that does weddings at unusual locations throughout Washington. It's called a pop-up wedding," I said.

"Now I've heard everything," said our driver, rolling his eyes. "Good luck. You'll need it."

Meg and I hauled ourselves out of the car and hustled to the sidewalk. Sure enough, Doug turned the corner, with Clarence on a leash and his parents in tow. He was wearing a light-blue linen suit with a crisp, white, buttoned-down shirt underneath. He'd initially insisted on wearing a tie, but I'd convinced him it would scream "wedding" and therefore draw unwanted attention inside the Sculpture Garden. After pointing out I wasn't exactly dressed for a stroll in the park, he reluctantly agreed. Even though his shirt collar was open, he was already sweating profusely under the hot, late-morning summer sun.

I'd gotten dressed after he left the condo this morning, so he hadn't seen me in my wedding finery yet. This was the so-called big reveal.

I opened my arms wide. "Ta-da! No fancy aisle required. Just a sidewalk on Seventh Street in downtown D.C."

"Stunning, nonetheless." He twirled me around for a 360-degree view of my dress. Clarence barked his approval.

Doug's parents followed behind him. Winston grabbed my right hand and kissed it. "What a beautiful bride."

Buffy almost knocked him out of the way. "Kit, I absolutely love the elegance. Is it Vera Wang?"

I shook my head.

"Oscar de la Renta?" she asked, a hint of hope in her voice.

"Nope."

Buffy looked at me expectantly.

"I bought it online from a woman who canceled her wedding," I said. "Never been worn, though!"

Buffy appeared as though she'd just been told I'd found the dress at Goodwill. "Well, it's certainly unconventional." She forced a cheery smile. "Nonetheless, it's striking." She added, "Particularly on you."

"Thank you," I said politely.

"It's a damn shame your parents couldn't make it," said Winston.

"They're on a month-long tour of Australia, hitting every possible vineyard," I explained. "They understand. We told them we'd recreate the ceremony with a justice of the peace the next time they roll into town."

Doug wrapped his arms around my waist. "It's a good excuse to get married twice. I don't mind."

My soon-to-be husband had a goofy grin plastered across his face. "This might be the happiest I've ever seen you," Meg said.

"I've never said these words, and I may not say them again," said Doug. "Meg, you are one hundred percent correct!"

As we were laughing, a younger woman with spiky red hair joined us on the sidewalk. She was slightly out of breath. "The

Hollingsworth-Marshall wedding, I presume. Are you ready to get this party started?"

Kendra was our pop-up wedding coordinator. Her company had received great reviews online. After the Continental Club murders, Doug and I decided we didn't want to waste any more time planning an elaborate wedding. We pondered elopement, but somehow that didn't seem right, either. Then a colleague at work had mentioned the idea of a pop-up wedding, and we quickly booked one of the last available days of the summer.

Doug's father extended his hand to Kendra. "Pleased to meet you. I'm Winston Hollingsworth, president of the Mayflower Historical Society and attorney-at-law. How does this whole pop-up wedding thing work?"

Worry lines appeared on Kendra's forehead. "Are you here to shut us down?"

"I apologize!" Winston bellowed with laughter. "I neglected to tell you my most important credential." He pointed to Doug. "I'm the father of the groom."

Kendra sighed in relief. "Thank goodness. Lawyers usually tell me what I can't do."

"Not this one. We want to get the show on the road," said Winston. "It's about time these two got hitched."

Kendra consulted the iPad she was clutching. "It says here that your friend Trevor is taking care of security."

"In a manner of speaking," I said. "He monitored the garden last week and figured out where the guard hangs out. He's going to chat him up and hopefully delay him from making his rounds in this part of the park."

"Genius!" exclaimed Kendra. "I love it when friends work together at weddings. We've never pulled off an uninterrupted wedding at the Sculpture Garden before. This just might be our lucky day!"

"What happens if security breaks up the wedding before they're married?" asked Buffy.

Doug shrugged. "We don't have a backup plan, Mother. Kit

has taught me to loosen up, if you haven't noticed." His eyes glittered with amusement.

"I noticed," said Meg. "You're only half the stick in the mud you used to be."

"Coming from you, that's a compliment," said Doug.

"Are you two ready?" asked Kendra.

Doug and I nodded. With Clarence in tow, he put his hand in mine, and we walked inside the Sculpture Garden. We'd chosen a secluded spot near the entrance, tucked behind the pyramid sculpture.

Kendra's partner, an equally hip-looking guy named Maurice, was waiting for us with a small book in his hands. "Welcome, Doug and Kit. We're under the gun in this location, so we should begin the ceremony immediately."

Winston, Buffy, Meg, and Clarence surrounded us as Maurice began the ceremony. Trevor could only hold off security for so long, so we'd chosen the abbreviated version. After a few pleasantries, it was time to exchange our vows.

"As I understand it, Kit and Doug have chosen to recite vows they have written themselves." Maurice signaled for Doug to go first.

"Kit, today is the happiest day of my life. I've waited for years to marry you. I promise to love you for all eternity. And I also promise to accept everything about you." He paused. "Even your sleuthing."

Meg giggled, and Buffy dabbed her wet eyes with an embroidered handkerchief.

Now it was my turn. "Doug, there were times when I thought this day would never come. But now it has, and I can't find the right words to describe the contentment I feel. I promise to love you unconditionally." I took a deep breath. "Even when you interfere with my crime-solving."

Doug smiled. Meg gave me his wedding ring, and I slipped it on his finger. Doug bent down and unzipped a small compartment attached to Clarence's collar. Inside he removed a diamond-studded platinum band and placed it on my finger.

Maurice clapped his hands. "Fantastic! By the power vested in me by the District of Columbia, I now pronounce you husband and wife. You may now kiss the bride."

Just as I leaned in toward Doug, out of the corner of my eye I noticed Kendra making crazy hand gestures in the direction of the pathway.

"But you'd better do it fast," added Maurice.

Clarence growled softly as Meg pointed in the distance. "Uh-oh. Wedding party's over."

A slightly overweight, balding security officer was heading right for us. "Stop!" he cried. "There are no weddings allowed inside the Sculpture Garden. You're in violation of federal government regulations!"

Doug and I looked at each other and kissed quickly. Filled with bliss, we grabbed Clarence's leash and dashed toward the gate, leaving behind us a trail of joyous tears and hearty laughter.

The Washington Whodunit Series

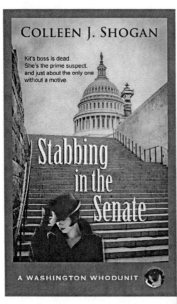

When Senate Staffer Kit Marshall stumbles upon her boss's dead body, she becomes the prime suspect in his murder. If she ever hopes to work on Capitol Hill again, she must prove she had nothing whatsoever to do with his death. And that means finding the real killer.

During a government shutdown, Kit's congresswoman boss is found standing over the dead body of a staffer she tangled with in front of the press. The weapon was the Speaker's gavel, entrusted to Dixon at the time. The killer knows Kit is on the case. Can she solve the mystery in time to save her job and her life?

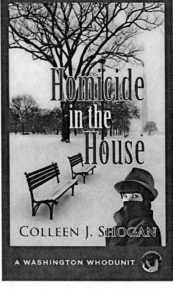

Photo by Glen Fuhrmeister,
GF Photography

COLLEEN J. SHOGAN has been a fan of mysteries since the age of six. A political scientist by training, she is a senior executive at the Library of Congress where she works on great programs like the National Book Festival. A proud member of Sisters in Crime, Colleen won a Next Generation Indie Award in the Best Mystery category for her first novel *Stabbing in the Senate*. She lives in Arlington, Virginia with her husband Rob Raffety and their rescue mutt Conan.

For more information, go to www.colleenshogan.com.

CPSIA information can be obtained
at www.ICGtesting.com
Printed in the USA
FSOW01n1858200517
34296FS

9 781603 813358